M. Maguire & Co.
Discreet Inquiries

PRAISE FOR THE MAGGIE MAGUIRE SERIES

**MORE MYSTERIES FROM THE
BERKLEY PUBLISHING GROUP . . .**

SISTER FREVISSE MYSTERIES: Medieval mystery in the tradition of
Ellis Peters . . .

by Margaret Frazer

THE NOVICE'S TALE	THE SERVANT'S TALE	THE BOY'S TALE
THE OUTLAW'S TALE	THE BISHOP'S TALE	THE MURDERER'S TALE
THE PRIORESS' TALE	THE MAIDEN'S TALE	

PENNYFOOT HOTEL MYSTERIES: In Edwardian England, death takes
a seaside holiday . . .

by Kate Kingsbury

ROOM WITH A CLUE	DO NOT DISTURB	CHIVALRY IS DEAD
SERVICE FOR TWO	EAT, DRINK, AND BE BURIED	RING FOR TOMB SERVICE
CHECK-OUT TIME	GROUNDS FOR MURDER	MAID TO MURDER
DEATH WITH RESERVATIONS	PAY THE PIPER	

GLYNIS TRYON MYSTERIES: The highly acclaimed series set in the
early days of the women's rights movement . . . "Historically accurate and
telling."—Sara Paretsky

by Miriam Grace Monfredo

SENECA FALLS INHERITANCE	NORTH STAR CONSPIRACY	THE STALKING-HORSE
BLACKWATER SPIRITS	THROUGH A GOLD EAGLE	

MARK TWAIN MYSTERIES: "Adventurous . . . Replete with genuine tall
tales from the great man himself."—*Mostly Murder*

by Peter J. Heck

DEATH ON THE MISSISSIPPI
A CONNECTICUT YANKEE IN CRIMINAL COURT
THE PRINCE AND THE PROSECUTOR

MAGGIE MAGUIRE MYSTERIES: A thrilling new series . . .

by Kate Bryan

MURDER AT BENT ELBOW	A RECORD OF DEATH	MURDER ON THE BARBARY COAST

MURDER
ON THE BARBARY
COAST

KATE BRYAN

BERKLEY PRIME CRIME, NEW YORK

MURDER ON THE BARBARY COAST

A Berkley Prime Crime Book / published by arrangement
with the author

PRINTING HISTORY
Berkley Prime Crime edition / June 1999

The Penguin Putnam Inc. World Wide Web site address is
http://www.penguinputnam.com

ISBN: 0-425-16933-2

Berkley Prime Crime Books are published
by The Berkley Publishing Group,
a division of Penguin Putnam Inc.,
375 Hudson Street, New York, New York 10014.
The name BERKLEY PRIME CRIME and the
BERKLEY PRIME CRIME design are trademarks
belonging to Penguin Putnam Inc.

PRINTED IN THE UNITED STATES OF AMERICA

10 9 8 7 6 5 4 3 2 1

MURDER
ON
THE BARBARY
COAST

ONE

>—◄—◆—⊙—◆—►—◄—

MAGGIE MAGUIRE WASN'T THINKING ABOUT HER caseload, nor was she thinking about the old days growing up with the circus. She wasn't even thinking that she'd nearly got herself and Grady killed last month in that Cutthroat Island affair. Well, not much. So far as she was able, she had only one thing on her mind: Quincy Applegate.

As he moved her around the Foxglove's dance floor, she thought how strong his arms were, and how wonderful he smelled, and how really, honestly handsome he was with that strong, square jaw and those long-lashed bedroom eyes. He'd seemed just the tiniest bit distracted all evening, but then, running Western Mutual was a demanding job.

She understood. She had a demanding job, too.

The music slowed and as he pulled her closer, she smiled dreamily into his lapel. Dear Quincy. So sweet. So stalwart. So *there*. He smelled of bay rum.

Then the orchestra began to play a lively number, and Quincy, making his usual flimsy excuses, led her back to their table. The darling. He just didn't know how to polka and was too embarrassed to ask for instructions. She didn't believe those stories about a bad back or a long day or a sore leg for a minute, although she was too polite to say so. And normally she would have brushed a kiss on

Quincy's brow and patted his hand, then grabbed Cousin Grady and polkaed till she dropped.

But tonight she followed along demurely, feeling a little schoolgirlish and giddy. This time, they'd had no Grady tagging along with his girl of the hour. It wasn't that she didn't care for Grady's company, but Lord! Three-fourths of the time he stuck Quincy with the check, and she couldn't keep track of his women! She was always calling them by the wrong name and Grady was always kicking her under the table or asking her, at the most inopportune moment possible, just what it was like to ride a horse standing on your head.

This evening, however, she'd received no bruises, only an attentive beau whose detachment had grown, rather than faded, over the course of the evening. So much for feminine charms. Now that she wasn't in his arms, lost in a tune, she wondered what he was up to.

"My dear?" Quincy held out her chair.

"Thanks, Quin," she said, and waited while he took his seat.

She smiled.

He smiled back.

She smiled some more.

He stuck a finger under his collar.

"Quincy?" she said sweetly, leaning forward and folding her hands upon the table. "Tonight has been lovely. A play, then dinner, and now dancing. . . . What do you want?"

Quincy's mouth opened, then closed again. "Why, Maggie!" he said, with just a little more indignation than was necessary. And a great deal more guilt. "What makes you think I—"

She reached across the table and put her hand on his. Gently, she said, "At the theater, you folded your program into a swan. Three times. During dinner, you kept tapping your fork between courses, and you made your napkin into a little Japanese kite. And here?" She gave his hand a squeeze. "Well, you're not quite *here,* are you, sweetie?" She eyed his cocktail napkin, which was two folds away from an owl.

He lifted his hand, taking hers with it, and pressed his lips to her knuckles. "Magdalena. Sorry. I'm just a little distracted." He turned her hand over and kissed the palm.

To take her mind off that palm-kissing business, which made her feel entirely too warm for her own good—and, well, a way she shouldn't be feeling in public—she said, "Tell me about it, Quin," and then extricated her hand. Gracefully, she hoped.

Quincy didn't even notice, drat him. "It's . . . it's . . . are you certain you want to hear about it, Maggie? I mean, right now? I don't want it to ruin the evening. I seldom have you all to myself, you know."

He tried to smile, but Maggie saw the strain gathering subtly in the corners of his mouth, and mentally kicked herself for waiting this long to ask. She suddenly realized why he'd asked her at the last minute, when Grady'd already made plans. This confession—or whatever it was— was supposed to happen, but not until later.

Well, she'd given it a shove down the hill. Best run to catch up with it.

She propped her head in her hands and looked him square in the eye. "Tell me, Quin."

"Well . . . I . . ." He patted his pockets for his cigarette case, located it, then brought it out. "Mind?" he asked as he fanned it open and took a cigarette.

She shook her head.

"It's just," he said, striking a match, "that I think better when I smoke."

His hand was shaking as he struck the sulphur tip. Whatever it was, it was more serious than she'd imagined. Embezzlement? No, she couldn't see Quin siphoning off cash from Greater Western Mutual, not in a million years! Not staid, honest-to-a-fault Quincy! And murder, of course, was completely out of the question. Dear Lord, he wasn't going to ask her to marry him, was he? Why, that would be simply—

"It's my friend. My best friend, Sutter Malone," Quincy said, snapping her back to attention. He'd left the case out on the table, she noted, and held his cigarette in templed fingers, the smoke rising in a blue curl.

"Go on," she urged, grateful that he hadn't popped the question. She could handle anything but that.

"Sutter and I went to school together. I'm sure you've heard me speak of him? Haven't I shown you and Grady any photographs?"

Maggie nodded. She remembered an old photo and a few newer ones of a thin, pale fellow, and a few stories, all of them about collegiate hijinks, which had had Quincy and Grady in tears and rolling on the floor, and had left her wondering if she'd missed the punch line.

"Well, it's Sutter's niece, actually. Trini. Short for Katrina. She's missing. Sort of."

Maggie sat back in her chair. "Sort of? How can a person be 'sort of' missing?"

She hadn't meant to be curt, but Quincy made a pained face.

As kindly as possible, she asked, "Quin, is this a very long story?"

He nodded. "Afraid so."

"All right, dear," she said, and out of habit signaled the waiter with a waving hand and a whistle. Quincy, she noted, was too distraught to cringe. It *must* be serious. "Whiskey for the gentleman," she said, as her internal "Maggie Maguire, Girl Detective" cogs slipped the rest of the way into gear. "Better make it a triple. And I'll have a large lemonade. With extra ice."

For starters, it seemed that Sutter Malone's family was quite wealthy. Quincy told her that upon old Seamus Malone's death, Sutter and his two siblings each received better than eight hundred thousand dollars. Sutter's older brother—Skipper Malone, Trini's father—had already passed on in a yachting mishap, and so the bulk of his estate passed entirely to Trini's mother.

Trini was always a strange child, he said. She was stunningly beautiful in face and form, and extremely bright, but she seemed to have had a very hard time sorting out her place in life. She was alternately headstrong and vocal, or meekly penitent, with no mid ground whatsoever. Sutter never knew, when he visited, whether he'd find her out marching for women's rights or the local antivivisection league, or at home, locked in a closet, starving herself for Jesus. On three occasions, her mother had been forced to physically restrain her from shaving her head.

"She's a very, well, *passionate* girl," said Quincy, over a syrupy Hungarian song. He stubbed out his third cigarette.

"So it would seem," Maggie said noncommittally, and wondered if he was basing that on any personal knowledge. Passionate, indeed! And why did the rich always have such bizarre names? Sutter, Skipper, and Trini? They sounded like a crew of acrobats! She said, "Go on."

Five months prior, it seemed, Trini had vanished from her home. The family had hired the Pinkertons, and they'd traced her to Chicago, where she'd fallen in with a group of religious zealots. Maggie made no comment on the Pinkertons—she had her own axe to grind with them—but listened raptly to Quincy's description of the Children of Golgotha, the religious group Trini had taken up with.

Secretive, mysterious, and guarding their converts jealously, they were led by a character called Brother Ascension, aka Darby Halstead, a former resident of Dannemora Prison in New York State.

"Doesn't sound too terribly promising," Maggie muttered.

"Wait," said Quincy. "It gets worse." He lit another cigarette, then fanned at the smoke.

Members, he explained, took menial jobs and turned their pay over to help run the "church" and support

Brother Ascension. They lived, sometimes six or eight to a room, in cheap boardinghouses, while Brother Ascension lived in comparable splendor. They had prayer meetings every night and worship three times a week and twice on Sundays, were expected to each bring a member a month into the fold, and spent their "spare" time on street corners, passing out handbills for the church.

The Pinkertons had picked up Trini as she walked to her sweatshop job at the Pinnacle Wireworks Factory, and forcibly removed her to a hotel. There she shrieked and ranted and carried on, demanding that she be released and allowed to go back to her "family," and finally had to be put under a doctor's care.

Suffering from scurvy and general malnutrition, she was sent home, under guard, to her mother in Boston. Two days later, she escaped by crawling out a second-floor window. It was assumed she had gone back to the Children of Golgotha and Brother Ascension, who had quietly pulled up stakes and moved his little religious order to parts unknown.

"So she wants to stay with them," said Maggie, twirling her empty glass on the table, making a pattern of the watermarks. "It's sad, but you really can't do anything. Not legally, if she's past the age of consent." She looked up. "I take it she is?"

"Unfortunately," replied Quincy, who held up his hand, the cuff link winking gold, and signaled the waiter for another whiskey. "You, darling?" He nodded toward Maggie's glass.

"I'm fine," she said. "I can see why you're upset about this thing, Quin. But if Trini is bound and determined to stay with this ... this cult, I don't see any way you can stop her."

"But that's just the point, my dear," he said, his brow furrowed. "I have to stop her. You see, her mother—" He stopped while the waiter slid his drink across the table. "Her mother was killed two weeks ago. They say it was a bungled burglary, but nothing of real value was taken.''

The orchestra was playing another waltz. Maggie made herself stop tapping her fingers in time to the music and hoisted an eyebrow, waiting.

''If this was the first time, I . . . Well, there have been others. I mean, other incidents of wealthy parents meeting with untimely endings. Two, that I know of. There may have been more. The majority of the young people—and they are all quite young—are from relatively wealthy families. Boys, plucked from college to work at hard labor to support this Brother Ascension character. Young girls, scraping their fingers to the bone instead of making their debuts.''

Maggie rolled her eyes.

''Well,'' Quincy added quickly, ''I suppose some of the girls might have been students, too. But the point is, Maggie, that people have died. And more to the point, their children—the Children of Golgotha—have died, too. A boy named William Sempler was run over in the streets not ten days after he made a will leaving everything to the Children of Golgotha and Brother Ascension. There was a sum of over one hundred and fifty thousand involved. And two years before that, a girl, Amy Proctor, 'accidentally' fell from a fourth-floor window a bit over a month after she signed the same bequest. That time, Brother Ascension came into sixty-two thousand and change. There have probably been more, but those were the two the Pinkertons had time to dig up.''

''So turn him over to the law. Surely there's enough evidence—''

''No,'' said Quin, shaking his head. ''That's just it. All of this is hearsay, Maggie. There's no hard evidence. The police can't do anything unless they actually catch him in the act. I just don't want the act they catch him in to be Trini's murder.''

He slumped back in his chair, as if exhausted, and wiped his forehead with a monogrammed handkerchief. ''We've

got to get her out of there, Maggie. She's to come into her
Malone inheritance in ten days, on her twenty-third birthday. Eight hundred thousand. There's another sum from her
mother, a goodly amount of money, actually, but she won't
have that until she's thirty-five. If she lives that long. The
thing is, I . . . I want to hire you. Sutter says the Pinkertons
won't touch the case again. I suppose they're afraid of a
lawsuit or some such rot.''

"Ten days?'' said Maggie, her brows arched. It *was* serious. If this Brother Ascension had killed for sixty-two
thousand, he wouldn't hesitate to do it again for over ten
times that amount! They had to act fast, but drat that
Quincy, anyway! He certainly didn't give a girl much lead
time. "Where in the world am I supposed to start?''

Quincy leaned forward. "But I found them!'' He looked
momentarily smug. "I found them down on the edge of
town. Well, not San Francisco proper. In Conquistador.
You know it?''

She nodded. Conquistador, despite its regal name, was a
failing community about ten miles south of the outskirts of
San Francisco. Nothing there but old miners and aging saloon girls and people passing through on their way to somewhere else. A couple of run-down hotels, two or three
saloons, a mercantile, and that was about it. Conquistador
was just a glorified stage stop, really, for people who
couldn't afford to take the train, or were coming from other
small towns with no railroad access.

"What in heaven's name are they doing there?'' she
asked. "And furthermore, what were *you* doing there?''

Quincy had the decency to blush, and Maggie had to
push down her *he's so cute!* response.

He said, "I was returning from Iron Creek, Maggie.
Business.'' He lifted his chin. "And I heard a porter—if I
can call the creature that—mention something about Mr.
Halstead to the desk clerk. 'That wouldn't be Darby Halstead, would it?' I asked, and he told me it was none of
my business, but yes, it was. To make a long story short,

I found where Trini was staying and I crawled in her window late that night—I thought I could get her out, you see. 'Uncle' Quincy to the rescue and all that," he added sheepishly, "except that somebody banged me over the head before I could figure out which bed she was in. I woke up on the stage the next morning, three-quarters of the way into town."

Maggie said, "When was this?"

Quincy didn't look at her. "I came into San Francisco yesterday, before noon."

"So they clubbed you the night before last?"

He nodded.

"Quin, why didn't you—" She stopped herself. She already knew. It was the same thing—things, really—that stopped too many people from hiring her until it was too late, or nearly so. The three *P*s: privacy, pigheadedness, and pride. In Quincy's case, she imagined it was more the privacy issue than any other. After all, those little odd jobs from his office at Western Mutual were her bread and butter. He knew she was very good at what she did, and he'd have had no compunctions about hiring her on his own.

No, the problem was that it was *Sutter's* relation who'd gotten herself into this mess. His best friend. And a man like Quincy didn't run around baring his best friend's private problems.

"All right," said Maggie. Behind her, she heard the rattles and scrapes of the orchestra packing up for the night. The crowd had already thinned out considerably.

"I'll pay your expenses and your standard rate," said Quincy. "By the day. Just get Trini out of that bastard's hands. It means a very great deal to Sutter, and consequently, to me."

"All right," repeated Maggie.

"And I'll throw in a bonus if you can get enough evidence on this Brother Ascension or Darby Halstead—or whatever his name is—to put him away."

"I said yes, Quin," Maggie said again, tilting her head. "It's all right. I'll take the case."

"You will?" he practically chirped. "I can help. I can take time away from the office and come down there and—"

"Just wait a minute!" Maggie said, holding up her hands. She hadn't seen him this animated since she'd proved Constantine Marco a fraud, and Western Mutual hadn't had to pay him that three hundred thousand dollar settlement.

"Quin," she explained, "they've seen you. You can't go down there again. Leave it to me, all right? Well," she added, thinking it over, "and possibly Grady."

"Yes. Yes, of course. But if you need me?"

She reached across the table and patted his hand. "You're the first one I'll wire. Do you want to go now?" she said then, twisting to reach for her shawl. "Most everybody else has. You can give me the rest of the details on the way home. And, Quin?"

He paused, his chair halfway pushed in. "Yes, dear?"

"You didn't have to go to all this trouble," she said, smiling. "I mean, the dinner and the play and all. You know I would have taken the case anyway."

He smiled, those delicious dimples sinking creases into his cheeks, and said, "I know, Maggie." He came round the back of her chair and held it out while she stood up. Then, taking her shoulders from behind, he whispered in her ear, "I know. But we get so little time alone, sweet." And then he kissed her neck and said, "Shall we go?"

Maggie scraped herself up off the floor and took his arm.

TWO

>—i—<♦>—<⊙>—<♦>—i—<

"**B**UT YOU WON'T HAVE TO DO A THING!" MAGGIE said, tossing a case of her favorite target-throwing knives into her small carpetbag. She was still dressed in her wrapper. "Just be there, that's all. Just in case." Then, "Ozymandias! Get out of there!"

Watching as the cat leapt from her bag to the floor and proceeded to clean his shoulder, Grady yawned. He'd come in at three—ah, Ramona of the dark eyes!—and Maggie'd stormed into his bedroom before the crack of dawn carrying on about Quincy and Conquistador and, well, he hadn't really listened. She had her . . . oh, what was the word? He was too groggy to think of it. Nerve, that was it.

"Then take Otto with you," he said grumpily, and squinted at the sun's first rays, just coming through the big office window and creeping along the tabletops. "It'll keep him away from my poor Edison."

The sun highlighted the top edge of the talking machine's trumpet, just one of the many pieces, large and small, neatly spread out on the table. Grady shuddered. "Or take Quincy! Take anybody but me! I'm going back to bed. C'mon, Ozzie."

He was halfway off the sofa when two small but powerful hands came through the potted ferns to grip his shoulders and pushed him back down.

"No, you don't!" said Maggie, behind him. "Grady, I

need you undercover. All you have to do is go down there and get a job cleaning spittoons or mopping—''

A chill, almost greater than he'd had for the dismantled Edison, overtook him. "Cleaning? *Spittoons?* You must be mad!''

She came around the couch and smiled. "Awake now?''

He crossed his arms with a "Humph!''

"It has to be menial,'' she soothed. "So you won't be noticed. And anybody who has more than a nickel to his name and stays around Conquistador for more than a night gets noticed.''

"Menial,'' he grumbled. He supposed he'd have to wear some sort of hideous rags. And slouch. Or have a speech impediment. "Tell me why I'm doing this wretched thing. And it had better be good.''

"Have a cup of coffee first,'' she said, returning to her packing. "And bring me one, while you're at it.''

When he returned bearing the coffee, he was fairly alert—well, as alert as anyone could be before six in the morning when they'd spent the previous evening and the best half of the night with Ramona Chardonelle. Maggie was just curling into a leather armchair, her packed bags at her side. He noticed she'd picked particularly shabby ones, and the largest of the two was none too big.

He handed over her coffee, then took a seat on the couch. "I'm waiting.''

He listened while Maggie filled him in on Quincy's dilemma. She talked for nearly fifteen minutes straight, and the only movement he made, aside from draining his coffee, was to lift the saucer higher to make room on his lap for the cat. By the time she finished, Ozzie was curled in his crotch, asleep, but Grady was wide awake.

"The man's a fiend!'' he said. "Maggie, you'd better be very, very careful with Darby Halstead. He wasn't in Dannemora for tipping tills.''

She set her coffee cup aside. "You're the one with the photographic memory. Tell me.''

It never failed. He supposed she'd want it all now. Closing his eyes with a sigh, and bringing the most recent printed information into his mind's eye, he began, "Darby Halstead, alias Dennis Harvey, alias Father Derek. Previously wanted for fraud, embezzlement, alienation of affection, gross misconduct, impersonating a priest, and murder. Convicted for manslaughter and fraud, served three years in Dannemora before being upgraded to trustee, gained early release for pious behavior." He opened his eyes. *The trained poodle strikes again*, he thought smugly.

Maggie looked thoughtful. "It's a long way from impersonating a priest to murder," she said quietly.

Grady shrugged. "Actually, I don't even believe that's a real charge. Priest impersonation, I mean. I think some overzealous officer of the law thought it sounded like one. Nonetheless, it isn't a big leap when you've impersonated one to gain the confidence of a rich old codger and his family."

"And then you kill them? Is that where the murder charges come in?"

"Precisely," he replied. "After, of course, you've coerced the old man into leaving everything to the Church. Your own private church. Through you."

Maggie twirled her coffee cup absently. "Must have been a trick. I mean, getting him to bequeath the money directly. Most people just leave it to the Church in general. Or to some specific order or other, I suppose. How'd he manage to get the charges down to manslaughter?"

Grady shook his head. "Smart lawyer? Maybe a smart lawyer and a dull prosecutor. Maybe somebody cut a deal. He didn't get the money, at any rate. Sounds like lately he's raking it in."

Maggie seemed to mull this over for a moment, then said, "What's he look like?"

"Tall," said Grady, conjuring up the description in his head. "About six foot three. On the thinnish side, about one hundred and eighty pounds. Balding on top—a little like Friar Tuck, but one-fourth the girth. Piercing blue eyes. Good-looking, but you wouldn't call him handsome. Charismatic, more likely. And what about this girl? Trini Malone, did you say? Odd name, Trini. Seen the brother's mug more often than I care to admit—"

"Oh, Grady," she chided.

He sniffed. "Well, your Quin can be a bore sometimes. All that college rah-rah and hoopla."

"Well, this isn't about Sutter. It's about his sister."

Maggie rose and plucked something from her purse. She handed it to him. It was a small, framed picture, hand-colored, of a stunning young girl with dark, setter-red hair. She wore a very simple white dress. With her bee-stung lips and luminous green eyes, she might have been on a magazine cover. He looked up reluctantly. "White dress. Confirmation picture?"

Maggie took it back. "Finishing school graduation. Taken a few years ago. It was the only one Quincy had. On second thought, keep it," she added, handing the picture back. "They'll probably search my bags, and it wouldn't do if they found it."

Grady stared up at her. "*Who'll* search your bags?"

"The Children of Golgotha," she answered, opening the carpetbag and wistfully taking out her knives, muttering, "I suppose these'll have to go, too."

"Maggie," he said patiently, "why will they search your bags?"

"Because I'm going to join them, of course. Now, there are some things I'll need you and Otto to do . . ."

That afternoon, after training to a town farther south then grabbing a stage back up to Conquistador, Maggie sat on a bench outside the Wells Fargo office looking dirty, ragtag, and dejected. At least, she hoped she did. She'd worn an old dress that had been ripped and patched many times, and done her hair in a simple, farm girl style with a few random tendrils loose and falling, for effect. She carried herself not with her usual straight-backed, head up, look-'em-dead-in-the-eye posture, but slumped and hunched. She gave, she hoped, every appearance that she'd been beaten down by life and was just waiting for the next blow to fall.

She'd been slouched there for a good hour, watching the street traffic and thinking that surely Brother Ascension or one of his flock would have seen her. After all, their hotel was just across the way. She was about to pick up her bags and trudge across the street, when a young man appeared beside her.

He was certainly clean, and although his simple work clothes were cheap, they were pressed. His blond hair was wet-combed into place, and there was a Bible tucked under his arm. One of the Children of Golgotha, if she didn't miss her guess.

Maggie, staying in character, cringed away from him. "What you want?" she exclaimed. "I didn't do anything!"

The boy backed up a step, dropped his hands to his sides, and said, "I won't hurt you. You just look like you need a friend, that's all." He smiled.

Maggie let her posture relax a little. "No, thanks. I don't need anything or anybody. I work for what I get, and don't you go gettin' any ideas."

The boy kept smiling. "Would you like a meal? I'll bet you're hungry."

She licked her lips but pointed at his Bible. "You read the Good Book, too? You're too young to be a preacher."

That smile of his never broke. "I'm eighteen. And I'm not exactly a preacher, but I like to help people who are down on their luck, the same way our blessed Christ Jesus ministered to the sick and gave nourishment to the poor."

She had her foot in the door. Now to get him to drag her through it. Leerily, she said, "God will provide, but I don't know that He sent you to feed me."

Still smiling that beneficent smile, he picked up her bags. "My name's Jim," he said. "Jim Smoller. There's a café just down the way." He began to walk. "They've got real good apple pie,'' he called over his shoulder.

"Hey!'' she cried after a moment, and loped to catch him. "Wait up!''

Maggie sopped the last of the gravy from her second plate with gusto, and popped the last piece of sourdough into her mouth. Leaning back, her eyes closed, she rubbed her stomach and said, "Good. That was fine.'' Then suddenly her eyes popped open and she sat forward, leaning across the table. "You *sure* you've got the money to pay for this?''

Jim laughed. During her meal, she had come to like him, although with reservations. She wondered if he had a rich family somewhere, and if they were scheduled to die, too, or if he was one of Brother Ascension's pawns.

"Don't worry about it,'' he said. "As you said, the Lord provides. And we have unlimited credit here.'' He hadn't eaten a thing, just ordered coffee while she plowed through two enormous plates of the saltiest beef stew she'd ever had the misfortune to meet. Having skipped lunch on purpose, she'd been hungry enough to eat a fried skunk when she started, but that second plate had nearly done her in.

"Can I have some more water?'' she asked, hoping he wouldn't offer dessert. "And who's 'we'?''

"My friends and me. We're staying at the Choice Hotel.'' He tipped his head toward the window. "You know, you never told me your name.''

"Sorry,'' she said, and wiped her hand on her sleeve before holding it out. "Maggie. Magdalena Obermyer, that is.''

He shook it solemnly. "Pleased to meet you, Miss Obermyer.''

She feigned embarrassment, and drew her hand back. "Just Maggie's fine,'' she said, "or Magdalena.'' *Are you forgetting the water, you grinning idiot?* she thought.

"All right,'' he said, the smile returning. "Magdalena, then. What brings you through Conquistador, Magdalena?''

"My grandfather," she said, looking out the window. It wouldn't be dark for six or seven hours. Grady should be pulling into town any time now. She turned back toward Jim. "See, Mama died and they took the farm, and Grandpa Otto's the only family I've got. I prayed for guidance, and the Lord told me to get myself to San Francisco, and I was doing just that except I ran outta money. Back home, Parson Grimsby took up a collection to get me set on the way, but two heathen jackals robbed me before I got twenty miles down the pike. So I just started walking."

She took a drink of her coffee. "They tell me San Francisco isn't far, though. 'Bout ten miles. I reckon I can walk that much farther, easy."

Jim shook his head. "That's just to the outskirts of town, Magdalena. It might be another fifteen or twenty, if you get turned around once you're in the city. Do you have his address?"

Maggie stared at her lap. "Not exactly." Suddenly, she looked up. "But he's a famous man, and real rich! He won't be hard to find." She let the barest hint of a question drizzle into that last statement.

One corner of Jim's smile quivered just a little, and she knew he'd taken the bait. "Well, Magdalena, if you don't mind my asking, if your grandfather is so wealthy, why didn't he help your mother with the farm?"

She didn't reel him in yet. Not all the way. She pursed her lips and looked out the window again. "Nobody told him. See, Papa ran off when he was just a kid and they never spoke again. I guess Mama got into the habit, too, and didn't even tell Grampa when his very own son died. I don't imagine he even knows about me being born, let alone Papa being married and all. I figure he'll be real welcomin' of some family news after all this time." She looked at him hopefully. "Don't you think?"

Jim patted her hand, a tad too enthusiastically. "I think you need some dessert. Waitress?"

She cringed inwardly, but tried to appear enthusiastic,

chirping, "Boy, oh, boy!" and covering, with her red-checkered napkin, the belch that unfortunately followed. She didn't think he noticed, since he was speaking to the serving girl.

Along with a new glass of water, which Maggie grabbed and drained immediately, the girl slid an enormous slab of apple pie onto the table. It was covered in what she had to assume was cheddar cheese, although hard to tell, what with it being so dry and congealed. She poked at it with her fork.

"It's all right," said Jim, mistaking her misgivings for politeness. He laced his fingers atop his Bible. "Eat up."

"Sure," she said, trying to smile, and sawed off a forkful. She had a feeling the sermon was about to begin.

"So tell me, Maggie," he began. "You mentioned Parson Grimsby. Are you a churchgoing woman?"

She paused the fork halfway to her mouth. "Of course!" she said indignantly. "What kind of person do you take me for? The Good Lord's led me this far, and I'm not about to forsake him at this late date."

"Do you believe that He is the one true Heavenly Father," Jim went on, "and that Jesus was and is His only son, sent to earth in corporeal form to be tortured and crucified and wash away the sins of mankind with his Blessed Holy Blood?"

Maggie let the indignation bleed from her face, put down the fork, and cocked her head stupidly. "I never heard it put all in a lump like that, but yes, I reckon so."

Jim smiled, and it was, she thought, the smile of a man about to talk an extremely grimy five-year-old boy into taking a bath and liking it. She didn't believe she liked him so much anymore.

He said, "Let's start a little slower, all right? One thing at a time. Maggie, do you believe God has a plan for each and every one of us?"

•   •   •

Jim led a bloated and uncomfortable Maggie up the street to meet his "friends" just as the San Francisco stage pulled up to the Wells Fargo office. On the hotel's threshold, she turned just in time to see Grady, dressed in rags, land on his backside in the dirt, and hear the driver call, "And *stay* off!"

Momentarily, she forgot her discomfort and bit her lips to keep from laughing.

"Magdalena?" said Jim, gesturing from inside, and she reluctantly turned her back and followed Jim inside. He nodded to the desk clerk, who had lowered his newspaper a few inches, and then motioned her up the narrow stairs.

They went along the second-floor hall, past closed doors and then open ones, each shabby cubicle containing five or six young men or women. They were all dressed like Jim, in cheap, look-alike clothing which was immaculately cleaned and pressed. The boys, like Jim, wore plain dark blue pants and suspenders, and lighter blue work shirts. The girls wore pale blue dresses, severe in design and buttoned up the neck, and their hair was gathered up under poke bonnets made of the same fabric. Each one was engaged in reading the Bible or tatting or mending or writing. Few looked up as they passed. She didn't spot Trini Malone anywhere.

It gave Maggie a slight case of the collywobbles to see so many young people, and all of them quiet. You'd think there'd be a few shouts or some laughter. At least a heated game of checkers!

Toward the end of the hall, Jim ushered her into a room much like the ones before, except that in this one, one of the girls was pressing clothes on a foldaway ironing board. Three baskets of clothing took up most of the available floor space. A flame flickered beneath a small metal plate at the girl's elbow, and when Jim quietly said, "God bless you, Sister Polly," she carefully set her iron atop it.

She turned toward them with a smile and a soft, "Yes? Oh, hello, Brother Jim. God bless." She turned and focused the smile on Maggie. "Have you brought us a guest?"

Sister Polly wasn't at all what Maggie had expected. A sour face, perhaps, or a sweating brow, or at least a sign of some annoyance at having to iron for all these people! But Sister Polly's face was as open as a spring meadow and as sweet as clover. She was blond, like Jim, and a woman of perhaps thirty-five or forty, but still quite pretty. And if her cheeks were flushed, it wasn't with the heat of ironing, but with joy.

"Indeed I have, Sister Polly," said Jim, at her elbow. "This is Magdalena Obermyer."

Maggie wiped her hand on her skirts, then stuck it out. "Pleased to meet you, ma'am."

Sister Polly folded it into both of hers and held it. "God bless you, Magdalena." Her smile never faltered, but her eyes flicked quickly down then back up, taking in, Maggie supposed, her shabby clothing. She drew Maggie forward a step and said softly, "Have you a place to stay the night, child?"

Maggie looked down, studying her shoes. Rather, her muddy work boots. "No, ma'am," she whispered. Then she looked up. "But I can work," she declared earnestly. "I can always earn out my keep. Or I can sleep on that bench across the way. It was fair comfortable, and God'll be with me. Don't you folks worry none."

Sister Polly was still holding her hand captive. She laughed softly, and said, "We won't hear of it, dear Magdalena. I believe we can make some room for you. Isn't that right, Sister Trini?"

In the corner, a girl looked up from her mending, a girl who it would have taken Maggie a long time to recognize, if all she'd had to go on was Quincy's photograph. At first glance she was just pale, but upon closer inspection a sickly grey tone lay beneath the fashionable pallor. She was far too thin, and all that gorgeous hair was tucked away beneath her cap. But she laid aside the shirt she was mending and stood, stepping toward Maggie with a smile. That smile was so similar to Jim's and Polly's that it could have been stamped out on a press.

"Certainly, Sister Polly," said Trini Malone, once the prettiest girl in Boston. She turned her smile on Maggie and, green eyes sparkling from that thin, gaunt face, said, "God bless you, Magdalena. Welcome."

THREE

><del>━━◆━━◯━━◆━━</del><

BACK IN SAN FRANCISCO, MAGGIE AND GRADY'S downstairs neighbor, Otto Obermyer, was just stepping into the lobby of a very different sort of hotel.

"*Gott in Himmel!*" he whispered under his breath, and then stood a little taller, remembering who he was supposed to be.

He strode between the tall polished marble pillars of the Majestic Hotel's entrance, considering that he shouldn't compare it to the habitat to which he was accustomed—two crowded and cluttered rooms at the rear of Hammacher's Toys—but rather to the palaces and museums he'd visited as a boy in Germany and Austria.

It worked. The lobby's glittering brass and glass and leather and marble didn't look so fancy-schmantzy anymore. No gilded trim? No fittings of solid gold or ivory or amber? Suddenly, he was slumming!

Head up, chest out, full of Germanic pride, he marched to the desk, followed by two porters struggling under his matching bags and trunks (borrowed, for the time being, from some lady friend of Grady's). He smacked the teak desktop with the butt of his silver-headed cane.

"Manager!" he called.

The clerk, who had been a scant four feet away, stepped over. "Sir?" he said, eyeing the cane and surreptitiously checking the desktop for damage.

"You have rooms for me?" Otto asked, looking imperious and trying to remember his lines, and suddenly worrying that he'd got the wrong hotel.

The clerk lifted a brow. "And you would be . . . ?"

"Otto Obermyer, *dummkopf!*" He said it with a bit more command than he'd intended, and several people turned to look.

"Oh, yes!" the clerk replied hurriedly, and pivoted a large, open register. He picked up a pen, dipped it in the well, and handed it to Otto, indicating that he should sign. "Yes, sir!" he said. "Your secretary telephoned, and we certainly do have a reservation!"

Otto took the pen and inscribed "Otto Obermyer" on the first blank line. He started to write "San Francisco" in the space for the address, but caught himself after the first *S*, muttered, *"Scheisse!"* and scratched it out. He wrote "New York City" in its place, then handed the pen back with a flourish.

The clerk said, "We have a very fine suite for you, sir," and took a key off the wall rack. "On the third floor. You have a spectacular view of the bay." He handed Otto's key to a bellhop. "If you need anything, anything at all, just call room service."

Otto perked up his ears. "Telephones, you have? In the rooms?"

The desk clerk colored slightly. "Well, not real . . . That is to say, it's more an in-house system. But it's the very finest!"

Just then, he felt someone tap his shoulder. He turned toward it, momentarily afraid he'd been caught and was about to be tossed on the street. Or asked to fix the pipes. But it was only Quincy Applegate, briefcase in hand.

"Herr Obermyer?"

"Ja?" replied Otto, trying to remember if he was supposed to recognize him or not. In fact, he almost hadn't. Maggie didn't bring her beau home often, and he wasn't always invited upstairs. This was too confusing.

"I don't suppose you remember me, Herr Obermyer," Quincy began. "Thomas Halliday. From the firm? I have some papers here that demand your immediate—"

Otto waved a hand. "*Ja, ja.* We get to that in a minute. Come you *mit* me up the stairs, Halliday." Then he turned to the bellboy and waved his cane. "Well? What do you wait for? *'Raus!*"

There was an elevator, as Quincy could have told him. As they slowly rose to the third floor, he imagined that Otto was just itching to get his hands on the mechanism. Wouldn't the Majestic be surprised to find the guts of its lift strewn over the lobby!

The bags were brought in, and the bellmen were apprised that Herr Obermyer preferred to unpack his own luggage, thank you very much. They were tipped and dismissed, and the moment the door closed behind them, Otto rushed to fetch a small bag, which he carefully set on the floor. Kneeling beside it, he popped the catch.

"*Ach! Schnitzel!*" he exclaimed, and lifted out Ozzie, who blinked his blue eyes against the light and then stretched before strolling off to investigate.

"You brought the cat?" Quincy asked incredulously. Who would bring a cat to a, well, whatever this was!

"All alone I am supposed to leave him?" Otto replied, struggling up from the floor. He brushed off his knees, then looked up. "So. In the lobby. I do hinky-dinky?"

Quincy had to think for a minute. "Yes. Yes, I see. You did just fine." He dug a paper from his breast pocket and unfolded it. "Now," he said, consulting his list, "I've planted a small story in the papers. Müller and Dorfer over at American Pacific agreed to help, and so has Conklin at the First Union Bank, as well as Mr. and Mrs. Thatcher."

Otto shook his shaggy head. "Pretty fancy. You got lots of friends in tall places, Quincy."

Quincy just looked at him for a moment, and then said,

"Oh, I see. High places. Yes. Well, no. Maggie gave me her contact at the paper. She sent me to the Thatchers, too. They're going to say you've always stayed with them before when you had business in San Francisco, which removes your need for a house in town. I understand that Maggie saved Mr. Thatcher's bacon a few years back in some stock swindle, so they were delighted to help. They've put out the word that their daughter has the mumps. Naturally, you're staying at the Majestic. Rather tidy, I thought."

In fact, it was the only really tidy thing about the entire escapade. Maggie had put it together so fast it made his head spin, and he still wasn't sure on the details. He liked things slower. More reasonable. More *civilized*. But getting Sutter's niece away from that monster, Brother Ascension, was of paramount importance. As long as Maggie understood it, he supposed that was all that mattered.

The sound of a soft, rhythmic ripping came from behind them, in the bedroom, and Otto called, "Ozzie? *Liebchen?* Don't make *mit* the toenails on nothing expensive."

Quincy cringed. He'd be paying for the damages. Which reminded him of the money. He reached into his pocket and said, "Otto?" Then, "Otto, don't you even think about it!" when he found the old toy maker staring at the wall-mounted telephone.

"Was?" Otto turned his head back toward Quincy. "Oh, not to worry. Take it to pieces, I won't. I just use it to telephone for . . . What you call it? Room service." He looked entirely too eager to give it a try.

With a sigh, Quincy handed him a thick roll of bills, which Otto immediately began to count. "Don't get too extravagant," Quincy cautioned, feeling a little ill. He could hear the cat in the bedroom, shredding something new and undoubtedly very costly. He said, "Couldn't you fit him with, I don't know, mittens or something?"

Still counting the money, Otto called, "Ozzie!" and the

ripping sound stopped. He looked up. "Why you give me so much money?"

"For meals," Quincy said. "For tips. For . . . I don't know. Throw it around. Just try not to throw all of it, all right?"

"*Ja,*" Otto replied, a little too noncommittally for Quincy's taste, and pocketed the roll. "I try."

"You know what to say if anyone should telephone or come here?"

Otto nodded. "*Ja.* I don't got no granddaughter. I got a son named Hardy, but he runs off, long time ago, and I don't hear from him no more. I also say I got the bad heart and the liver disease, and I take pills." He patted his pockets and drew out two clear glass vials, one containing white pills, the other, blue. "White sugar pill for heart, blue sugar pill for liver.

"The Thatchers are my friends of the bosom," he went on, "because I get Mr. Thatcher started in business long time ago. I don't stay *mit dem* this time because their little girl who is called Florence, she has the mumps. This is not a good disease for an old man. I say I got holdings in Mr. Müller and Mr. Dorfer's railroad—"

"Which is?" Quincy butted in, staring at his paper and trying to keep up.

"The American Pacific," Otto said from beneath beetled eyebrows. "You gonna let me finish? Grady told me good, you know."

"Sorry," said Quincy. "Go on."

"I say I got holdings in the railroad, like I mention when you interrupt me. I say I got holdings in a lot of companies, ships and iron and ladies' garments and tin for to start, and I don't know how much money I got, but last counting was two million, about. Mr. Alfred Conklin, at the First Union Bank, does my accounting and has my will. You are Mr. Thomas Halliday, and you work for Müller and Dorfer in accounting department."

Quincy grinned. The old man had it down, all right.

"And who is your doctor in San Francisco?"

Otto threw up his hands. "*Ach!* Sorry, I forget. In San Francisco, *mein* doctor for the heart is Dr. Hedrick. He visits me every other day on account I got such a bad ticker. Who you gonna get for him, anyway? Dis whole thing make my head go dizzy."

You're not the only one, Quincy thought, but said, "Some friend of Grady's." He hoped the modicum of distaste he had for any friend of Grady's didn't show in his face. Not that he didn't like Grady—sort of—but some of his friends were a tad on the shady side. More than a tad, actually. Best to be leery, just on general principle. "He'll drop by later today," he added. "His name is . . ." He ran a finger down the paper. "Mr. Bedside Blevins."

Otto opened his mouth, but before he could speak, Quincy said, "That's all I know."

Otto settled broad hands on his knees. "So. What we do now?"

"Well," said Quincy, stuffing the paper back in his pocket and standing, "I'm going back to the office. And you? You wait. And stay away from the elevator, too."

Otto lifted a brow.

"Just . . . just don't take anything apart, all right?"

Otto looked slightly annoyed. "*Ja, ja,* Mr. Worrywart."

A quick flicker of movement beside the windows caught Quincy's eye, and he looked over, looked up. With an expression fast slipping into resignation, he added, "And Otto? Would you please remove that cat from the drapery?"

FOUR

➤━┿━◆━◉━◆━┿━◄

MAGGIE SAT WITH BROTHER JIM AND SISTERS
Polly, Edwina, and Trini at a small corner table.
The Conquistador Café was crowded tonight. Less
than a handful of people she assumed to be travelers, two
or three locals, and the Children of Golgotha. She counted
twenty-six altogether, although Brother Ascension hadn't
yet made an appearance. They never referred to themselves,
at least in public, as the Children of Golgotha—a good
idea, she thought. Brother Ascension must have a morbid
streak, naming his followers after the hill of the crucifixion.

Dinner conversation had been next to nil, and since their
party took up most of the available seating, there was a
macabre atmosphere to the café. Even the "outsiders," as
Brother Jim called them, spoke in whispers, and every once
in a while stole a gaze in their direction.

Well, Maggie thought, taking another forkful of salty
corned beef—they had all had corned beef hash—*I suppose
they do look bizarre. Like students of an overage parochial
school. Or a prison outing.*

Having too recently eaten the café's heavy-on-the-salt
cuisine, she picked at her food, moving it around on her
plate. Trini, she noticed, did the same. Twice, she saw the
girl sneak food into her napkin instead of her mouth. No
wonder she was so gaunt. Well, that would be Quin's problem—or Sutter's—once they got her out. Her problem was

preventing a murder, not putting a stop to slow suicide.

The others at the table didn't seem to notice what Trini was doing, though. Intent on their dinners, they ate like the condemned, focused entirely on their plates.

Sister Polly and Brother Jim finished scraping up the last morsels at about the same time, and Sister Edwina a moment later. Trini sat back from the table, rubbed her stomach, and smiled. Maggie followed suit, and Brother Jim said softly, "Sister Trini eats like a bird, but I'd think you'd be more hungry, Maggie."

She held her hand to her throat. "I'm full up to here, Jim," she said, grinning, then lowered her voice. "Reckon that stew stuck to my ribs!"

He smiled at her. That smile everybody wore was starting to become annoying. He said, "Next, we have prayer meeting. Would you like to join us, Maggie?"

She pursed her lips. Prayer meeting meant Brother Ascension would make an appearance, she hoped. She said, "I believe I'd like to. Is there a church round these parts?"

Sister Polly touched her shoulder lightly. "God isn't only in churches, dear Maggie. He's wherever His Holy Word is spoken."

"Oh," said Maggie. "Then where do you—"

"You folks done?" said a familiar voice. Grady!

She didn't look up while he snatched her plate away.

"Yes, thank you," said Jim, focusing just above her shoulder. Then he lowered his eyes to hers. "We'll have prayer back at the hotel."

Out of the corner of her eye, she saw Grady drop a crumpled bit of paper beside her chair. "That's fine with me, Jim," she said, and elbowed her fork off the table.

She dived to pick it up—and the paper, too—but Sister Polly beat her to it and laid the fork atop her own plate.

"Thank you, Polly," she said. Grady, now across the table loading Jim's plate and silverware on a tray, glared at her. She glanced down. The paper was still there.

All around her, chairs scraped back. The Children of

Golgotha were rising. They began to file toward the door. Jim rose, too. "Shall we?"

The others rose, and Maggie did, as well, then suddenly stooped, pulling loose her bootlace with one deft finger. At the same time, she scooped up the paper.

"Just a second," she said, carefully retying the lace while Sister Polly waited. She gave it a last tug, then walked out with Sister Polly, Grady's note burning a hole in her palm.

She had no time to read it, for they immediately trooped back up the street and across it, then climbed the stairs in silence, two abreast. To the back of the hall they went, and began to file into a room. Maggie whispered to Sister Polly, "I gotta use the outhouse!" but Polly only pressed a finger to her lips and shook her head sternly.

Suds! thought Maggie, who was itchy to get a gander at that note. She managed to slip it into her pocket as Sister Polly shepherded her through the door and inside.

The room was larger than the others she'd seen—a good thing, since en masse, the Children of Golgotha would never have been able to fit into a smaller one. As it was, they were packed like sardines into the furnitureless room. There was a light up front, but she couldn't see its source for all the bodies.

And then the Children of Golgotha began to sit down on the bare pine floor. She watched as they sat, seven or eight people at once, row by row, as if by military standards. When it was her row's turn, Sister Polly put a hand on her elbow and guided her down into place.

She could see now that the room did hold some furniture. At the front, a space the width of the room and perhaps five feet deep had been left clear, and at one side a kerosene lamp rested on a small, plain table. One wooden chair sat in the center of the clear space. The room also had two doors—the one she'd come in, and another, at the opposite end of the same wall, up toward the front.

One of the boys in the first row—she couldn't tell who he was—said, "Silent prayer."

Everyone bowed his or her head obediently, and Maggie followed suit, folding her hands the way Sister Polly did. *How long does this part last?* she wondered, flicking a gaze to the right, then the left, from the corners of her semi-lidded eyes. *Five minutes? Five hours?* Suddenly, she felt very sorry for anyone who really *did* have to use the outhouse.

The minutes plodded by. Her left foot had gone to sleep and her right one was threatening to do likewise when, at the head of the room, the same boy who had told them to pray said, "Amen." And then, after a pause of perhaps ten seconds, he said, "Rise for the coming of the new dawn."

Everyone said, "Amen," but nobody stood up.

"Rise for the rebirth into life everlasting of holy men."

"Amen," said the throng.

"Rise for Brother Ascension."

This time after an "Amen," the room rose as one person, and Maggie clambered to her feet along with them, eager to see just what this Brother Ascension—this stealer of children, this murderer for money who turned perfectly normal young people into windup toys—looked like. But she couldn't see a thing over all the blue-bonneted heads and blue-shirted shoulders in front of her. Shifting from foot to foot, trying to once again establish the flow of blood, she heard him—at least, she thought it was him—come into the room. She heard footsteps cross the floor, then stop.

"God bless," said a surprisingly pleasant voice. Brother Ascension's?

"God bless," answered the room, and everyone, Maggie included, sat down with a loud *thump*. Belatedly, she wondered if the floors were reinforced.

Brother Ascension sat at the front of the room, in the single chair. He wore a long hooded cloak, almost a monk's robe, really, except that it was light blue: the same sky shade as the boys' shirts and the girls' dresses. She couldn't make out his face, for it was hidden in the shadows of the hood.

"I bring you glad tidings," he began, and his voice was soothing, musical. Almost hypnotic. "Our brothers and sisters who have gone ahead have this day sent word that they have made a place for us."

Maggie's stomach lurched. They'd gone ahead? To where? Heaven? What was he going to do, talk them all into jumping off the roof?

"Sister Mae and Brother Michael send word that a modest lodging has been located in San Francisco," he said, and Maggie let her breath out. She hadn't realized she was holding it. "There are quarters connected," he continued, "which will make a splendid meeting hall. Brother Michael reports that jobs wait for most of the men on the docks, and the women have been found pleasant labor, as well. He that labors in the Lord is content."

Everyone said, "Amen."

Maggie was wondering just what sort of pleasant labor he had in mind for the members—scaling fish twelve hours a day, perhaps?—when he said, "I see we have a guest."

They all swiveled round to peer at Maggie. Sister Polly touched her arm and whispered, "Stand up, child."

Maggie rose clumsily, remembering to stay in character. She clasped her hands in front of her and timidly said, "Howdy, sir."

Brother Ascension shifted slightly. Now she could see his jaw, but little else. He said, "God bless you, my child. Have you a name?"

"Maggie," she said haltingly. All this jumping up and down was making her feel a little dizzy. "Maggie Obermyer."

"Margaret," said Brother Ascension, drawing the word out like a bale of silk fabric.

"Um, actually . . . well, it's for Magdalena, sir. The Maggie, I mean."

Several soft gasps rose from the floor, but she kept her

eyes on Brother Ascension's chin. He said, "Ah. Magdalena."

"It—it's from the Bible," she offered, in a stutter she hoped would be taken for nervousness.

Toward the front, a girl said softly, "Is it a sign, Brother?"

The room took up the word, echoing it like a muted buzz. All around her, she heard, "A sign! A sign!" and she flicked her eyes over the crowd, letting them widen as she did.

"Sir?" she said, giving every appearance of fright. She stepped back toward the wall and brought her clasped hands to her chest, cowering slightly.

Brother Ascension raised his hand, and the buzzing stopped. "All in the Lord's good time, Sister Ruth," he said to the first girl who'd spoken, and then he turned to Maggie. "Come here, my child," he said, holding his hand toward her.

Maggie looked to the left, then the right, and finally said, "M-me?"

"Yes, child," said Brother Ascension, and Maggie couldn't help thinking that he could have made a good living as a mesmerist. "Don't worry," he coaxed. "No harm will come to you."

Gingerly, Maggie picked her way over the crowd. She was dizzier than she'd thought, and stepped on a couple of hands before she reached the front of the room. He had risen to meet her, and when she looked up, she could see his face.

He looked, well, peaceful. Not like a murderer, not like a con artist, not like a man who'd spent time in Dannemora Prison. Of course, she reminded herself, the best con men never looked crooked.

He had fair hair, from what she could see of it, and was clean shaven with a strong, solid jaw and a slightly aquiline nose. But his eyes were the thing that really caught her attention. Ice-blue with an absolutely riveting stare, they

fairly sizzled out of his face. She found even she couldn't
look away, that gaze was so intense.

The thing was, she didn't feel the least bit threatened by
him, though she knew she should. Brother Ascension was
a dangerous man, but he put out nothing but kindness and
love in such a way that she could almost physically feel it.
His eyes drew her in deeper and deeper, bathed her with
generosity and an understanding so intensely warm and su-
pernatural that—

She dug fingernails into her palms as hard as she could.
The pain wrenched her out, like a frayed rope tugging a
drowning woman from the water just long enough to fill
her lungs for the last time. In that brief moment, she did
the only thing she could think of. She let her knees buckle,
and collapsed in a swoon.

She hit the floor reminding herself, behind lidded eyes,
to look upward. She did it just in time, for not a second
later she felt someone pull her lid open, then drop it again.

She heard Brother Ascension say, "Brother Jim and
Brother Clarence? Would you please take this poor sister
to my room? I'll wish to talk with her after we finish prayer
meeting."

Maggie felt herself lifted—rather clumsily, too—and
carried. She sensed, rather than felt, the doorway when they
passed through it. The clump of her bearers' boots on
wooden planks changed suddenly to a soft footfall on thick
rugs. She was laid upon a mattress—goose down?—her
skirt was tucked carefully round her ankles, and then she
heard them leave.

She waited a few moments after the door clicked closed,
just in case it was a trick and one of them had stayed inside
the room. To do what, she wasn't sure, but a girl couldn't
be too careful. But besides Brother Ascension's murmurs
coming through the closed door, there was silence.

She slit open one eye.

By the light of one lantern, turned down low, she saw
that she was in one of the smaller rooms, about the size

she was to share with five others. This one wasn't shared, though. There was only the one bed, beneath her.

She opened both eyes and sat up. The room was simple, with a minimum of furnishings. A bed, a chifforobe, a small bureau, a simple wooden chair. Where was all this splendor that Brother Ascension was supposed to live in?

She stood, weaving a little, and opened the chifforobe. More blue robes. Pants, shirts: all plain. The top drawer contained more clothing, the middle drawer extra Bibles and religious tracts, and the bottom drawer, bottles. Not whiskey bottles, but all sorts of unlabeled bottles of varying shapes and sizes.

That was odd, she thought as she staggered back to the bed and perched precariously on the edge. Was Brother Ascension ill?

She must have been a great deal more exhausted than she thought, for she nearly fell over. *Wake up, Maggie!* she thought, and pinched her forearms. It helped a little. Yes, she was certainly tired. The train and the stage had done her in. She was getting too old for this game. Either that, or Brother Ascension's eyes had lulled her closer to sleep than she'd thought.

But was he really all that bad? Trini Malone was starving herself, that was certain, but everybody else seemed so blasted happy to be here! Brother Ascension was a born mesmerist, and perhaps he had done a turn in prison, but couldn't it be that he was on the level this time? Just because somebody was a little cracked didn't mean that person was a criminal. And the death of Trini's mother could have been a tragic coincidence, plain and simple.

Brother Ascension was one scary son of a sea serpent— she'd grant Quincy that much—but it was the wrong kind of scary. And his eyes were so kind! As for his followers, they were a nice bunch. Well, a little too overregimented, but she supposed some parents would be happier to see their children with Brother Ascension than off throwing rocks through windows or sticking up the corner druggist.

She thought of all that setting up they'd done back in San Francisco. Well, that she'd had Grady and Quincy do. She thought about all the people she'd gotten involved, and groaned. She hoped Otto was making the most of the room service at the Majestic, because his days there were numbered.

She'd figure out how to separate Trini from the herd and then get her back to Quincy, but that was as far as she was going to take this thing. No flimflamming Brother Ascension, who had turned over a new leaf as a do-gooder. A crazy do-gooder, but a do-gooder, nonetheless.

She crooked her mouth to the side, *hmph*ing under her breath and thinking up nasty things to say to Quincy while she dug in her pocket for Grady's note. She found it, pressed it flat against her thigh, then held it closer to the lamp. It read:

Urgent we meet behind café. Ten p.m. G.

So much to go through for such a little message! *Urgent my foot!* she thought, crumpling the paper again. She had it halfway to her pocket when reflex took over; she popped it in her mouth. It wouldn't do at all if the Children of Golgotha went through her pockets and found it.

She was just swallowing the last of it—and sleepily wondering why on earth Grady had used so much paper when a third the size would have done—when she heard the door opening. There wasn't time to lie back on the pillows again, so she gripped the bedclothes on either side of her legs and assumed a cowed position. She'd started it, so she supposed she'd have to play it out, at least in front of Brother Ascension.

After all, she thought with a yawn, you never could tell about people, not really.

"Ah!" he said, closing the door behind him. "You're awake, my child." He pushed back his cowl to reveal a perfectly normal balding head. Smiling a perfectly harmless smile, he bent to the lamp. "Let's have a little more light, shall we, Magdalena? And do sit up," he added kindly. "We're here to help you, not hurt you."

FIVE

G RADY PACED BACK AND FORTH IN THE SHADOWS
behind the Conquistador Café, grumbling under his
breath. Ten-thirty, and she still hadn't arrived. It was
probably 10:35 by now, and the only sounds in the whole
of the town were muted piano banging and the occasional
shout or laugh from the saloons down the street. One street,
all in a straight line, that was Conquistador.

Again, the thought entered his head that he should go
and have a look for her. Maggie was always so punctual!
Well, sort of. Actually, come to think of it, not at all . . .

And, again, he reminded himself that he didn't have the
slightest idea what room she was in. He'd watched her go
into the hotel with the others, but that was as far as it went.
He wouldn't know where to start looking. He pictured himself going from room to room.

"Excuse me, madam, but have you seen a—"

Then she'd scream, and he'd be arrested and probably
hanged, for God's sake, and not even in decent clothes.

Perhaps Maggie *couldn't* come. Maybe there was some
sort of get-together or something. Maybe she'd fallen
asleep or into a trance or—God forbid—into a twitching
fit under the influence of—

"Psst! Grady!"

He spun around, and nearly bumped into her in the dark.

"It's about time," he growled. "And don't sneak up on me!"

"Stop it," she said. "I wasn't sneaking." Faintly, he saw her put her hand to her temple. "Can we go somewhere where there's a little light?"

He took her arm and led her to the end of the row, where they could at least see the glow cast into the street by Conquistador's saloons. "What's wrong?" he said as he sat her down on an upended crate. He pulled one out for himself, brushed it off, and sat down opposite her.

"I've got the most terrible headache, Grady," she said, and rubbed at her temples. "I feel sort of . . . odd. Must be that lousy café food. Too much salt or something. Can salt give you a headache?"

"I'm not surprised your head hurts," he said. "But it's not the salt. Your Brother Ascension poured enough dope in your dinners to stagger an ox."

She sat up straight, and he saw her cringe with the effort. She must really have a pounder if she was complaining about it. "Brother Ascension?" she said. "But he wasn't at supper."

"Of course not. I wouldn't have eaten that hash either if I'd stirred a pint of that stuff into it."

Maggie's eyes narrowed. "What sort of stuff?"

Grady shrugged. "Good question. He walked in the back door big as life, said hello to the cook like she was his favorite auntie, and asked where the food for his flock was. Once she showed him, he dumped the bottle in the hash."

"Right in front of everybody?" Maggie asked slowly. "Grady, what was *in* the bottle?"

"Well, I certainly don't know!" he sniffed. "I'm not a chemist, for God's sake! But it was a clear liquid, and it was in a brown glass druggist's bottle, unmarked. I asked the cook, and she said he brings it before every meal. Special vitamins, that's the story. Mrs. Miggins—that's the cook—seems quite taken with him. Said they thought he was a crackpot when he and the youngsters first pulled into town, but he's such a nice man, and quiet, too. That's a quote. He pours that stuff on every meal, breakfast, lunch, and dinner. By the way, I noticed he took his dinner out before he doctored the rest. Added a steak and eggs to it, too.''

Maggie appeared to mull this over, then lowered her head and began to rub the temples furiously. ''Gad!'' she said. ''I can't think!''

Grady helped her up. ''Come along,'' he said. ''You need coffee.''

She paused in her head-rubbing long enough to look up at him. ''And where, pray tell, are you going to get coffee this time of night? The café's closed, and I can't go into a saloon. Somebody'd see me.''

''And report to Brother Ascension,'' he said, pulling her along. ''Don't worry, Mags. I left the back door to the café unlocked.''

By the time an hour had passed, Maggie had downed nearly a pot and a half of black coffee in the kitchen of the Conquistador Café and made three trips to the two-seater out back. In between, she'd told Grady the story of her afternoon and evening with the Children of Golgotha. She was feeling more herself now. Even the headache, while still present, had faded from a thudding pain to a faint, needling sensation. Just enough to be annoying.

''Good galloping gravy!'' she said, pouring herself another cup of coffee. ''It's a good thing I didn't eat much dinner. I'd have been roped, tied, and singing 'Alleluia' while they threw me in the river.''

''Not to mention the fact that you would have been draped in blue,'' said Grady dryly. ''Personally, I think green's more your color. You want eggs? Some food'll make your head feel better.''

Maggie looked up. ''I could eat. What time is it?''

''Close to midnight,'' he replied, peering at his pocket watch. He peeked into the guts of the stove, then closed it.

"Well, they banked the coals. Settle for a sandwich?"

"I guess." She stared at Grady's back while he searched through the café's large cold box. Once again, he'd pulled her beads out of the grinder. If it hadn't been for him, she would have risen in the morning, sat down to breakfast, and spent the rest of her (probably short) life smiling beatifically and handing out leaflets.

She rubbed her arms to put down a sudden rebellion of gooseflesh, just as Grady slid her plate across the gingham tablecloth. "Thanks," she said, and she meant it for more than just the cheese and lettuce sandwich.

Grady seemed to understand. As she took an enormous bite, he gave her a smile and sat down across the table from her. "No charge. I'm not allowed to take money." He began to polish his glasses. "So how'd you manage to get out here alone?"

Maggie nodded and held up one hand until she'd swallowed. "I just pretended to pass out again. Trust me, it wasn't that hard. I tell you, that man's eyes . . ." She shuddered again. "I thought Brother Ascension would just call someone and have them haul me out. But no. First, he went through my pockets."

She took another bite, and around it said, "He found the stuff on Otto. The phony clipping, I mean. The one I had Sam, down at the print shop, do up special to look like it was a couple of decades old." Grady cocked a brow, and she swallowed, saying, "I must've done it on my way out of town. Sorry. Brain's still a little fuzzy."

She took a sip of coffee. "That was in the same little packet with my phony birth certificate and the picture of your parents—"

"I still don't know why we had to use *my* parents," Grady interrupted.

"Because the picture was handy," Maggie replied. "Because they had it taken in front of one of those cheap backdrops that traveling photographers used to haul all over the countryside."

By the annoyed look on Grady's face, she could tell she shouldn't have said "cheap," but she was too exhausted to make reparations. "Don't worry," she said, hurtling ahead. "I wrote 'Hardy and Francine Obermyer' on the back in pencil. It'll erase. Anyway, he went through my pockets and then he carried me over to Sister Polly's room. And then he carried out my carpetbag. He brought it back about a half hour later and then I snuck out." She picked up the sandwich again. "Good thing I took my knives out. Let me tell you, it's not easy to pretend you're asleep when you're really *wishing* you were sleeping but you can't. Oh, never mind. My palms will never be the same."

She looked at the one that wasn't full of sandwich. It was black and blue, with tiny crescent-shaped cuts from earlier, when she'd had to feign passing out. She turned it toward Grady, who remained silently grumpy.

Well, she'd try changing the subject. "What do you do here, anyway?"

"You don't really want to know, do you?" he said, leaning back. His glasses were on his nose again.

She studied him for a moment. Actually, she didn't really want to know, but he looked like he'd burst if he couldn't lodge his complaint—probably a whole chain of them—so she said, "Yes, I do."

He folded his hands over his chest and the ratty shirt that covered it, and assumed a long-suffering expression. "I wash dishes. Thousands of them. I bus tables and scrape plates, and then I wash *them*. Not just once, mind you, but over and over and over. I have washed three thousand, four hundred and thirty-seven dirty plates, cups, saucers, glasses, soup bowls, tureens, frying pans, saucepans, roasting pans, pans that I have no idea what they were used for except that they were filthy, ladles and pitchers and pieces of flatware since I landed in this culinary establishment—if you can call it that—this afternoon. By this time tomorrow, I won't have any fingernails at all! And when all the plates were washed, I mopped the floors, wiped down the counters, took the trash out back, and—I'm certain you'll be delighted to know—cleaned the goddamned spittoons.''

He paused for effect, and he looked so melodramatic that Maggie had to bite the inside of her cheek to keep from laughing. ''All this,'' he continued, ''for the princely sum of exactly one dollar a day, of which I will only receive eight cents for this day's work because I had a little accident with a stack of dishes.''

His hand had gone to the tabletop, and his fingers drummed in annoyance. ''I have to open the place at six in the morning. And I sleep there.'' He pointed to a pallet on the floor between crates marked Gibson's Blue Ribbon Flour and Mother's Canned Lard. ''I am also the night watchman.''

''My goodness,'' said Maggie, doing her very best to swallow a laugh. ''Grady, I think you're underpaid. But you don't have to worry about your fingernails vanishing.''

''They're being eaten away, Mags! Lye soap!'' He leaned forward and waved red, peeling fingers under her nose. ''It's criminal, I tell you.''

For a moment she felt, well, awful. Grady had such wonderful hands: the nimble, long-fingered, graceful hands of a pickpocket. Ex-pickpocket, anyway. He always took such good care of them. And so she took an extra measure of satisfaction in saying, ''Well, you can stop doing it this minute. I heard Sister Polly talking to one of the others. They—I mean, we—are leaving tomorrow.''

He said, ''I'll have to think about it. I'll lose my eight cents, you realize.'' And then he snorted. ''Just how are they going to leave? On whose six stagecoaches?''

Her mouth was full of cheese sandwich again, but she managed, ''They've got a lot of people. They must have wagons of their own.''

''Maybe,'' said Grady. ''But what I want to know is how you intend to keep from starving to death. They'll be watching you, you know. I won't be able to get any decent food to you if you leave town. Where are they going, by the way? I doubt there's any place worse than this. And you haven't said a word about Trini.''

Maggie swallowed. A cheese sandwich had never tasted so good. If only he'd quit interrupting her! She said, ''San Francisco.''

Grady's brow wrinkled. ''Is that good or bad?''

Maggie stopped the sandwich halfway to her mouth. ''I don't know. Trini's fine, at least for the time being. And I don't think they'll be watching all that closely. I don't think any of Brother Ascension's followers know he's keeping them doped. Nobody watched us at dinner, anyway. And Trini's starving herself. She didn't touch her meal.'' She paused a moment. ''Are the baked goods safe? I mean, you say this concoction is a liquid . . .''

Grady nodded. ''Eat bread to your heart's content. I hadn't thought of that.''

Maggie took a gulp of coffee, draining the cup. ''Good. Whatever it is, people must get used to it. Jim and Polly and the others practically ate the pattern off their plates, and it didn't have any discernible effect. Other than that they're so blasted *nice,* I mean. But I ate just a little, and it knocked me for a loop.''

''Probably loses the brunt of its blast after a time,'' Grady said, nodding. ''Although it must have some effect. Otherwise, why keep feeding it to them?''

Maggie concurred.

''And how in blue blazes is he getting it? Conquistador's a small town, and—''

''The bottles,'' Maggie cut in. ''He's got a drawer full of druggist's bottles. Sorry,'' she said with a shrug. ''Just remembered. The thing I can't figure,'' she went on, ''is whether our little Trini's purposely trying to kill herself, or if she's taken fasting for Jesus to new heights. Or whether she caught on to them somehow, and she's attempting to sober up and get away. But if it's the latter, then why in the world did she come back?''

Grady shook his head, then stood up and got the coffee.

Pouring her a fresh cup, he said, "I haven't a clue. But then, that's your department, isn't it?"

"Grady?" she said. "I'm sorry about your hands."

He put the pot on the table, sat down, and looked at his fingers. Then, smiling just a little, he slumped back in his chair. "That's right. Throw the dog a bone."

She started to protest that she was doing no such thing, but he stopped her before she got a word out.

"Oh, go on, Mags," he said. "They'll heal. Now, finish your sandwich."

Nimbly feeling her way, Maggie shimmied up the corner porch post, then hauled herself up, onto the overhang's roof. She made her way quietly to her window, peeked over the sill to make certain all the women were sleeping soundly, then slipped over the sill. An instant later, she had silently pulled off her dress, and wearing her underwear, she slid between the covers of the corner bed, next to Trini.

It was fixed. Grady was to wire Quincy in the morning and alert the crew that they were coming. She'd thought that only Brother Ascension would make the trip—he, or possibly one of his henchmen, if he trusted anybody that much—but now they'd have the whole batch of them in town. She hoped they were up to it. And she hoped there'd be bread with breakfast tomorrow, since it was the only thing she could eat without fear of turning into the village idiot again.

Trini rolled toward her, and instantly Maggie closed her eyes and pretended to be sleeping.

"Where did you go?"

Maggie opened her eyes to find Trini staring at her. Maggie, speaking as quietly as Trini had, said, "You're having a dream."

But Trini wasn't the mouse she'd seemed earlier. Those enormous green eyes narrowed, and she repeated, "Where were you?"

"Outside," whispered Maggie. "Having a smoke, Miss Nosy Parker."

Trini's mouth tightened. "Leave," she whispered. "Leave tomorrow, and stay away." And then she turned away, unresponsive to Maggie's hand on her arm.

"Trini! What do you mean?"

SIX

>──┼──◇──◎──◇──┼──<

S HE HADN'T EXPECTED TO WALK. AFTER A BREAKFAST
of fried potatoes and pancakes and toast—of which
she could only eat the toast, since she knew the pan-
cake batter was easily doctored, and the Lord only knew
what was mixed with that grease the potatoes were swimming in—all of the Children of Golgotha had started north,
toward San Francisco.

It wasn't that it was so far. There was only a distance of
ten miles from Conquistador to San Francisco's city limits,
and she supposed that she could have walked it, if pressed,
in three or four hours. That would have put her in the city
before noon.

Except that Brother Ascension had a wagon heaped with
supplies and pulled by the slowest horses west of the Mississippi. Except that the Children of Golgotha walked even
slower than those horses did, and the wagon kept having
to rein in and wait for stragglers. Except that her boots hurt
and it was hot and her clothes were dirty and sticking to
her, and she was sure she was going to end up with a rash
and blisters.

To top it off, they stopped for lunch in the exact middle
of nowhere, and the only offered sustenance was a kettle
of cold beans, brought from the café in Conquistador.

Maggie filled her growling stomach with water, then
dumped her plate behind a rock.

They finally straggled past the city limits at about three o'clock, with Trini and several of the other weaker members riding the wagon with the supplies. Maggie, who was supposed to be unaccustomed to whatever it was that Brother Ascension dumped in their food, had pretended to faint before mid-morning. She'd been in and out of that blasted wagon all day.

It was dark by the time they finally reached their goal, and Maggie was worried. She hadn't expected to see Grady following them: he'd have taken a stage later in the morning. But she had rather expected to catch a glimpse of Quincy.

Somehow, she'd rather hoped that Quincy would magically find her, and that she'd spy his friendly face peeking at her from a crowd or a storefront. Oh, well. Tomorrow she'd have to manage to send a message to his office, or perhaps Otto's hotel, and let them know where she was. That was, if she was allowed to stay with the Brother's flock.

She suspected she would be, for all day long, during the times she was given permission to ride in the wagon and squatted in its bed behind Brother Ascension's back, one or another of the sisters had read to her from the Bible. And then they'd given out with a discourse on what that chapter or verse had *really* meant. They were giving instruction and edification to a lost soul, she supposed, but if she'd been free to, she would have given them an argument as to their interpretation.

She hadn't heard a peep out of Brother Ascension. He rode alone on the wagon seat, exchanging a brief word now and then with one of the boys, but that was all. About halfway through the morning, she had started calling him— to herself, of course—Brother Pompous Ass.

Where they had finally come to a halt was on the outskirts of the Barbary Coast district. Odd, she thought, that he should pick a place on the Coast, but then, what better place to choose if you were going to have someone killed, and have it appear accidental? In a section of town where there were plenty of people who'd knife a body for drink money, nobody was shocked by—or really interested in—murder, least of all the police.

Several times since they had entered town, she'd given thought to simply grabbing Trini. They could walk off into the crowd, and nobody'd be the wiser. Unless Trini yelled. Of course, she could always knock the girl cold and drag her off, but some bystander was bound to complain. And once they came into the Barbary Coast, some smart boy was bound to yank them into an alley and try to roll them.

Not that Maggie couldn't take care of herself. She could, and very well indeed. But she had Trini to think of, too, and so she trudged along obediently.

The Seawitch Hotel looked as if it had been in dire need of painting for at least ten years. Dressed simply, like the boys, Brother Ascension pushed open the flaking front doors and ushered them into a tiny lobby decorated with a crooked and aging print of a sailing ship and a wall clock.

A nondescript young man, in the uniform of the Children of Golgotha, greeted Brother Ascension as they crowded in. The two spoke for a moment in whispers, and then the boy turned toward the waiting Children.

"God bless," he intoned, smiling benignly.

They all answered him in kind—Maggie, too, mouthed a "God bless"—and then they followed him up the complaining stairs. Brother Ascension remained in the lobby.

Maggie was assigned to a room at the back with five other girls, including Sister Polly, who'd been her shepherd—or her watchdog—for the day. She'd lost track of Trini. She'd been unable to speak with her all day. The one time she'd managed to catch Trini by herself, when they stopped for lunch, the girl had turned her back without expression and walked away, toward the crowd.

"When's supper?" she asked Sister Polly, who was unpacking a simple bedroll. All the Children carried them.

"Very soon, God willing," Polly replied. There was that

smile again. "Are you staying with us, Magdalena? Now that we've reached San Francisco, I mean. I thought you were wanting to find your grandfather."

For a bunch of people who hardly spoke a word, news certainly traveled fast. She supposed Jim would have told Brother Pompous Ass—no, she had to start calling him Brother Ascension again, or she'd slip, sure as shooting. Well, Jim would have told Brother Ascension her story for certain, but she was fairly surprised that Polly knew it. And if Polly knew, everyone probably did.

"Yes," she said, and moved over for another girl, who was trying to get to the window. "I reckon I do. But I kinda wanted to stay with you folks a bit. I mean, you're all so smart and everything. I never had anybody explain it to me like you folks."

That was certainly true. She'd never in her life heard anybody put Christ into six different books of the Old Testament eight times in one day.

"That Jesus, he sure got around," she added admiringly.

It surprised her when Polly suddenly hugged her, but she recovered in time to beam at her.

Softly, Polly said, "He has many names, Magdalena. He is with us always. He is the before and the after, the now and the eternal."

Maggie said, "Sister Polly, I like hearing you talk. You're real kind, to just pick me up off the streets, a total stranger and lookin' like something the cat dragged in, and lettin' me listen." She stopped to feign a yawn, then continued, "I'd admire to stay on a bit, if you'd let me. I want to hear more. And after all, I might not find my grandpa right off the bat."

Polly smiled contentedly, and one of the other girls clasped her hands before her and softly said, "Praise be. Welcome, Sister Magdalena."

But Polly turned and, the slightest hint of a stern quality creeping into her voice, said, "Sister Rebecca, we must speak with Brother first."

Rebecca, a frail thing with mousy brown hair, flinched almost imperceptibly. But Maggie saw. It was as if she'd been struck. Then the girl smiled and said, "Of course, Sister Polly. Of course we must consult Brother first."

"Magdalena?" said a male voice from the open doorway. It was Brother Clarence. He was smiling. He said, "Brother Ascension wishes to see you."

Grady sat across the street from the Seawitch on a flour barrel, mopping his neck and watching for Maggie.

He'd had a wretched day.

First, the stage driver must've told them in the office not to let him on or sell him a ticket, because the agent booted him out before he could say a word. Who'd think a man would get so riled up—and hold a grudge!—over a harmless little game of three-card monte?

He could have rented or even bought a horse, but seeing as how he'd almost rather eat one than ride it, he'd managed, two hours after Maggie left, to finagle a ride with a teamster hauling grain. But the teamster had turned off the main thoroughfare about five miles outside of town, which left Grady stranded in the middle of the road.

After a good ten minutes of feeling sorry for himself (and being passed by two other wagons and another stagecoach), he came to the sorry conclusion that the only way he was going to get where he was headed was to put one foot in front of the other. So he'd followed the tracks of Maggie's mob. It had been astoundingly easy—nothing to this tracking business at all!—up until they reached the town limits. And then it had been, "Have you seen a gang of people, all in blue?" so many times that he was hoarse.

At least, he thought, readjusting his seat on the flour keg, *the Children of Golgotha have the courtesy to stick out like twenty-five or thirty sore thumbs. . . .*

The flour keg upon which he took his ease was out front of Best Dry Goods, right across the street from the Seawitch, and Grady cast an occasional dirty look over his shoul-

der. This was for the proprietor, who could not spell to
save his life, but who nonetheless (and with squeaking
chalk that set Grady's teeth on edge), kept correcting the
next day's specials. So far, the chalkboard listed the "milld
flowr—fancie grade," "kideny beens," and "gud flake
sope."

The proprietor caught him looking and said, "Hey, you!
How d'you spell raisins?"

"R-a-i-s-i-n-s," replied Grady matter-of-factly.

The proprietor shook his head. "Aw, you can't spell fer
shit, neither," and carefully printed out "Razens."

"Perfect," Grady said dryly as he turned back toward
the Seawitch. They'd lit the gaslights by that time. His eyes
flicked over the second-story windows again. Lights had
been lit and he could see young men and women dressed
in blue passing back and forth in the glow behind the glass,
but no Maggie.

He felt the hint of a finger sliding deftly into his back
pocket and, quick as a snake, reached behind to catch it. It
was such a reflex action that he barely realized what he was
doing until he'd yanked the fellow around the barrel and
into the lantern light.

He sighed. "Better polish up the act, Stanley," he said
wearily. "I don't even *have* a wallet."

Stanley "Bedside" Blevins, his pudgy features gone
from horror to surprise to bored indifference within the
space of perhaps a half second, shook his arm free indignantly. In a voice dripping with not-quite-authentic Britan-
nia, he said, "Grady, old chum, no one outside of you and
Louse-head Louie would have felt that in a million years."
He straightened his sleeve and gave a little twist to the cuff.
The silver cuff links twinkled. "Where *do* you buy your
clothes? You look dreadful. Didn't recognize you at all.
And I thought you were someplace down south."

"Was," replied Grady. "And now I'm not." He checked
over his shoulder and found the proprietor of Best Dry

Goods just going inside, the bell jingling. The "Closed" sign flipped over. The shade was pulled.

Hopping off the barrel, Grady ran his fingers quickly along the chalkboard's tray and found what he was looking for.

Blevins arched a brow.

"Half a second," Grady said, and walked across the street on feet that hurt more than he remembered. On the sidewalk out front of the Seawitch, he picked a thick post opposite the front door. Pressing firmly on the chalk, he drew a heart with an arrow through it, and then inside, wrote "M. M. + G. M." That ought to let her know he'd found her.

Of course, he couldn't be certain she'd see it, or that somebody wouldn't scrub it off before she had a chance to. Although, looking at the dingy hotel with its peeling paint and filthy windows, he doubted that would be the case.

Well, he thought, going back across the street, *I'll come back in the morning.* He hoped she could find something safe for dinner. Personally, he was going to eat an entire steer. He stepped up on the sidewalk, tossed the chalk into the tray, and to Blevins, said, "Walk with me."

The two men began to move out of the district, walking from one gaslit pool of light to the next. Grady said, "You've been to the hotel?"

"Hotel?" Blevins said, his angelic baby blues on a ripe mark up ahead.

Grady ground his teeth. Bedside Blevins was a keen man on the con, but he was a sucker for an easy purse. And too often, those easy purses turned out to belong to members of local law enforcement. Blevins might not look like it, but he'd only been released from prison three weeks ago.

Grady said, "Pay attention, Stanley." He was envying the man his suit: dark blue with a pin stripe, and exquisitely tailored. They surely didn't give him that when he walked out of jail. And he was always so bleeding jovial! He looked like a Santa Claus, if Santa had been a prosperous young businessman about town. Minus the beard, of course. "The Majestic," Grady said, remembering himself. "Have you been to see Otto yet?"

"Yes," Blevins said, "I have." He doffed his hat to the mark as they walked past, then hissed, "You're not paying me enough to pass up these golden opportunities, old boy."

Grady stopped and Blevins stopped with him. "Oh. And I suppose *I* looked like a golden opportunity?" Grady ran a hand over his patched shirt and underneath one saggy suspender. He gave it a twang, and instead of thudding back against his chest, it drooped down further. "Honestly, Stanley. You won't be any good to us at all if you're in jail. If you've got any wallets on you, dump them now. And don't go pinching any more!"

Blevins had the gall to look offended. "My dear boy! What do you take me for?"

Grady sighed. "Just dump them."

Blevins stared back at him for a moment, a study in wounded innocence. Stanley could have gone on the stage, he was that good. And then he reached into his breast pocket and fanned out three wallets.

"Oh, all right," he said. "Just trying to keep my hand in." With a flick of his wrist, he tossed them toward the mouth of an alley. A stray mongrel grabbed one immediately and trotted off with it. "Greedy bastard," muttered Blevins. Then he shouted after the dog, "There's nothing in it!"

"Thank you," said Grady. He started walking again; Blevins, silver watch chain glinting, beside him. "Otto doing all right?"

"He'll be fine. Don't know as I can say the same for your fancy boy. What's his name?"

"Quincy App—No, Halliday. Thomas Halliday. That's what he's using."

They had walked their way to a main thoroughfare, and Grady was certain that when he got home—if he ever got home—he'd take off his shoes and find there was nothing left of his feet but two shapeless masses of bloody pulp. The two men came to a halt beneath a gaslight, and Grady flagged down a cab.

While the driver pulled his horse to the curb, Grady said, "We may have a bit of a problem, Stanley. He's brought the lot of them to town. They're putting up at the Seawitch."

"Wondered why your backside was parked across the street," Blevins said good-naturedly, and reached across Grady to open the cab's door. "And?"

Grady shrugged. "It may be nothing. I just thought you should know, that's all. I might have to call for reinforcements. Johnny Fargo in town?"

Blevins screwed his chubby, angelic features into a scowl. "On the up side of three-to-five for battery, poor sod."

"How about Tommy Two-Tone? Or Boston Pete?"

"Pete's in pocket," Blevins said, as Grady climbed gratefully into the cab. "Don't know about Tommy. I'll ask around." He closed the door.

Grady leaned out the window. "All right. You know where you can find me. And, Stanley? Stay out of trouble for just a little while." To the driver, he stuck his thumb over his shoulder and said, "Back up the hill a few blocks, I'm afraid."

As the cab slowly negotiated the thinning evening traffic for the U-turn, Blevins called to him from the sidewalk. "Take a bath, Maguire. You need one. And by the way, I believe I planted a wee seed in the harridan's ear the other night."

Grady, hanging out the window, yelled, "What? Whose ear?"

Blevins didn't answer. Instead, he held up a coin purse. A coin purse that looked a little too familiar.

Groaning, Grady slapped his pockets, and found one in particular a little too flat. He leaned out the window again and shook his fist down the hill at Blevins, who laughed and shouted, "Admit it, Grady—I've still got the touch!"

Not more than forty-five minutes later, Grady was freshly bathed and sitting at his desk in his dressing gown. His feet were in a bucket of cold water, a freshly poured tumbler of bourbon was at his elbow, his supper was sending enticing smells from the kitchen, and he was still annoyed with Bedside Blevins.

"Lift *my* purse, will he!" he mumbled to himself, drumming his fingers on the desktop. It was spotless, once he flicked off a few motes of dust. Maggie's looked as if it had played host to a very tiny, localized earthquake.

He supposed he should phone up Otto and Quincy, to check in and bring them up to date. And to make sure Otto had the cat, who hadn't so much as poked his nose out. A glance at the clock told Grady that he had exactly twelve minutes until his dinner was ready to come off the stove. Enough time, he supposed.

He lifted the telephone's earpiece. "Good evening," he said, once the operator came on line. "Could you be so kind as to ring the Majestic Hotel for me, please?"

While the connection was made, he grinned. That Stanley. Thought he'd got away with something, didn't he? Well, he'd discovered by this time that there was nothing in that purse but a few coins. Grady's smirk turned into a chuckle. The real wallet—his "just in case of an emergency" money—had been down the top of his boot.

"Majestic Hotel," came a tinny voice, at last, through the earpiece. "How may we be of service?"

Grady felt the prickle of a thrill. It never ceased to amaze him, this telephone. He said, "Yes, hello! Could you be so kind as to connect me with Mr. Otto Obermyer's suite, please?"

SEVEN

> ❦

BROTHER CLARENCE HAD COME FOR HER. SHE'D AL-
ready determined that he and Sister Mae and Brother
Michael—the two scouts Brother Ascension had sent
ahead to San Francisco—seemed to be the only people in
"uniform" who weren't flying on Brother Ascension's
happy juice. Clarence never took meals with them, and Michael and Mae had to be trusted enough to travel apart from
the group. Of course, they could smile as blankly as the
rest of the Children of Golgotha. But sometimes, when they
thought no one was looking . . .

Brother Ascension's magic elixir was just like her papa's
old Indian Remedy with a few added ingredients, she supposed. Like laudanum. Or something worse. Maybe a mixture.

But she was more concerned with the fact that Clarence
and the other three weren't smashed on it. Well, she had
her doubts about Sister Polly. Unlike the other three, Polly
ate heartily of the drugged foods at every meal, but they
didn't seem to affect her as they did the other Children.
Maggie wondered if a body could develop an immunity to
them over time.

So Brother Ascension had at least four sober followers.
Probably someone to do his dirty work: throwing people
out of windows, for instance.

She peeked through doorways as she followed Clarence

down the long hall. No Trini. No Trini. Again, no Trini. She must be somewhere in one of the rooms toward the front.

"Here we are, Magdalena," Clarence said, opening the door for her. He was one big grin. He was also tallish, perhaps six feet or a little better, brown-haired and muscular, with a small white scar through his right eyebrow that gave him a dashing look, like a German who'd fought too many duels. Fairly good-looking, too, although she'd long since learned that looks could be deceiving. Actually, he made her skin crawl. Something about his voice.

But she smiled at him, aping that benign expression she'd seen too many times in the last thirty hours. She said, "Thanks, Brother Clarence," and walked past him into a small, simple room dimly illuminated by candles.

Brother Ascension came to his feet as she entered. He was no longer attired in the simple blue shirt and trousers he'd worn all day, but had changed into the cowled robe again, and Maggie thought, *He's got his working togs out. Better be on your toes, old girl.*

Brother Clarence pulled a wooden chair from somewhere in the shadows and set it at the foot of the bed. Then he stepped back against the wall and folded his arms.

"Sit down, Magdalena," intoned Brother Ascension, and his voice was positively drenched with the milk of human kindness.

"Yes, sir," said Maggie, and perched on the wooden seat. Her palms were already scabbed and sore from last night's near fiasco. They'd do the trick for her again if he flashed those blue eyes and started sinking her into a trance. But then, she hadn't eaten his doped food all day. Just a piece of toast at breakfast, and that was it.

Her stomach, which had gone past growling to complaining to full-fledged hurt, would distract her if nothing else did. And, she supposed, he was accustomed to victimizing much weaker prey. She doubted he felt he had to try too hard.

Brother Ascension laid a hand briefly on her head, then sat down opposite her, on the bed. Their knees almost touched. He cupped his with his palms and leaned forward.

"Do you prefer Maggie or Magdalena?" he asked.

It took her by surprise. She said, "Doesn't matter. I'll answer to either of 'em, sir. I . . . I sorta like the way everybody says Magdalena, though." She looked at her lap, feigning shyness.

Again, he touched her, and this time his hand settled on hers, just briefly. His hands were so big! And they didn't look to have done much manual labor, either, she thought, bringing herself up from an increasingly relaxed state. Mesmo the Magnificent, her father's mesmerist, had told her about "stroking" long ago. Something about touches in certain places that dropped a person's guard, sort of like gentling a pony or trancing a chicken. She, herself, used to go round the carnival, putting all the chickens and ducks to sleep, much to her father's chagrin.

Tricky bastard, this Brother Ascension.

He said, "Then Magdalena it shall be." The words flowed out of him like warm taffy. "Do you like it here with us, child?"

Still looking at her lap, she nodded and said, "Yes, sir. I admire it."

"But you wish to find your grandfather, too. Isn't that true?"

Again, she nodded.

"Magdalena," he said, his words wafting over her like a summer breeze, "I can help you find your grandfather. I can help you reconcile with him. Would you like that, my dear?"

She looked up quizzically, as if she didn't understand. "Sir?"

"I can help you patch things up with him, if they need patching. Mend your fences. Would you like that?"

Her eyes grew wide. "Yes!" It came out as an excited whisper filled of hope.

Brother Ascension smiled, and there was a faintly predatory air about it. She supposed that she wouldn't have
noticed at all if she'd had his Baked Bean Surprise at lunch.
He patted her hand again, this time letting his fingers linger
a little longer.

"I—I just want him to know about me," she offered
shyly, looking into his eyes. Good gravy, but they were
blue! *Quick, think about something awful!*

She whispered, "I think, that is, I think kin . . . relatives
. . . should . . ."

"That's right, child," said Brother Ascension softly, at
the same time reaching out to touch her hair, her shoulder.
Comforting touches, light touches. Quietly, he continued,
"Did the sisters give you Bible instruction today, Magdalena?" He stroked her arm.

"Yessir," she breathed. *That's right, Maggie, just stare
into his eyes and think about dead, smelly things.*

"Dear Sister Polly tells me that you might like to stay
with us." He picked up her hand and slowly, rhythmically,
began to stroke her wrist.

Her eyes fluttered once, twice. "Y-yes." *Dead chip-
munks. Giant ones. With maggots. And how the Sam Hill
does he know what I told Polly five minutes ago?*

"You're welcome to stay, you know." Now he was
stroking her hand. "It's been a long day. A very, very long
day."

You slimy sack of ripe road apples, she thought. Her
head lolled, and she moved her mouth to say yes again, but
nothing came out.

"Sleep now, Magdalena. It's all right. You can go to
sleep now."

With that, Maggie closed her eyes the rest of the way
and let her head roll down until her chin rested on her chest.

"That's right, Magdalena. Sleep. Rest." Brother Ascension carefully put her hand back in her lap. "If you can
hear me, child, say yes."

She just managed it.

"That's very good. Now, I want you to rest until I come back." His tone became a little more demanding. "You won't eavesdrop on my conversation, will you, Magdalena?"

"N . . . n . . ." she whispered with great effort.

"Excellent. Now deeper."

She slumped forward slightly.

"Deeper, Magdalena."

She overdid the slumping and began to topple from the chair, but hands caught her and lifted her and moved her to the bed.

"She's a good subject," began Brother Clarence's voice.

"Wait," said Brother Ascension, somewhere at the foot of the bed. And then he spoke again, this time next to her ear. "You feel nothing, Magdalena. No pain, no discomfort, no pleasure. You feel nothing."

She felt her dress being pulled up, and then fire in her calf. It was all she could do not to flinch, to cry out, to sit up and fling the son of a bitch through the wall. But she didn't. She just lay there like a corpse and pictured those chipmunk maggots having their way with Brother Ascension.

Fortunately, it didn't last more than a second. Suddenly the fire was gone—what had the bastard used, anyway? A darning needle?

"She's out," said Brother Ascension, although she noticed he didn't have the common decency to flip her skirt back down. And then she heard Grady's voice in her head, asking her why on earth she'd think that a murderer would have any decency, common or not.

"Nice legs under those clodhoppers and rags," said Clarence. "I'd like to see her dressed up. Maybe we could have a little party."

Fine, thought Maggie, still limp as a rag, her leg throbbing. *You be the donkeys, and I'll pin new tails to you. With a railroad spike.*

"Later, Clarence." Someone sat down on the bed, and

when next he spoke, Maggie knew it was Brother Ascension. "We have to work fast, considering what you've told me."

What? thought Maggie. *What have you told him, Clarence? We just got here. How could you have had time to tell him anything?*

"Well," said Clarence, "all I know is the old kraut-eater's plannin' on leaving town in three days." He scraped the chair back and sat down with a small thud. "He's got a bum ticker. Pills all over the joint."

"I must say," said Brother Ascension, "Michael worked remarkably fast this time."

Maggie thought, *Atta boy, Sweeney!* She was surprised that the story he'd planted for her had made the paper so soon. Brother Michael had apparently already visited the hotel and told Clarence all about it.

Then Brother Ascension stood up, jouncing the mattress slightly. "All right," he said. "I'm going to work on her. Send Polly in."

She was wondering just what Sister Polly was going to do when she heard the chair being moved again, then Brother Ascension's voice, very near.

"Magdalena? Now I want you to listen. Listen very closely. I am going to tell you secrets, secrets about our Lord known only to a very few over the centuries. And secrets about yourself, secrets even you don't know. Don't try to speak. Just nod if you hear me."

Her eyes still closed, she nodded once, more than anything wishing that she could rub her leg. Or pull down her skirt. The man was a sadist, not to mention a Peeping Tom!

"These are secrets just for you, Magdalena," he continued. Maggie heard the door open and close. Polly? "These are secrets you must keep, for they are holy secrets, known only by myself in this century, and now by you. Nod if you understand."

Maggie nodded, and a second later felt someone fussing

at her clothes. No, not fussing, taking them off, right off her back!

"Now, Magdalena, first I shall explain the Mystery of the Rebirth."

Her dress was gone, and that damn Polly—if indeed it was her—was untying her petticoats! What were they doing, stripping her? She'd have given anything to just sit up, all of a goddamn sudden, and punch them both in their smug and smiling faces.

"Do not confuse this with the Miracle of the Resurrection. No indeed. You see, the Christ has come to earth many times in many guises. You believe this with all your heart."

Behind her eyelids, Maggie thought, *You've been eating a few too many of your own magic beans, buster,* and then cursed herself for the reminder of food. Hands removed her first petticoat, then her second, and she began to worry in earnest that there was some kind of horrid initiation for which she had to be naked in front of everybody.

"Twelve times in the Old Testament the Christ comes," Brother Ascension went on. "He comes as magician, as priest, as humble shepherd . . ."

Thank God she left my underwear! Maggie thought with relief as the fingers moved down to her old work boots.

". . . as Philistine, and as King most high of Israel," continued Brother Ascension. "You believe this steadfastly, Magdalena."

She'd been so concerned about that naked-in-front-of-everybody business that she'd lost the middle part of his sentence. Probably a goatherd or two in there, mixed with a date picker and Bob, the camel salesman.

What a load of cabbage!

"And each time," he went on, in that deep, honeyed voice, "he has chosen a woman to ease his body and his mind, to feed him and clothe him and see to the needs of his followers. To lie with him and—"

"Darby!" hissed a woman. It was Polly after all, and

she was distinctly out of character. "Don't you dare. I won't have you screwing the flock, you son of a bitch. Not again!" she whispered, yanking the first boot from Maggie's foot with such force that the laces snapped around and stung her calf. As if that thing he'd stuck in it wasn't enough. And he was going to do *what* to the flock?

"Oh, Christ," he grumbled under his breath, before he gathered himself and said, in dulcet but rather hurried tones, "Sleep, Magdalena, sleep deeply until I say your name again."

And then Brother Ascension got up and went to the foot of the bed, where he and Sister Polly proceeded to have, Maggie thought, a most interesting quarrel.

EIGHT

>━┤━◆━❍━┝━◄

BY EIGHT O'CLOCK THE NEXT MORNING, GRADY HAD spoken with Otto and Quincy and the Thatchers, and Müller over at American Pacific. He had ministered to his aching feet, read three newspapers, and scrubbed the kitchen, and at present was outside Best Dry Goods. This time he had dressed up as a mustachioed street tough. He lounged against a post in the morning light, slowly peeling a very small apple with a very large knife.

It was important that he stand in the sunlight, so that Maggie could see him easily. And he knew she'd recognize him behind the false mustache. She'd given him the plaid flannel shirt six years past for his birthday. Something of a joke, really, because he'd said at the time—well, for weeks, actually—that he'd never in a million years wear the wretched thing, and why on earth had she ever thought he'd wanted one, anyway?

He kept on complaining about it so long, in fact, that about two months after his birthday when they were walking down the street and he'd started harping on it again, she'd simply tossed him over her shoulder and into a pile of garbage. And not very fresh garbage at that. Very flatly, she'd stared at him for a moment, and then she'd said, "Enough. All right, Grady?"

And smiled. And walked off whistling.

He gave an involuntary shudder. He really should warn Quincy about that temper of hers. . . .

He peeled the apple and ate it, eyeing the door across the street. He had just reached for another when the storekeeper—who he remembered from the night before—grabbed his wrist. "You payin' for that, mister?"

It was on the tip of his tongue to say, "Only if you can spell it!" but he caught himself. Digging into his pocket for his coins, he growled and made a face at the shopkeeper, then flipped him a nickel.

The man studied it. "Two more of 'em, or you want change?"

"Two more," Grady grumbled, remembering to look menacing, and stuck two more apples from the barrel into his pockets.

The shopkeeper turned his back and stepped inside, but not before he added, "Your lip hair's fallin' off."

Grady pressed his fingers to his upper lip. Drat the luck! Not enough spirit gum, he supposed, and certainly none in sight. He was about to yank it all the way off, but just then, the Children of Golgotha made their appearance.

Two by two, they filed out the front door of the Seawitch, up the sidewalk, then turned the corner and proceeded toward the docks. He searched the ranks for Maggie or Trini. At last he spotted Trini Malone, or thought he did. The girl's face was gaunt and distorted, but he thought he saw a glint of green from those eyes. Too bad they all wore those poke bonnets; if he'd seen her hair, he would have known for certain.

After the girls, the boys emerged in the same manner, walking like so many doped lemmings. They moved slowly and with heavy feet. Some of them stumbled; the girls, too. But they all had the same expression, as if they were moving through treacle, and for some reason found it pleasant.

After the last boy had turned the corner, he realized that Maggie hadn't come out with them, and he felt an uneasy twitching deep in his belly. He hadn't seen Brother Ascension, either, but maybe he didn't make it his business to show up for early morning roll call.

Or maybe he'd done something very nasty with Maggie. Maybe he'd managed to drug her after all, and then he'd hoodooed or mystified or heebie-jeebied her or whatever it was he did, and she'd spilled the beans and they were going to kill her—or maybe torture her first and then kill her!

I knew I should have hung around last night! he thought angrily, and forgetting the drooping mustache, he suddenly stood up very straight. Well, they by God wouldn't have Maggie's fingernails to pull out! Not his Maggie, nothing of the kind! He stepped down onto the street, hands curled into fists, and had already lifted his foot to take the first marching step into the fray when a voice hissed, *"Grady!"*

He wheeled around so fast he lost his balance and had to catch himself on the hitching rail. Hanging from it, his face screwed up, he said, "M-Mags?"

There was a figure in the doorway, a figure in the shadows just past the light. "Grady! Get in here!"

Scrambling, he pulled himself up and hurried inside, where Maggie took his arm and dragged him like a disobedient dog through the store and out into the alley.

"Honestly!" she said, once they'd closed the service door behind them. "You've got to start paying more attention. I practically did cartwheels!"

"You did no such thing," he replied, too indignant to remark upon the fact that she still had her fingernails and didn't look to have been flayed. "And besides, you were behind me. I was watching the street. And come to think of it, how did you know I was here if you didn't come out the front?"

She leaned back against the brickwork and crossed her arms, and only then it struck him that she was dressed in blue, just like the others. She'd been accepted into the fold, then.

"Because we got up at six," she replied, "and by six-thirty we were marched into the lobby and next door to the

meeting hall for breakfast. I saw your love note. Clever,''
she added. Then, "Did you bring any food? I'm starving.''

Grady divested his pockets and came up with a cold beef
sandwich and a slightly squashed apple fritter, along with
the apples he'd just purchased, and handed them to her.
"You eat. I'll talk.''

She had already torn into the sandwich, and nodded,
grunting.

"First, I phoned Otto over at the Majestic.''

Maggie raised a brow.

"He's fine. Ozzie's fine. Did you know he was taking
the cat?''

Chewing, she made a face at him.

He said, "Anyway, he can't be sure, but he thinks there
was something fishy about the porter who brought his supper last night. As you instructed him, he's been leaving the
room on the excuse of fetching his wallet. He peeked round
the door, and this fellow rummaged through the medicine
tray, checked out the bar, and took a kick at Ozzie.''

Maggie swallowed. "He didn't connect, did he?''

"Halfway up the drapes before mid-swing of the boot,''
he said with a smile. "It probably wasn't anything but a
snoopy employee, but—''

Maggie held up her hand. Around a mouthful of sandwich, she said, "Description?''

"Brown-haired,'' said Grady. "Brown-eyed. Medium
build.''

"About five foot ten?'' Maggie cut in. "Nice-looking?''

Grady crossed his arms. "You know, I haven't the
slightest idea why I bother telling you anything.''

"Michael. Brother Michael, that is.'' Maggie stared at
the wall past his shoulder. "That was awfully fast. I mean,
for the story to get into the paper. And for them to find
it!''

"Hasn't been in the paper yet,'' Grady said. "I know. I
looked.''

"Then how?''

"Beats me," replied Grady. "But Mrs. Thatcher said that her stableman said—"

"How is Catman Culhane these days?"

Grady frowned. "He likes it that there aren't any bars on the windows at the Thatchers', thank you. Eat your fritter." He stood silently until she bit into it, and then he said, "Catman told her that yesterday afternoon, some girl came past the stables—you have to pass their stables to get to the house, you know—and inquired after work up at the house. Scullery work, she said. When he told her not to bother, she stayed around to talk. Inquired very discretely about Otto. He said she was a real pro."

Around the fritter, Maggie mumbled, "And the Catman would be just the fellow to know that. The girl would have been Sister Mae, unless I miss my guess. I'll be hanged as to what tipped them off though."

Suddenly, Grady slapped the side of his head. "Stanley!" When Maggie looked at him quizzically, he added, "That's Bedside Blevins to you. He said something yesterday, about having planted a seed . . ."

"Must have been it," she said, taking another bite. Around it, she added, "Ask him." Then she pointed at him with an index finger. "See? I told you you'd wear that shirt someday."

"Mind if I finish?" said Grady, deliberately ignoring the little dig about the shirt. "Anyway, regardless of who she was or how she got there, Catman told me he very discretely gave her the scoop on Otto—the scoop Mrs. Thatcher told the help to spread—and worked his way around to who'd sent her. Didn't say a word, of course. So then he asked her . . ." Grady paused. Maggie didn't need to know everything. "Well, she slapped him and made her exit."

Maggie snorted and nearly choked on her pastry. Grady patted her back. "I guess she believed him," she finally managed to say.

"Yes, it appears so," he said, moving back to lean against the wall. "Lovely frock."

"Thanks," she said. "All the best people are wearing them. Your mustache is falling off, by the way."

"Oh, bother." Grady sighed, then pulled it the rest of the way free. The blasted thing. He didn't know why he'd troubled with it.

As he poked it carefully into his pocket, she continued, "And that was the driest fritter I've ever had in my life, Grady. Where'd you get it? Peterson's Day Old Bakery?"

He *had* bought it at Peterson's, but he'd hardly admit it now. "I notice you ate it."

Maggie scowled. "When you're starving," she said, brushing crumbs from her bodice, "you'll eat anything. Unlike you, who'll eat anything anyway." She looked up. "Can you bring me some dinner? And what time is it?"

"Eight-thirty, and yes, I can. What time? And what's going on in there? How'd you get out? Did you talk to Trini yet?"

"Good gravy," she said, "so many questions." Sitting down on a crate, she stuck her legs out before her and said, "Maybe about ten or eleven, for dinner. Unless something happens, in which case I don't know. I'm supposed to be in my room, writing a letter to dear Grandpapa. I slid down the drainpipe, for your information, and I've got about twenty minutes to get back. You'd be surprised."

Grady lifted a brow. "About what's going on," he asked, "or about Trini?"

"Both."

At a quarter to ten that morning, the private phone in Quincy Applegate's office rang. He nearly knocked it over getting the mouthpiece off the hook, then anxiously said, "Yes?"

Five minutes later he hung up, the sweat beading on his brow. This sort of thing was an everyday occurrence to Maggie and Grady, but for him, it was, well, nerve-wracking. He wasn't a bit sure he could pull off his part, small as it was.

He snatched the handkerchief from his pocket and ran it across his forehead, reminding himself that Sutter, sitting back there in Boston, was probably worried white. No, not probably—definitely, what with poor little Trini still being in the clutches of that Bible-thumping monster. And Sutter didn't know the half of it. If he'd been aware of the new information Grady had just imparted, he'd have lost his mind with worry.

Steeling himself, Quincy picked up the telephone. His hand had never left it, being locked around the neck of the beast like an iron cuff.

"Number, please?"

"Majestic Hotel," he said, then quickly added, "No, cancel that. Sorry, operator. Get me—" He pulled a slip of paper from his desk and glanced at it. "Get me Beacon seven-four-eight, please."

Grady had given him three people to phone up. He'd call Otto last, putting off the cat damage report as long as possible.

After a short wait, he heard the buzz as the phone at the other end rang. The call was answered immediately by a pleasant enough woman.

"Good morning, First Union Bank. How may I direct your inquiry?"

"Alfred Conklin, please," he said. Thank God his voice was still reasonably crisp and businesslike. By rights, he should sound like warm aspic. He ran his handkerchief around the back of his neck.

"Good morning. Mr. Conklin's telephone," said a male voice. His tone was very young and very eager: Hodgekins, the secretary. Or was it Hopkins? "May I help you?"

"Conklin, please," said Quincy. "Tell him it's Thomas Halliday, from American Pacific." Why should telling lies—even to people to whom it made not the slightest difference—make a fellow sweat so?

Oh, horseradish! He wasn't going to be convincing in the least! When the time came, he'd probably let them all down: Maggie and Sutter and Otto and Grady and—

"One minute, Mr. Halliday."

—and Trini and even Mr. and Mrs. Thatcher (didn't they have a policy that was up for renewal?) and that horrible Blevins fellow and—

"Conklin here." At least Alfred's voice was as solid as ever.

"Alfred, it's Quincy."

A pause. "Yes, I'm aware of that, Mr. Halliday."

Quincy rolled his eyes to the ceiling. "Sorry, Alfred. The walls have ears and all that. Grady just phoned, and—"

"Certainly, Halliday. Did you want those documents sent to Mr. Müller or Mr. Dorfer at the railroad offices, or would you care to come get them in person?"

What? Why was Alfred Conklin acting as if he was, well, *acting*? And then it dawned on him. He hunched over, looked to the left and right in his empty office, then whispered, "Are you saying they're there? Are they there *now*?"

"Yes, that would be splendid," said Conklin, as cool as an iced cucumber, and Quincy suddenly remembered that Alfred won more than his share at poker. A good bluffer made a good liar. "I'll expect you at ten-thirty, then. Good morning."

This time, Quincy didn't bother to mop the sweat that trickled into his collar. He hung up the phone and immediately jiggled the receiver again, this time asking the operator for Grady's number.

"They're there now," he half-shouted after Grady picked up. "They're at the bank!"

NINE

> ━╾┼╼◆╾⊙╾◆╾┼╼━

NOT TWO MINUTES AFTER MAGGIE HAD SHINNED HER way up the drainpipe and crawled through her hotel window, a key had rattled the door. A second later, Brother Ascension had stepped into her room, all smiles, to check on her progress with the letter.

"Not yet, sir," she'd said with a hint of a blush—nice touch, she thought, if she did say so herself—and a yawn, which she covered with her hand. "I'm just so . . . I guess I'm sleepy or something. I keep nodding off. But I'll get it done, I promise."

Brother Ascension had smiled benignly and told her to take her time, but that he was going to see her grandfather at noon, and he'd need the letter by then. And then he'd gone away, locking the door behind him again.

He was suddenly very big on locked doors.

It was now nearly eleven o'clock. She'd finished her letter to Otto—a young girl's plea to her long-lost grandfather for an audience, that was all—and sat beside the open window, thoughtfully juggling her last apple, a cheap glass paperweight she'd found in the room, and the pincushion she'd pulled from Polly's open sewing bag.

She was thinking about Sister Mae, one of Ascension's little information finders, and the girl who'd turned up at the Thatchers' looking for information. Sister Mae was petite and red-haired and fine featured except for her nose. It looked to have been broken at least twice, and it had been none too dainty to begin with. She smiled right along with the rest of them, but at dinner last night Maggie had caught her in earnest conversation with Brother Clarence. A conversation too earnest—an argument, really—for anyone who was drugged. Or honest.

She'd caught just a snatch of it. "... and when them bulls ketched Bob, I says—" was all she'd heard before Clarence caught her looking and hushed Mae, but it was enough. Maggie had smiled foggily—after all, wasn't she freshly released from her first "session" with Brother Ascension?—and moved along.

It was Mae who'd gone to the Thatchers', she was sure of it. What she couldn't figure out was how Mae had known to check there.

She stopped juggling for a moment, catching the apple and the pincushion in one hand, the paperweight in the other. Well, maybe it *had* been something Bedside Blevins had done or said. Whatever it was, it was done.

Trini. Now there was a mystery! She wasn't starving herself, after all. At breakfast, she'd taken a small orange and eaten it—gobbled it, really—and a piece of toast, which was gone in three bites. But she'd just moved her oatmeal around in the bowl, and spooned some into her napkin. The same thing Maggie had done.

Trini wasn't drugged. She was terribly thin, but she wasn't fasting. She'd told Maggie to go, to get out.

Why on earth was she staying?

Out of loyalty? Why not eat the food if you were so damned keen on Brother Ascension and his methods? Out of lack of an alternative? Trini had a loving uncle, even if she had no immediate family left. For all Maggie knew, the girl still thought her mother was alive.

She started the objects moving again. Apple, paperweight, pincushion, apple ...

If Brother Ascension thought for one minute that Maggie was going to be his "wife"—or his whore—he had another

thing coming. After that fight he'd had with Sister Polly
last night, he'd pledged that he wouldn't. But after Polly
had finished dressing her in clothing Maggie had come to
think of as "Ascension blue" and left the room, he'd re-
planted the suggestion.

She was supposed to be Mary Magdalene to his Jesus,
with the extra added bonus that she was to sleep with
him—on command, like a trick dog. And then she thought
that even a dog wouldn't sleep with Brother Ascension, if
that dog was in its right mind.

Polly had been with him a long time, she supposed. A
lot of that argument could have passed as one between a
husband and wife, or at least a brother and sister. They
reminded her of a sort of evil version of herself and Grady,
actually.

And Polly must be immune to the drugs. She'd eaten
heartily at every meal, but she didn't seem to show any
effect.

A key rattled in the door, and Maggie quickly shoved
the apple in her pocket and slid the paperweight and the
pincushion onto a table. She stood up just as Brother Clarence opened the door.

There was a leer in his smile as, one brow arched, he
asked, "Disappointed?"

Grady picked up Brother Ascension outside the bank. Folding his newspaper, he crossed over California Street—
hardly an easy task, considering the congested snarl of midday traffic—and quickly strolled after him, roughly three-
quarters of a block behind.

Ascension wasn't alone. There was a young woman with
him—a buxom, freckled redhead with a nose so crooked
that it was noticeable from across the street—and a young
man: brown hair, medium height, husky build. This must
be the Brother Michael that Maggie had mentioned, and the
woman had to be Sister Mae.

Ascension and his associates moved briskly down the

sidewalk to the intersection, where a cable car was just stopping, and climbed aboard.

Grady had to sprint for it. He leapt a man tying his shoe, long-jumped over a terrier on a leash, knocked a man sprawling, and only just managed to leap aboard at the last minute.

Panting and mopping at his forehead and thinking ugly thoughts about Maggie—who was doubtless relaxing in relative comfort at the Seawitch—he traded grimaces with the conductor and walked to the back. Three rows behind Ascension and his minions, he eased toward a window seat.

He moved immediately after finding something decidedly sticky on it, though. For a nickel a ride, you'd think they'd clean the blasted things more often! Wiping at his hand with a handkerchief and cursing children who bought penny candies or spun sugar just before they got on the car, he found a relatively nonsticky seat, opened his newspaper, and raised it just high enough so that he could peer over the top. He then set into a serious study of the back of Brother Ascension's balding head.

Today Ascension was attired in a black suit. Somber, but stylish. The young man and woman with him weren't in the sect's uniform, either. Mae wore a high-necked, deep purple dress, and Michael was in a brown tweed suit. What, he wondered, had they tried to pass themselves off as when they visited Conklin's office?

He supposed Quincy was getting the answer to that right now. Quincy. He frowned. Why had Maggie allowed him to become so involved in the case? Well, he knew the answer to that, unfortunately. But Jesus, Mary, and Joseph, the man was going to trip them all up!

Maggie had picked a fine time to go gaga over somebody's dimples. Not that she wasn't already gaga, he reminded himself. Oh, she hid it well enough, but she'd have to bury it down a mine shaft in South Africa to keep it from *him*.

Three stops later, Brother Ascension got off the cable car

and immediately flagged a cab, which then set off at a brisk trot in the direction of the Barbary Coast. Grady, however, remained seated. Mae and Michael had remained on the car, and at the moment he was more interested in seeing where they were headed than following Ascension back to the Seawitch—which was, he assumed, his destination.

No, he'd just tag along with the terrible two.

The car started again in the usual manner—with a jerk as the hook caught the moving cable—and he turned his newspaper's page to the society section. One eye on the couple up front, the other on the paper, he read again the story Maggie's reporter friend had planted.

INDUSTRY MAGNATE OBERMYER VISITS CITY AGAIN read the headline. It wasn't much of a story, but he'd managed to get American Pacific and the First Union Bank in there, not to mention the Thatchers. And he'd said that Mr. Obermyer was staying at the Majestic Hotel on account of little Florence Thatcher having the mumps. Very nice.

A little after the fact, perhaps, but nice.

Two stops later, Mae and Michael got off. Grady stepped out the rear door and followed them up the street. He didn't have to walk long, though, for they hailed a hack. He caught one for himself, and after telling the driver, ''Follow that cab!''—he loved saying that—he settled rather uncomfortably with his head out the window, eyeing them through the traffic.

They'd only gone about six blocks when he suddenly realized where they were headed.

This is becoming very interesting, he thought to himself. *Very interesting indeed!*

Back on the Barbary Coast, Brother Ascension—aka Darby Halstead, aka Dennis Harvey, aka Father Derek—walked away from the Seawitch Hotel patting his pocket, which contained Magdalena's birth certificate, her photo of the loving parents, and her letter to her dear grandfather. He smiled.

Quite a piece of luck, finding her in Conquistador. Pretty little thing, and so lost and helpless. He'd guessed her at twenty, but her birth certificate had said twenty-two. Thoughtful of her to have brought it along.

Perhaps he'd quit after this one. After all, her estate would bring him well over the two million dollar mark all on its own, and wasn't that what he'd aimed for in the beginning? Now he'd end up a good bit over it, counting the money from the four that had preceded her. Not even counting Trini Malone's fortune!

He was mildly concerned about Trini. She seemed awfully thin. He'd been worried, when he first noticed, that she wasn't eating enough of his concoction. She seemed docile enough, like a little lamb: a little lamb to the slaughter. At this rate, he might not even have to lead her to the knackers—just wait until she starved herself to death.

Of course, first he needed to get the paperwork finished. So much bother, all this paperwork. But it had to be done lest the transaction not be legal.

This time he snorted through his nose, a half laugh. Legal!

Well, tomorrow he'd give his usual speech and then take Trini to see a lawyer. She wouldn't make any trouble. They never did after an extra blast of his special mixture.

He dodged a sailor who had the bad fortune to be tossed out of a bar (and watched as three rough-looking fellows dragged him into an alley), and shoved away the two crib girls who propositioned him.

He sniffed the sickly sweet scent of opium wafting from a Chinese whorehouse and was tempted, but walked on.

Another half block and he had walked himself out of the Barbary Coast district—Clarence had chosen it, probably at Mae's bidding. A Bowery girl, she probably felt right at home amongst the detritus of society.

He didn't though. He was rising above it. He was also going to move the group in a day or two. Nothing fancy, but at least to a section of town that was marginally respectable. Just in case Obermyer checked up on them.

He flagged down a cab, climbed aboard, and sat there, still lost in thought.

"Mister? Where to?"

He looked up. "The Majestic, if you please," he announced grandly.

The cabby sighed. "Majestic Hotel, Majestic Theater, or—?"

"Majestic Hotel, and hurry," he said, cutting the man off, and slammed the panel between them.

The door opened again with a snap. "And I ain't gonna do nothin' faster than a trot," said the cabby, his face backlit by the sky. "I ain't killin' ol' Nugget, here, just because some fare's got a whim. That ain't all right, you can climb out now."

He absorbed this with a certain degree of exasperation but said a curt, "Fine." And slammed the panel closed again.

As the horse clopped along Pacific Street, he thought it was too bad the cable cars didn't come this far. He rather enjoyed them. At least they didn't talk back. He wondered just how crippled the city would be if a fellow was to go to the main station and blow up the cable car barn, steam engines and all. Something could be done with the chimneys, he supposed . . .

Well, time enough to think on that later. Just file it with the rest of his schemes. He'd have them to toy with once he retired from the God business. He was growing weary of it anyway, weary of all this preaching and Bible thumping, and worse, having to read the damnable thing in order to preach from it. He'd been "thee'd" and "thou'd" to death.

Very soon there'd be no more Brother Ascension, no more Father Derek, just plain old Darby Halstead, living like a king in Europe. The south of France, perhaps. Or England. In England, at least, he wouldn't have to learn an entire new language. Of course, he could always hire peo-

ple to interpret for him, he supposed. With Magdalena Obermyer's fortune plus Trini Malone's money plus what had
come to him before, he'd have better than three million.
Three million? It was unheard of!

It was also, he thought, a good thing Mae had disobeyed
his orders and gone into that bar. A little eavesdropping
was good for the soul, he supposed, and when she told him
what she'd heard, he hadn't had the heart to punish her. He
had, in fact, given her a fifty-dollar bonus. Probably already
spent it on booze, if he knew Mae.

There was a big shot in town, she'd said, name of Obermyer, and wasn't that the man he'd wired them about?
Between the noise from the Hawaiian sailors with their
whores at one table and the Panamanians with their whores
at the next, she'd managed to overhear a fellow at the bar—
his back was to her, but he was fat, she said, and she'd
seen him slip the purse from one of the Panamanians. A
fellow after her own heart.

She hadn't caught much, but she'd caught the name, and
something about some people named Thatcher, up in the
high-tone part of town, and something about the First
Union Bank.

The next morning, all on her own, she'd put on her
housemaid's rags and found the Thatchers', and had herself
a long and very edifying chat with their stableman.

He snorted again. Mae wasn't much to look at from the
neck up, but when you glanced down, she could be extremely persuasive.

And she had been.

Otto Obermyer was a frequent houseguest, she'd learned,
but he wasn't staying with the Thatchers on this visit. It
seemed one of their precious little rug rats had the mumps.
No, he was staying at a hotel. Either the Palace or the
Majestic, the stableman thought. Obermyer's money came
from railroads and a number of other ventures, and the First
Union handled his finances.

And then that idiot, Michael, had taken it upon himself

to determine the correct hotel. It would have been fine if he'd stopped at that, but he'd knocked out a bellhop and delivered Obermyer's dinner!

He had his doubts about Michael's mentality—cobbling hotel employees over the head with a blackjack!—but in this case it had worked out for the best. Michael just wanted to please him, like a lapdog. A stupid, simpering lapdog, but a lapdog nonetheless. At least he was loyal.

And now, this morning, he'd found the little clip in the paper, and then they'd visited the bank. It backed up Mae's story nicely, and put the lid on the honey-pot, so to speak. A lonely, sick, fabulously wealthy old man, estranged from his only son and probably pining for company, and now good old Brother Ascension would present him with the granddaughter he never knew he had. Ah, the pathos! How heart-wrenching!

They'd both be so grateful! And Obermyer wouldn't mind that his granddaughter wanted to stay with the Children of Golgotha. After all, hadn't they brought her to his attention? Hadn't they cared for her in his absence?

Well, maybe he *would* mind. Maybe he'd want to take Magdalena with him. But there were certainly a number of expeditious ways around that.

He studied his nails for a moment, considering the alternatives. A drop from the third story, a convenient heart attack—Michael had said he'd seen heart pills—an unfortunate "accident" in a dark alley . . .

Well, he wouldn't obsess on it too much in advance. No use plotting strategies until you found out the borders of the playing field.

Mae and Michael were off to the train station on other business, business he should have been attending to in person, except that this Obermyer thing had come up, and he was too excited to pass on it. Besides, the whole thing annoyed him, although quite a bit less than it had earlier in the game.

Splitting Trini's money with a partner wouldn't be so tragic if he also had all of Magdalena's.

Money was such a lovely thing.

But then, Polly was worrying him. Getting a little too bossy, wasn't she? That scene last night while she was dressing the girl! Why, she might have damaged Magdalena's trance!

Inside the privacy of the cab, he suddenly laughed. Fat chance of that! Between the dope and the trances and her naturally unsuspicious nature, Magdalena was under his thumb for good and all. Such a sweet girl, with such a sincere, pretty, unsuspecting face. Twenty-two wasn't that old, and she didn't look it. He liked them young, but he'd make an exception for her.

Perhaps not quite yet, though. He'd draw out the suspense. Oh, her expression when he'd popped into her room this morning! Full of yearning and worship and barely concealed passion—if she had any understanding of the word yet—all under a milky glaze of drugs.

She was ripe, all right, but he'd make her wait. Not just because it would be all the sweeter, but because he wanted to make sure she was back in her grandfather's good graces. And he wanted to make certain that she'd stay loyal to his little group.

But that Polly!

I should never have married her, he thought, frowning out the window at the street noise and the passing people and storefronts. *I shouldn't have wed her at all. Can't dope her into submission anymore. You give her a stronger dose and it only makes her meaner. She just smiles more while she tongue-lashes me, that's all. And the money! She squirrels it away, "invests" it, she says! Well, once I get this Obermyer business tied up . . . And don't forget Trini. Can't pass on Trini's fortune, old boy. But once we're finished, I'll take Polly's neck between my bare hands and—*

The cab stopped. "Majestic, sir," called the driver.

Brother Ascension gathered his wits about him, patted

the papers in his pocket again, then dismounted the cab.

He tossed up the cabby's fare—with no tip—and pulled the worn Bible from his pocket. Gripping it firmly, he faced the facade of the Majestic Hotel and smoothed his waistcoat. Then, head up and chest out, he strode between the marble pillars, singing under his breath, "Oh, hosanna, oh, don't you cry for me, for I come from Jesu Christi with a banjo on my knee . . ."

TEN

>——I—◆—◯—◆—I——<

A T TWELVE NOON ON THE DOT, MAGGIE WALKED
into the dining hall. Since the others had been given
sack lunches and sent off to the docks, she expected
to be alone. That was not counting Brother Clarence, who
kept leering at her from the corner of the room. It was
discreet, but she knew a leer when she saw one.

Apparently the Children of Golgotha were the hotel's
only guests, for she hadn't seen anyone else. She assumed
Brother Ascension—or Brother Michael or whoever—had
booked every room.

When it wasn't filled with blue-dressed young women
and blue-shirted boys praying or eating, the dining hall was
still decidedly depressing. Constructed of thin, wide planks
of raw lumber tacked to a flimsy frame, it was unpainted
and weathered, even on the inside. She could see light between the boards.

The sounds of the Barbary Coast filtered between the
planks, too. Catcalls, loud laughter, glass breaking, the occasional scream or roar or howl. Maggie directed herself to
ignore it, which wasn't easy—normally, she would have
been out in the street, breaking up fights and investigating
the screams.

She wasn't afraid of a bunch of drunken sailors or wily
cutpurses. She'd been caught in brawls a few times over

the years and had always managed to get out in one piece.
More or less.

One time up north, a few years ago, it had been those
four big lumberjacks in Harper's employ. She'd knocked
one of them silly, and ducked just in time to let number
two deliver a roundhouse to number three. When the fourth
one grabbed her from behind in a hold she couldn't break—
they were enormous men, after all—she'd simply kicked
the approaching number two in the belly with both feet.
The impact knocked number four to the ground as well as
knocked the air out of him, and he'd let go of her.

Of course, she reminded herself that it helped tremen-
dously that Grady had popped in the door at just the right
moment—with a shotgun. Bless his heart. She wondered
what he was up to right now.

But now she had to act stupid, had to act drugged and
adoring and pious and meek. And on top of it all, she had
to act like a lady, what with Clarence watching her every
move.

A bored, mustachioed waiter brought her lunch: a ham
sandwich. Now this was encouraging! She peeked between
the thick slices of bread, lifted the ham, and found nothing
ominous, nothing Brother Ascension—or Clarence—could
have squeezed joy juice into, at any rate. Except perhaps
the mustard. She scraped out the greater share of it, then
put the sandwich back together, remembering to fold her
hands and pray for a minute or two before attacking it.
Clarence was watching, after all.

When she was just starting the second half—and it had
turned out to be a disappointment, more gristle and fat than
meat—she heard someone else entering the dreary dining
hall. She turned to find Trini and Sister Polly headed toward
her.

This was an unexpected boon! Trini looked bedraggled.
Polly looked radiant. Perhaps Polly would get out of her
hair after lunch. She wanted, more than anything, to have
a long, serious, private talk with Trini.

Polly held out her arms. "Ah, Sister Magdalena!" She gave Maggie, who had risen, a hug. Then she pulled out the chair next to Maggie's, motioned Trini into a seat at the other side of the table, and said, "God bless you, Sister! Sister Trini was taken with a spell of dizziness, so I walked her home. Isn't God's handiwork a glory this fine day?"

Through the boards, the noise and the flickering images outside betrayed some poor fellow getting bashed over the head with a bottle. Maggie smiled and said, "Yeah, it sure is, Sister Polly," as from the corner of her eye, she watched the basher roll the bashee.

Polly gestured at the waiter and said, "Two more, please?"

Maggie looked across the table at Trini, who was studying the rough wood table. "How're you feeling, Sister Trini?"

Trini looked up with sunken eyes, smiled thinly, then lowered her gaze again.

"If you don't mind my saying, you look poorly." Maggie shoved her plate across the table. "Takes the folks in the kitchen a coon's age to bring anything out. Why don't you have mine, and when yours comes, I'll take half of it."

Trini said, "Thank you, Sister Magdalena," and eyed the plate with suspicion.

"Sorry, but I scraped the mustard off," Maggie said, hoping the girl would understand. "It's there on the plate, if you want it back."

Trini chewed on her bottom lip for a moment, peered inside the sandwich, and at last picked it up and took a bite. "Good," she said, chewing, and gave Maggie a grateful smile. She'd understood, then.

Sister Polly reached over and put her hand on Trini's. "Sister," she said kindly, "are you forgetting to thank Heavenly Father for His bounty?"

Trini blushed, put the sandwich down, and bowed her head.

Polly turned to Maggie. "Did you remember, Sister Magdalena?"

"Yes'm," Maggie said, nodding. "I sure did. He's been awfully kind to me lately, what with bringing me to meet you folks, and now bringing me to San Francisco to meet my grandpa Otto. I reckon Brother Ascension's with him right now. My grandfather, I mean."

She managed a little blush at the mention of Ascension's name, by picturing him naked. It always worked. "I thanked Him extra good," she went on. "Brother Clarence was here. He watched me." She pointed toward his chair, but he was no longer in it. Sometime during Trini's internal debate over the sandwich or Maggie's speech, he had left.

Polly's eyebrows had furrowed, but her mouth was still smiling. "I believe you, Sister Magdalena," she said, and patted Maggie's shoulder.

As the waiter slid two more sandwiches on the table, Maggie did her best not to cringe and to hold her smile. She said, "God bless you all to pieces, Sister Polly."

While Polly was engrossed in prayer over a mostly-gristle-and-fat ham sandwich, Maggie said a silent prayer for Otto, who was probably face-to-face with Brother Ascension right now.

And she wondered where that big creep, Clarence, had gone off to.

The knock came as no surprise to Otto. They'd phoned up from the front desk to announce his latest visitor, and he and Bedside Blevins (who'd only arrived five minutes earlier) were set.

Coatless, Otto reclined on the couch, an afghan over his knees and hoping to *Himmel* he could make it through this without disgracing Maggie and Grady. And without ruining the case for Maggie's young man and thereby getting that Trini girl killed.

"Ready?" Blevins asked, halfway to the door.

That Blevins, never batting an eye! Cool like the Alps

in winter, that fellow, practically ice. Otto said a little prayer that he wouldn't make some colossal error, and then added that if he slipped, could Blevins maybe be fixing it? He looked up at Blevins—no, he was supposed to be Dr. Hedrick! *Scheisse!* Already he was making mistakes, and they hadn't even started yet!

But he looked up anyway and said, "*Ja.* Let him in."

Blevins opened the door, saying in a loud voice, "Honestly, Otto! These constant interruptions aren't doing you any good. In my opinion—"

"*Ja, ja,* Hedrick," Otto replied, doing his best to ignore the tall, balding man who stepped through the door. "I got a good idea what your opinion is. But I came here to do business. Business can't be waiting on your opinion."

As Blevins threw up his hands, Otto turned toward the stranger. "Herr Ascension, I am assuming? What business you got to conduct with me? I am a busy man with a bad heart and a worse doctor."

Then he scowled at Blevins, who said to Brother Ascension, "Can you talk some sense into this old fussbudget? I can't!" Blevins dropped into a chair, grumbling to himself.

Otto said, "Well, young man? What you got that's so important? They tell me you say it's 'imperative' that you see me. You got two minutes." He took out his pocket watch and stared at it, saying, "Begin . . . now."

This was easier than Otto'd thought! All he had to do was pretend to be his *Grossvater* Ingo, with his fierce dueling scar and his discipline, slapping his boot with his riding crop as he scolded a much younger Otto.

"—urgent matter, Mr. Obermyer," Ascension was saying.

His eyes on the watch, Otto practically felt his *Grossvater* Ingo's dueling scar appearing over his eye and puckering his cheek as he announced, "One minute, thirty-five seconds."

Ascension remained calm, however. "It has come to my attention that you once had a son, by the name of Hardy, whom you disowned many years ago. By the way, I'm *Brother* Ascension, founder, leader, and spiritual advisor to the Golgotha Universal Church.''

Otto glared at Brother Ascension for a second, then said, ''I don't got no son. And I never heard of this church.'' He glanced over at Blevins and said, ''And you think crazy *I* am?'' To Ascension, Otto cocked an eyebrow. ''One minute, fifteen seconds.''

''It has also come to my attention,'' Brother Ascension continued, as if he were above mockery and was the sole provider of the truth, ''by way of my official capacity as advisor to the Children of Golgotha, of course, that your son married and sired a child before his death. This child is with me, here in San Francisco. I have brought her to you.''

Otto let the watch fall into his lap. ''*Ein minute.* What means this?''

Immediately, Blevins—that was to say, Dr. Hedrick—was at his side, taking his pulse.

''I mean that you have a granddaughter, Mr. Obermyer. A lovely, charming granddaughter. Her name is Magdalena, and she is staying with my flock.''

Otto, who'd been holding his breath so that his face would turn red, pushed Blevins aside and railed, ''Get back! Why are you poking me into my grave? You think if you take the pulse, it would keep me alive? And you!'' He pointed at Ascension. ''I have no son named Hardy, no son at all! How can I have a granddaughter with no son? Answer me that!''

Ascension's tone suddenly dropped three notches to become almost overwhelmingly persuasive. ''Herr Obermyer, denying the girl exists won't make her go away.''

He sank to one knee beside the couch, his Bible clutched to his bosom. He took Otto's arm. Blue eyes bored into Otto's. ''You did have a boy named Hardy,'' he said softly. ''A beautiful boy with blond hair and twinkling eyes. He laughed and played, as all children do. He ran to you with bruised knees and scraped elbows. He was proud when he did well in school, because he did it for Papa. There was a time when you were his God. You want to take his only daughter to your heart, don't you?''

Suddenly, Otto wasn't sure what to do. He was supposed to tell the lies he'd rehearsed, but the man's eyes were . . . He managed to open his mouth and whisper, *"J-ja."*

"Let me bring her to you tomorrow, Mr. Obermyer," Brother Ascension continued in the same melodious tones.

Like water, thought Otto, staring into those eyes, listening to that voice. *Like warm water pouring over me. Warm water with music in it.* He blinked slowly, then said, *"Ja.* Tomorrow, you bring her."

Abruptly, Ascension's eyes were gone, and Otto was staring at the wall. He heard Blevins say, "Stop that! Stop whatever it is you're doing, Retention!"

Otto looked up just in time to hear him correct the doctor. "Brother Ascension, if you don't mind, sir."

"Whatever."

Ascension said, "There's no need to become distraught, my good man. I was simply—"

"Oh, I'm aware of what you were doing, Brother Apprehension," Blevins said sternly. "Stop it."

"That's Ascension," the tall man replied with just a hint of testiness. "I was only trying to—"

"Well, it'll be enough!" Blevins interrupted. "Mr. Obermyer is not a well man. This folderol is doing him absolutely no good, and may be causing serious harm!"

"Stop making *mit* the arguing!" Otto shouted, and he surprised himself as much as the other two men. Both turned to stare at him.

He gave his head a shake, as much to clear it from the aftereffects of Brother Ascension's warm-water eyes as to gather his wits about him. He pointed his finger at Ascension and said, "You be standing back from me. You got funny eyes *mit* a hex in them. No making with the soft talk like a lover, *verstehen*? And, Hedrick, you medical misfit."

He glowered at Blevins. "You stop grabbing me every five seconds. Now," he said, turning back to Brother Ascension, "you got maybe some proof that what you say is truth?"

Ascension flicked a smug smile at Blevins, and produced a slim envelope from his pocket, which he handed to Otto with a flourish. "Certainly. Her birth certificate. A photo of her parents. And a letter she wrote, asking to see you. And I assure you, sir, I was making no—"

"Quiet!" said Otto, all stern Germanic precision once again. *Grossvater* Ingo had the better of him. He made a show of thumbing open the envelope and studying the top paper. He couldn't remember if he was supposed to have his heart seizure now or later. Or maybe he should have had it before? And where in the donkey's spots had Ozzie got to? He looked up from the birth certificate, turned his head toward the bedroom, and called, *"Schnitzel? Kommen Sie hier!"*

A soft mew came from the next room, and then Ozzie strolled in, blinking, and Otto cooed, "Ach, *Liebchen,* did I wake you?"

He turned toward the other two just in time to see Blevins mouth, "See? Sick!" at Brother Ascension.

"Sick I'm not, Doctor Hedrick," Otto said, and turned to the photograph. "Well, not so crippled-up as you put on. You got one of my shoes in the grave already . . ." Ah, weren't Grady's *Vater und Mutter* handsome? So in love, they looked! But it was supposed to be a photograph of his imaginary son Hardy and Hardy's unknown *Frau,* so he frowned.

He flipped the page and studied Maggie's penmanship for a while. And finally, he held out the papers to Ascension, who took them. "How I know you don't get the picture from somebody?" Otto asked, one hundred percent *Grossvater* Ingo. All he needed was a monocle and a military commission. "Or that this girl is a real, what-you-call? McCoy? How I know she isn't some . . . some . . ."

Struggling for the word, he looked to Blevins.

"Con artist is the term I believe you're looking for," Blevins replied, apparently disgusted with the whole business, or at least Ascension's part in it. Such an actor! "That is, if you were searching for a polite term. Now, why don't we take our medicine like a good—"

"Herr Obermyer," cut in Ascension, all pleading eyes and posture, like a supplicant in a religious painting. "I assure you that the child wants nothing more than to meet you, to be allowed to—"

The phone rang, and Otto struggled up from the sofa, waving off Blevins, and answered it curtly, glad for the interruption. If only he could remember when to clutch his chest!

It was Maggie's young man on the other end, which didn't make matters any better. That Quincy fella was all stirred up about something or other, and he was in the lobby.

Otto thought, *Gott in Himmel!* and then, remembering at the last moment that Quincy was supposed to be Halliday, said, "*Ja,* I see you now, Halliday. A small problem I have got that maybe you could straighten out." And then he clicked off before Quincy had a chance to respond.

He turned toward Brother Ascension. "So, Brother Ascending-to-the-Throne or whatever your name is, now I got a bright young man coming up to this room. He is an attorney, so you watch your *P*'s and *W*'s."

Blevins leaned down, offering a spoon and one of several bottles of medicinally labeled colored water. This one was green. "Otto," he said sternly, "take your medicine."

Otto grabbed the spoon. "Quack," he grumbled while Blevins poured the "medicine."

ELEVEN

>∻⊢⊹⊙⊹⊣∻<

"**N**OW YOU GO TO YOUR ROOM AND REST, SISTER Trini," Polly said as she finished tying her bonnet. "Promise me you'll rest. You'll be in my prayers as I work."

"Thank you, Sister Polly," said Trini, her head down. "God bless."

"God bless you both," Polly said with a smile, and then she was off, blithely stepping over drunks on her way down the street.

Maggie took Trini's arm and led her into the lobby, whispering, "Come upstairs with me."

But Trini shook her arm free and snarled, "Leave me alone!" with considerably more strength than Maggie would have thought the girl possessed.

Trini pushed past and was halfway up the stairs when Maggie caught her again. "I just want to talk to you, Trini," she hissed. "That's all. I want to know what's going on." Quickly, she glanced up the stairs for any sign of the missing Brother Clarence.

Trini shrugged her off again, and Maggie had half a mind to just toss the little snip over her shoulder and carry her to her room and *make* her talk. Ingrate! Besides, she couldn't weigh even ninety pounds. Skinny ingrate!

But she tamped down her frustration and caught Trini's arm again, jerking her back a step. "Listen to me," she whispered, her lips near Trini's ear. "You don't eat the food, so I assume you know it's doped. You only pray when you know someone's watching. You won't look anyone in the eye."

Nervously, Trini tried to back down the stairs, but Maggie wasn't letting go of her this time. "Just what are you doing here?" she said softly but a little angrily. She took a breath, willing the temper from her voice, and again lowered her face to the other girl's ear. This was a risk she'd have to take. She said, "I know about Boston, Trini. Why'd you run away again after the Pinkertons found you? You were safe!"

Suddenly, Trini stopped struggling. She stood for a moment, still as statuary, then turned her face to Maggie's, her green eyes wide. "Who *are* you?" came the barely audible reply.

"A friend," whispered Maggie. "You need help more than you know."

"No," said Trini, and pulled away again. Maggie kept her grip, but the girl hissed, "I don't need any help!" and yanked her arm away.

This time Maggie let her go, for she heard bootsteps approaching in the hallway above. Brother Clarence's, as it turned out. Trini rushed past Maggie, brushed past Clarence, and was gone. Somewhere upstairs, a door slammed.

"Have a nice lunch, Sister Magdalena?" Clarence said from the top of the stairs. That same everlastingly rotten smile was on his face.

"Yes, thank you," Maggie replied, remembering that she had better swallow her distaste. For the time being, she had to be Maggie the Polite, Maggie the Pious. Maggie the Sheep. Later on she could turn into Maggie the Wildcat and take a crack at Clarence.

The thought broadened her smile considerably.

She climbed the stairs and passed him, for he didn't budge until after she'd gone by, and headed for her room. Clarence was close behind.

"Have a nice rest, Sister Magdalena," he said as she stepped inside. "Brother Ascension should be back in about an hour with news from your grandfather. I suggest you read the Word and ponder the truth within." There was that leer again, creeping into the corners of his smile. "God bless you, dear."

"God bless," repeated Maggie as he closed the door between them. She heard the key turn in the lock, then the sound of his retreating footfall, then nothing.

Wonderful, she thought, and plopped on Sister Polly's bed. *Just dandy.* She could pick the lock easily and slip out, even search all the rooms if she had a mind, but the only room worth the trouble was Brother Ascension's, and she'd already gone through his things back in Conquistador.

I could find Trini and try to talk some sense into her, she thought. *Or shake some sense into her.*

But to do that, she'd have to go through each room on the floor. She doubted Trini would reply if she went around whispering at every keyhole. Contrary little witch.

No, I shouldn't say that, she told herself as she got up and took a glass from the bureau. She poured out a drink from the pitcher and drained it. The ham had been awfully salty, and she poured another and drank half of that. The Seawitch must shop at the same place that the Conquistador Café did.

The laugh bubbled out of her without her permission, and she immediately covered her mouth with a hand. She couldn't stop snickering into her palm, though. Salt! Now, that was funny! The All-Salt, All-the-Time Supply House, catering sardines, salt-packed beef, tuna, ham, and pickled eggs to bad restaurants everywhere! It was a riot! She'd have to tell Grady!

This time she didn't bother to hold back the laughter, and collapsed again on Polly's bed, sloshing water as she scootched back, wrinkling the covers. *That's it, Maggie, old girl,* she thought, taking another swallow that drained the glass. *Give 'em hell.*

"Nope!" she said aloud. "Give 'em heaven!"

This struck her as hysterical, and she was doubled over with laughter when it hit her. She stopped laughing. She held the empty glass at arm's length, staring at it in disbelief as it slipped through her fingers, bouncing from the mattress to the floor, where it shattered.

The water. Clarence had slipped Ascension's elixir into her water during lunch.

Damn it!

She lurched to her feet, only half-feeling them beneath her, and went to the door, rattling the knob ineffectually, unable to think how to unlock it. Her feet went out from under her, and she hung on the knob, clutching at it with fingers that no longer felt the pot metal knob between them.

She opened her mouth and screamed, "Trini!" before her hands failed her, and she slid into blackness.

Quincy marveled at how utterly painless this whole procedure was, once a fellow got the hang of it. Who would have thought that lies would roll so easily off his tongue?

Of course, it helped having Otto and Blevins on his side, even if they were arguing at cross purposes. As smarmy as he had found Blevins, he had to admit that the man knew precisely what he was doing. Even he—not that he was the best judge, mind—would have immediately taken Blevins for "Dr. Hedrick." Never would have questioned it.

He'd been lied to quite a bit, but that was the nature of the business he was in. If a fellow's wife's jewelry was stolen or his house burned down or his art collection went missing, he was bound to exaggerate its value. But that was a common sort of lie. In the office, he was suspect by nature, and when he had his doubts about a fellow's story, he could always hire Maggie to get to the bottom of it.

But he was rarely suspicious of regular people. Regular people? Now, why should he think that? It made him wonder just how many times he'd been lied to and had blithely gone on, none the wiser.

Brother Ascension had been asked to step out into the hall for a moment, where Quincy was certain the Holy Ear was pressed to the door. At the moment, he was positioned so that his body blocked the view from the keyhole. Ascension could hear everything but see nothing, and Quincy and Blevins were castigating Otto loudly.

"Otto," Blevins continued, calmly helping himself to the brandy, "I can't believe you're going to allow this . . . this *charlatan* to lead you around by the nose!" He took a drink, gesturing at Quincy to take up the conversational slack.

"Think of your reputation, Mr. Obermyer!" Quincy cried, in what he hoped was a tone on the edge of hysteria. "Your son has been, well, dead for years! Do you want the whole town to think you're—you'll pardon the expression, sir, but do you wish them to think you're an old fool? These people are after your holdings, pure and simple. They're gold diggers! There is simply no way that this woman can be your granddaughter. I beg you, listen to Dr. Hedrick. Think of the railroad. Think of the ironworks. Think, Mr. Obermyer, of your folio!"

Blevins, who'd downed his brandy and moved on to studying the pictures on the walls, added, "Otto, if you go through with this, I'll not be responsible for your health. Halliday's correct, although he's overlooked one salient point."

Quincy rolled his eyes. He thought he'd covered it quite well, thank you. He was beginning to think that Blevins was a bit of a ham.

"This girl cannot possibly be your grandchild," Blevins continued, straightening a watercolor, "and building it up in your mind—in your heart, Otto—when it must lead to inevitable disappointment? This is most dangerous indeed." He lowered his voice ominously. "It could well be fatal. You know very well how weak your heart is."

Oh, good point! thought Quincy. *Touché! Brother Ascension is probably drooling on the carpet right now!*

"Gentlemen!" Otto cried, scaring that blasted cat off his lap. The old man turned to apologize to it or catch it or something, but Blevins caught his attention in time. Otto frowned at him but went on without skipping a beat. "Halliday, you're right when you say you aren't my lawyer for real. But you're the closest thing I got out here. You work for Müller and Dorfer at American Pacific, and I own fifty-one percent of American Pacific, so for me you work, also. Maybe more than them."

Otto snapped thick fingers at the cat, who had begun to sharpen its nails on the brocade sofa. The cash register in Quincy's head went *ding-ding-ding*.

"So you shut up your mouth, Halliday," Otto continued. "This is my decision to make. Your job is to clean up after me if I make mistake." He stopped snapping his fingers and began drumming them. The cat stopped scratching the sofa—much to Quincy's relief—and readied itself to pounce.

Otto continued, "I know they report Hardy dead in that blast only a year after I throw him out. Or he leaves. Whatever. But don't you think I remember? Don't you think I have the grief? How can a man forget his only son, when he's turned that son away, and the son of a gun blows himself up in a mine shaft before his papa's pride can . . ."

Otto's voice broke then, although Quincy thought it might have been more from the cat's claws snagging his fingers than from being immersed in his part.

While Otto freed his bleeding hand and settled the cat on his lap again, Blevins filled the void.

"There, there, Otto," he soothed. He was pouring himself yet another brandy. Did he have a hollow leg? "You see? This is exactly what I was talking about. Your pulse is racing!"

"You get away, Hedrick!" Otto snarled at Blevins, who was across the room at the bar. "Stop *mit* taking the pulse! Is normal for a man to be excited when a fella tells him out of the clear blue sky that he might have the grandchild, no? So maybe Hardy doesn't get himself killed. Maybe he got the what-you-call. Ambrosia.''

"Amnesia,'' Quincy and Blevins said at the same time.

"*Ja.* That,'' Otto said. "Or maybe he tell those men to just say he's dead because he knows it would hurt me. Maybe he goes off and gets married and has the daughter.''

"Otto . . .'' interjected Quincy, mainly because he hadn't said much in the last few minutes and he was feeling left out.

"No, Halliday,'' interrupted Otto. "I not gonna brook no argument. I want to have the look-see at this girl. If she's my blood, I'm gonna know like that.'' He snapped his fingers again, which happened to be the ones that had just stopped bleeding, and grimaced.

"If she isn't,'' he said, studying his fingers with a frown, "you can do what you want with her and the Bible man. Put in jail or something. If my blood she is, then you can start making me up the new will. Hedrick?'' he said, and Blevins looked up from his brandy. "Hedrick, open the door up and let Brother Assertion back in here.''

"Otto,'' said Quincy, in pleading tones, "they sent you his watch. They sent—''

"I don't care what they sent, Halliday,'' Otto broke in, right on cue. "Now, you move backside out of the way, let Hedrick open the door.''

Grady emerged from the railroad depot on the heels of Mae and Michael—and the man whose train they'd waited for. Pretending to fumble in his pockets, he paused a moment on the steps, then climbed aboard a cab. "Palace Hotel,'' he told the driver, and slumped back in the seat, utterly dejected.

Maggie wasn't going to like this at all. And Quincy? Well, *he* wouldn't be the one to tell him. Quincy was bigger than he was, for one thing, and he was liable to punch anyone who brought him this particular bit of news.

He'd let Maggie tell him.

Up there ahead, somewhere in the snarl of cabs and freight wagons and buggies and horsemen, was the problem. He'd overheard Michael give their driver his orders, so he wasn't afraid of losing them in traffic. He just wished to heaven he'd never followed them in the first place. He should have let Maggie find out. Better yet, he should have rigged it so Quincy would see for himself. Quin could hardly slug himself now, could he?

Drat the luck, anyway!

The cab arrived at the Palace and pulled into the queue in the circular courtyard. Disgusted, Grady climbed out. Mae and Michael and the man they'd picked up at the train depot were just going in the doors, so he tarried with the driver's fare a moment, then dawdled at the newsstand, all the while keeping them in sight.

They had completed their business and gone upstairs by the time Grady crossed the lobby to lean against the long front desk.

"Excuse me?" he said, gesturing at the beanpole of a clerk who had signed them in.

"My name's Mr. Adolphus, sir. May I help you?" He was as polite as the hotel was grand.

"Sorry, Adolphus," said Grady. "That fellow who just went up the stairs. Think I know him. That wouldn't be old Billy Simpson, would it, from St. Louis? Those his kids with him?"

Adolphus tilted his head. "No, sir, I don't believe so. The gentleman checked in alone. I believe the others were just walking him up to his suite. I could check, if you like."

"If you wouldn't mind."

Adolphus walked a few feet down the big desk, Grady following on the other side, and studied the guest register. "Afraid not, sir."

"Well, now, that's a real shame," said Grady, fairly reeking of dejection. "I could have sworn it was old Billy. Would've bet money on it."

Adolphus's patience was obviously wearing thin. He

said, "Sir, look for yourself," and spun the oversized book toward Grady.

"Well, I'll be!" Grady said, shaking his head. "John Dobbs, from Chicago. Why, he could be Billy's brother!"

Adolphus smiled thinly, and Grady tipped his hat and walked across the lobby and outside, to the court, where he slumped against a post.

John Dobbs from Chicago, my mother's footstool! he thought dismally, and then angrily.

It didn't fit with the story Quincy had told, via Maggie. The wild Trini taking up with Brother Ascension, hiring Pinkertons, the capture, shipping Trini back to her mother, the escape . . .

It was rotten, rotten down deep.

Quincy would never believe them, if he knew Quincy. The man was on such a straight and narrow track that a railroad could have run on him. No, he'd likely knock somebody's lights out.

Because somewhere up there, making himself at home in the Palace Hotel under the assumed name of John Dobbs, was Quincy's best friend in the world, and Trini's dear uncle.

Sutter Malone.

TWELVE

T HE DAY WAS LOVELY, WARM AND SPARKLING, AND
Maggie was boating. Quincy was with her, as well
as Grady—what was Grady doing out here?—and
there was another man, too, a man who was rowing with
his back to her, although she had the strangest feeling that
if he turned around he'd have beautiful blue eyes.

Then the wind rose suddenly, and the streamers from her
hat lashed across her face.

"Grady," she said, "stop it!" even though she didn't
for a moment imagine that Grady had made the wind come
up or the streamers sting her. Then she did believe it, because the streamers turned into a hand that slapped her
cheek again, and she grabbed at it—who ever heard of a
hat with hands for ribbons!—and missed. And opened her
mouth to give Grady a good what for, when someone said,
"Magdalena!"

She tried to say, "Pretending you're a woman won't
help, Grady!" but it came out, "Retennin' yo womwon
hep."

What? And then she realized her eyes were closed. She
tried to open them with a snap, but it seemed someone had
sealed them with wax.

Someone was shouting at her again. "Magdalena!" A
woman. Was someone drowning?

She tried to call back, "I'm coming!" but it passed her

lips as clotted gibberish. She tried to open her eyes again.

This time she succeeded, to a degree. Through slitted eyes, she saw that Trini was in the boat, too. Straddling her, in fact! And their little rowboat had gotten much bigger, because she seemed to be in the bottom, and the sides went up so high that she couldn't see the water for the boards.

"Magdalena!"

There came that hand again, and this time Maggie caught it by the wrist. No, she'd caught a chair leg. "Qu—quiii—," she mumbled.

"Good," said Trini as she clambered off Maggie's stomach and to her feet. "You're awake. What was it, anyway? Did he put it in your water?"

She heard Trini pick up the pitcher and saw her walk past—the only things in focus, at present, were the girl's feet. Maggie heard a *slosh* as Trini threw the contents out the window and into the river. Water? No, the alley. No lake. No Grady. No Quincy. No boat.

Where the hell was she, anyway?

"Be careful," said Trini, who was suddenly behind her, lifting her shoulders. "There's broken glass all over the floor. Oh, come on, Magdalena! Help me!"

Maggie moved her feet somehow, and the next thing she knew, Trini was hovering over her and she was sitting in the chair beside the window. "I'm going to try to sneak some coffee, all right?" she said. "Don't try to get up! You'll fall in the glass. Understand?"

Numbly, Maggie nodded. Good old what's-her-name. Trini. Good old Trini, helping her out of the boat and to shore. But as she heard the door open, then close again softly, she stared stupidly at her lap and wondered who in the devil Trini was, and how she knew her name. And furthermore, why had Trini tied her into this chair?

It was much too difficult to think about.

Her eyes drifted shut again.

•   •   •

Brother Ascension left the Majestic Hotel in a curious state. He was excited, for that doddering old dimwit, Obermyer, had overridden the arguments of his doctor and his lawyer, and agreed to see Magdalena tomorrow at one p.m., on the dot.

But Brother Ascension was annoyed, too.

Magdalena had told him her father had died only a short time ago, yet Obermyer seemed to think he'd died when he was just a lad—twenty-four or twenty-five years back, before Magdalena was born! Somebody wasn't telling the truth. It couldn't have been Obermyer, for he was certain Obermyer couldn't have known he was out in the hallway with his ear plastered to the door.

He was firmly convinced that the conversation he'd heard had been a truthful one. That idiot lawyer, Halliday, had stood in front of the door. If they suspected him, if they thought he was peeping and they were staging the conversation for his benefit, wouldn't Halliday have moved? Of course he would have! They would have acted out the scene.

But they hadn't.

He admitted that he'd had some doubts. It was a little too convenient that Magdalena just happened to pop up when they were ten miles out of Frisco, a little too convenient that Gramps just happened to be in town. But now he was willing to forget that coincidence. Not because Halliday had stood in front of the door, not because their conversation had been so jerky that it couldn't possibly have been rehearsed, and not because everything had checked out at the bank.

He believed because of this little difficulty, this little timeline annoyance, with Maggie.

No one would be stupid enough to cast serious doubts on a member of their own scam. Magdalena had to be real because her story was too flawed to be phony. Obermyer and his clowns were for real, he was absolutely positive.

So it was Magdalena doing the lying, or possibly her

father. Maybe good old Hardy had faked his own death to
get Obermyer off his back. "Can't say I'd blame him," he
muttered as the cab clopped along.

That had to be it. After all, the other alternative was
almost ludicrous! That Magdalena, this docile little slip of
a child, would try to con him! Him!

No. Impossible. The drugs would have seen to that: laudanum to deaden the will, processed coca leaves to excite,
the essence of specially grown hempweed to heighten the
senses while calming the brain and the reflexes, a touch of
the extract of a certain type of cactus which caused hallu-
cinations.

He blended it carefully, in just the proper combination
to keep his children docile, happy, and easily suggestible,
yet able to work. They didn't realize it, but they stayed
with him not for God, but for the drug. How many times,
over the years, had one or another of the little morons
packed up and left, only to come back to him after a day
or two?

"God's punishing me for leaving, Brother Ascension!"
they'd say, looking green and sickly, and quite obviously
suffering from withdrawal symptoms. The laudanum
caused that, bless its heart. If opium had a heart, that was.
"Please forgive me," they'd whimper, "please take me
back!"

And he had, of course, after due thought. "Ask for God's
forgiveness, not mine," he'd say, all benevolence and
Christian charity, "for mine is already granted."

One meal with the flock and their happiness was restored
like magic, and they were certain it was because they were
once again in the good graces of Christ Almighty, and
tagged for heaven's shute.

The simpletons.

Magdalena seemed particularly sensitive to his little mix.
Seemed. That would be the operative word. He'd been so
sure she was drugged that first evening, and then again last
night! Nobody could withstand the hat pin test without a

twitch unless they were mesmerized, and no one could have been mesmerized so easily unless they were drugged. It would take an extraordinary individual to—

He sat up straight. He was so accustomed to these featherbrained debutantes and college boys—or the stupid farmspawn he used for padding—that he'd never before considered the possibility that one of them might be on the game and out after her own prey. What if Magdalena was out to con Obermyer out of his fortune—and trying to con him into taking her to him? After all, she'd have more credibility in the protection of a man of the cloth, wouldn't she?

She probably didn't have the slightest idea he was running a scam when she joined—although now he was certain that she must know, if she'd figured out that it wasn't a good idea to eat the food. No, not necessarily. Maybe she *was* eating it, and—

He slapped both hands against his forehead and pummeled it with the sides of his fists, as if he could get his brain to work better by thumping it.

"I'll wait until I get back to the Seawitch," he said finally to the empty seat across from him. "I'll get the truth, one way or the other."

Maggie's head lolled to the side again—and Trini slapped her. Again.

"St—sto—" mumbled Maggie, one eye open.

"Drink," Trini said, and shoved the fourth cup of coffee—that Maggie remembered, anyway—in her face.

Maggie took a sip—at least its temperature had sunk below volcanic—and said, "S'not helpin'. Wanna slee."

"It is, too, helping," said Trini. "Drink some more, unless you don't care to see this Grady person again."

Grady? Had she talked about Grady? What else had she talked about? She struggled with the coffee, and Trini helped her lift the cup to her lips. She drank it in three swallows (although most of it went down her front), then handed it back. "More."

She didn't know when she had placed Trini. She just knew that she knew her now. And that she'd been talking.

And that this was a very bad place to talk.

Trini handed her a fresh cup. "That's all there is," she said. "I can't chance another trip to the kitchen."

"Grady?" Maggie whispered, and finally willed open her other eye. She had a curiously superior sense that she'd be able to juggle eight balls if she had them. She'd come up with an ingenious plan whereby—*Stop it!* Trini was holding the cup at her lips. Maggie drained half of it, then whispered, "Wha . . . what'd I say?" *Please, let me have done as little damage as possible . . .*

Trini sat back on the bed and rubbed her temples. "You mentioned somebody named Grady. And somebody named Quincy, too. You seemed to be sweet-talking this Quincy."

Despite herself, Maggie felt heat rising in her face. She lifted the coffee to her lips and hit her chin. Trini helped her with the logistics, and she gulped it down before, with great effort, she asked, "Anything else?"

Trini shook her head. Her gaze was flat and level, and Maggie couldn't read anything into it, except perhaps a slight annoyance. God, her eyelids were so heavy! She was afraid to blink, lest they not open again.

"Well," Trini said, her expression finally changing to what Maggie thought might be embarrassment, "you, um, you did talk about someone else. You kept fussing with your skirts and saying, um . . ."

Maggie stared at her. Actually, since she was afraid to blink, she couldn't help but stare.

Trini took it for a command, however. "You kept saying, 'Not now, Ozzie!' You said it a lot."

Maggie was flooded with a relief almost as palpable as the drugs still washing over her system. "An' tha's all?"

Trini looked away, but she nodded.

Ozzie. The cute little buzzard. You could put your whole face in his furry little tummy, and . . .

Maggie tried to pinch her own arm and missed the first two times. *Got to stay on track, you feeble-brained idiot!* she thought angrily, for her thoughts were becoming more lucid than her speech. And then she said aloud, "Where'd . . . where'd he put it?"

Trini turned toward her, her face beet-red. "Who? Put what?" Obviously, she was still back at Ozzie.

"You . . . y'know . . ."

Maggie stopped mid-sentence and they both turned toward the door. Bootsteps echoed in the hall outside.

The drugs forgotten for the moment, Maggie lurched to grab at Trini's arm—and missed by a foot and a half, her torso dropping over the armrest of her chair. She'd intended to ask her why on earth she'd come back to Ascension, but Trini was already praying loudly.

"Help this poor girl shed the devilment of alcohol, O Lord!" Trini said as she helped set Maggie straight in the chair. "Help her fight this mighty curse which has fallen upon her." She arranged Maggie's arms. "Help her rid herself of the devil and all his works." She sat back on the bed and bowed her head.

"Help her cast Satan from her body. Lord, I beg you to fling from her the evil spirit of whiskey and wine—"

Maggie managed to hiss, "Don' sign . . ."

"—which has crept in upon her in the outer world in her foolishness and youth. Cast out—"

". . . any . . . thing."

"—this spirit of demon rum, and—"

Brother Ascension opened the door, with Brother Clarence close behind. Trini stopped praying. Through the one eye which had stayed open, Maggie lazily regarded the two men filling her doorway—they looked like a couple of carnival bouncers who had just answered the call of "Hey, Rube!"

Maggie let her eye close again. She felt her mouth drop-

ping open. Oh, it was good to close her eyes! She only
hoped she wouldn't have to pretend too long. She had to
get some more coffee. She had to try juggling those eight
balls . . .

"Brother Ascension, God bless you," came Trini's
voice. "And bless you, too, Brother Clarence. I'm so glad
you've come at last. I fear Sister Magdalena has . . . Well,
it grieves me to say it, Brother, but I fear she's . . ." Trini's
voice lowered. "She's been drinking. She was passed out
when I found her. I tried to—"

"There, there, Sister," said Brother Ascension.

Maggie heard the bed boards creak as Trini got to her
feet. Or maybe it was the boat listing to one side. And how
clever of Trini to say she was drunk! Of course, she could
have guzzled white lightning all day and never felt it, but—
Say, was this what it was like to be drunk? She imagined
it might be pleasant if all these people would just leave her
alone.

"You're excited, Sister Trini," Ascension went on. "Go
to your room and rest in the peace of Jesus. This evening
is leaflet night, you know. Brother Clarence and I will see
to Sister Magdalena."

Maggie tried to open her eyes, but the lids were stuck.
She heard the door click closed—behind Trini, she assumed—and then the smooth scrape of a heavy object on
wood. *Fight it,* she told herself, but she felt her mind sinking into confused but happy thoughts of rivers and trick
ponies and high-wire acts and boats.

"The whole pitcher?" came Brother Ascension's whisper. "How much did you put in there, anyway?"

That was right, the pitcher! She vaguely remembered
Trini tossing the remaining contents out the window. The
window to the sky, the window to the stars, the window—
Stop it, damn you!

"Just a half of one of those little bottles," Clarence said.
"I thought—"

There was a sharp smack of flesh hitting flesh, the sound

of a body hitting the wall and slithering halfway down it. "How many times do I have to tell you, don't think!" came Brother Ascension's voice, still a hiss, but a very angry one. "You could have killed her, you idiot! That's as much as I throw in a whole stew pot for twenty-five!"

Twenty-five? Twenty-five what? Now that Trini had departed, Maggie had lost all sense of anything being imperative. The boat was rocking again. Such a nice boat. Nice waves, nice sun, nice—

Hands clasped her shoulders and shook her. Oh, botheration!

"Magdalena?" Brother Ascension's voice. So annoying. "Can you hear me? Open your eyes, my child."

All on its own, Maggie's head rolled slowly downward until her chin was on her chest, although she was thinking that if Brother Ascension didn't unhand her pretty darned quick, she'd tell her father and he'd sic their jaguar on him, and *then* he'd be pretty dad-blamed sorry he messed with the Maguires!

"Damn it!" he said under his breath. He twisted her face from side to side. "Completely senseless!" Then he suddenly thundered, "Clarence! Make yourself useful. Go downstairs and refill that coffeepot."

"But—"

"And bring a broom to clean up this glass. Now!"

Then an arm—decidedly strong, decidedly male— Quincy? Grady? No, Brother Ascension, blast it—swooped under hers and lifted her up on her feet.

She wanted to go back on the boat. No, she wanted to put somebody in jail. Who was it now? Quincy? Never Quincy. Oh, that was right, the preacher-man. Teacher-man. Feature-creature-leacher-preacher—*get hold of yourself!* The man who had scooped her up out of the chair. Good old Ascension.

They really shouldn't be walking in the boat, should they? Not safe. And wasn't there something about eight . . . eight . . . juggling something?

"Damn it, Magdalena, walk." The grumble and jerk roused her somewhat. Brother Ascension was dragging her around the room, or the boat, or wherever they were. "And wake up. Don't you *dare* die before I show you to Obermyer!"

THIRTEEN

G RADY WAS ABOUT TO GIVE UP AND CALL OUT THE troops, such as they were. Over the thin background noise of clanking bottles and laughter and loud talk echoing through the alley behind Best Dry Goods, he struck another match and peered at his watch. It was 11:40. Maggie should have shinnied down that drainpipe ages ago! Her beef Wellington was cold as a hammer, and after all the trouble he'd gone to getting it!

Besides, as jaded as he was, even *he* didn't like to stand around in a dark alley on the Barbary Coast in the middle of the night.

He glanced at the dark heap he'd dragged behind a pile of garbage. The slow, rhythmic rise and fall of the shadow told him the Frenchman who'd tried to mug him was still unconscious. Well, he wasn't sure the oaf was French, but he'd bleated, *"Merde!"* just as Grady slugged him.

He gave a little tug to his cuffs, stood a tad straighter. The drunken fool—actually thinking he could roll Grady Maguire!

He turned again toward the narrow view of the Seawitch Hotel which the alley's mouth afforded him. Still nothing except that same fellow, dressed in Ascension Blue (as Maggie had dubbed it), who lounged against a post just outside the front door. Perhaps he was the reason Maggie was late. Maybe she couldn't get round him. He wondered if he shouldn't pick up the basket and take a little jaunt around the back of—

"Grady?"

He spun on his toes, fist cocked, and nearly decked Maggie, who'd snuck up behind him. She hadn't sounded at all like herself.

He slapped his forehead and hissed, "Good Lord, woman! You could warn a fellow when you're coming the long way round! And stop pussyfooting!"

She didn't say anything. He watched as her narrowed eyes searched the mouth of the alley, twenty feet beyond his shoulder, and then she slumped down on a crate—out of the hotel guard's line of vision, he noticed. Her head dropped into the cradle of her hands. Something was very wrong.

"Mags?" he said. He, too, stepped out of the man's line of sight—although it was highly doubtful he could see anything past the alley's opening, and they were better than twenty feet back. Kneeling beside her, he said, "Mags? What is it? And who's that ape over at the hotel?"

She spread her fingers and peeped between them. "Brother Clarence," she said, her voice unnaturally thick. And, if he didn't miss his guess, it contained no small degree of distaste. "Food first, Grady. Explanations later."

Something dreadful had happened during the day. But as troubling as this was, he knew better than to prod her. She'd tell him when she was ready. So he simply said, "All right," and settled the dinner basket in her lap. "Sorry it's cold. It was piping hot when it left Henri's, but *some* people insist on being late for dinner."

Even this humble attempt at humor didn't get a rise out of her. She only mumbled, "S'all right," and began peeling back the napkins.

"I'll tell you about my day, then, shall I? While you eat?"

She nodded wordlessly.

He glanced again at the Frenchman in the garbage to

make sure he was still out, then around the stack of crates at Brother Clarence, and then proceeded to convey the highlights of his morning and afternoon. He was only up to the part where he'd decided to let Brother Ascension go his way and follow Mae and Tweed Suit when Maggie's head suddenly jerked up.

He heard the noise and ducked just in time, blindly kicking straight out with one leg—a little trick he'd learned from Maggie—and almost simultaneously was treated to the sound of ripping fabric and the grunt of an enormous Hawaiian sailor, into whose bulbous stomach he'd just rammed his boot.

The sailor looked surprised—or so it seemed in the darkness—and crumpled to his knees. When it looked like he wasn't going down all the way, Maggie handed Grady a small plate, which he immediately cracked over the man's skull.

The plate shattered. The Hawaiian went all the way down and stayed there.

"Aloha," muttered Grady, before he turned back to Maggie and said, "I sincerely hope he wasn't just asking me for the time."

Maggie, completely engrossed in her dinner, said, "Had a knife," around a mouthful of something or other. Then she glanced over and added, "Best kick it away. Left hand."

"Nice job, Grady," Grady mumbled while he hunted through the shadows. "Lovely, Grady. Thank you, Grady. You're so kind, Grady, old boy."

Maggie looked up from her dinner. "What are you muttering about?" she asked.

Grady rolled his eyes. "Nothing, dear." And then he found and picked up the blade. It was a nasty-looking thing, a serrated hunting knife with a blade ten inches long. "Dear Lord," he said with a shudder, and tossed it gingerly to the foot of the Frenchman's garbage pile. "Closer to a broadsword than a knife."

"You'll have to pay Henri's for that plate," Maggie said. She wasn't listening to him at all. "What were you saying? Where did you track Mae and Michael?" She sounded a little more chipper—the sight of him engaged in physical battle always perked her up as much as it distressed him. But she still wasn't her old self. Why, any other day she would have shoved him out of the way to have a go at the Hawaiian herself!

Well, no, she wouldn't. She probably would have let him try, and when (and if) he bungled it, she'd have made that face at him and said, "No, Grady, like *this*!" And demonstrated.

Good thing he hadn't bollixed it up. She didn't look like she was much in the humor for giving lessons on self-defense.

He decided to forgo relating his little trip to the station until later, and instead told her about the meeting with Otto, Quincy, and Blevins at the hotel.

"Quincy's taken hold better than I expected," he admitted, somewhat baffled. "Really seems to enjoy it, actually. He kept saying, 'Good show, old man!' or 'By Christmas, that was brilliant!'—practically shouting it, for God's sake—while Bedside Blevins hit the high points of their interview with Ascension." He shook his head and grumbled, "I thought I'd have to gag him a couple of times."

"Quin or Blevins?" Maggie asked, then chuckled softly. The thickness was mostly gone from her voice, and it seemed she was getting her sense of humor back. This encouraged him momentarily, then just as suddenly he plunged into depression. The only thing he had left to tell her was that bit about Sutter Malone coming to town, and he was dreading it.

He opened his mouth to say, "Mags, there's one more thing . . ." but she beat him to it.

"Grady?" she said. She was finished with her dinner, and tucked the napkins and silver and plates back into their basket. "Do you realize you've split your pants?"

He grabbed his crotch, then his backside. "Damn and blast!" he breathed. How was he going to get home now?

But Maggie didn't care, because the next thing she said was, "I had a little accident this afternoon. Trini Malone saved my life, I think. Strange, that girl. She's got a sense of, well, a sense of purpose. That's the best I can explain it. I'll be damned if I know what that purpose is, though, and it's driving me crazy."

Grady waved his hands. "Wait. What do you mean you 'had a little accident'?"

Maggie leaned past him, apparently checking on Clarence again. Grady turned to look, too. He had moved from the edge of the sidewalk to the bench, and stared down Pacific Street. His face in profile, he scowled.

"Charming fellow, this Clarence," he commented. "Friend of yours?"

Maggie sighed. "So close that I let him dope me eight or ten people's worth."

Grady cocked a brow. "Huh?"

"He doctored the water," Maggie said. "Put some of Brother Ascension's damned junk in it. There was ham for lunch and I was thirsty, and . . ." She sighed. "It was a stupid, stupid thing. Anyway, later on, while they were walking me all over creation and pouring forty gallons of coffee down my gullet, I heard Brother Ascension tell the idiot that he'd put enough for twenty-five in my pitcher."

"Twenty-five? *People?*"

She waved her hands. "I only drank a glass and a half. Trini pitched the rest out the window. You know how I can drink like a fish and it never phases me until the next morning? Well, this stuff does *not* work that way."

Grady would have laughed if the situation weren't so deadly. Brother Ascension had killed before and was likely to kill again unless they stopped him. He didn't have any data on this Clarence thug, but it seemed likely that he was bent on killing Maggie by accident, if no other way. At least they'd walked her and filled her up with caffeine. Brother Ascension couldn't lose her now, what with Otto taking the bait. But while she'd been drugged, she might have said anything.

Frowning, he said, "Maggie, think hard. Did you say or do anything, anything at all that might—"

"No." She wasn't looking at him, but watching Clarence instead. "If I said anything at all, I said it to Trini. She found me first. Without her, I might have died like one of those poor sods they're always dragging out of Sing Chung's back room. You know, I have this horrible feeling that Trini thinks I'm having an affair . . ."

She leaned back against the bricks of Best Dry Goods rear wall, apparently satisfied that Clarence's attention was riveted on something up the street. Grady thought it might be a fistfight, since he heard the appropriate cheers and catcalls.

"Are you all right now?" he asked gently, choosing to skip over about her supposed affair.

"I expect so," she said, "but I wouldn't want to go through that again. I've passed enough fluid for three horses."

Grady snorted, couldn't help it, and Maggie grumped, "Go ahead and laugh, you sadist. At least I found out Trini isn't on their side." When Grady arched his brows, she added, "I'm not sure she's on our side, either. And no, I didn't let on. I think she's on her own mission. Just don't ask me what the hell it is, because I don't know. I don't even know if she knows her mother's dead. Some detective I am." She leaned forward again and frowned, saying, "You'd best do something about Laughing Boy, there."

The Hawaiian was waking up. Quickly, Grady looked around for something to crack him over the head with. When all he came up with was a palm-sized rock—you'd think there'd be a stray brick around when you needed it!— Maggie stuck a hand into the dinner basket and handed him another plate. A larger one, this time.

"This is going to cost more than the food did," Grady muttered, and broke it over the Hawaiian's skull with a much larger (and more satisfying) crash than the last one had. A half second later, the fellow crumpled to the ground again.

Grady let the segment of plate left in his hand drop to the ground, where it, too, shattered. He really ought to tell her, he thought, and now. He cleared his throat. "Mags," he began, "there's, um, something you should know."

"Oh, good gravy!" she hissed, breaking in. "Here comes Clarence."

He wheeled toward the alley's mouth in time to see Clarence's bulk silhouetted in the streetlight as he strode across the street toward them. *He heard the blasted plate break,* Grady thought angrily, and a rustle came from behind him. He hoped it was Maggie, hiding. She couldn't afford to be discovered.

Clarence stopped in the opening of the alley. He leaned in slightly, his head moving from side to side as if he were searching for something. He made a visor of his hand and leaned in.

Grady took a deep breath and said loudly, in his best imitation of a Cockney accent, "Bugger off, mate, 'less you're lookin' for more a the same."

"W-who's down there?" called Clarence. Obviously, he wasn't too bright. Everybody knew that was the *last* question you should ask a total stranger in a dark alley—especially an alley on the Barbary Coast, for God's sake! But not good old Clarence. The fellow was built like an ox—he obviously had the brain to go with it. He took another step forward.

"Puddin' Tame, that's me name," said Grady, in what he hoped was a sarcastically teasing but ominous tone. It'd probably be lost on Clarence, but still, a fellow liked to keep his hand in. "Ask me again, and I'll 'ave your kidneys for me breakfast. C'mon, y'stupid git. Let's see 'ow y'bleeds."

When Clarence just stood there, Grady took a chance. In one quick movement, he stepped to the garbage heap and retrieved the Hawaiian's knife, then stepped back to the middle of the alley, holding it out to the side where Clarence could see it. He knew that all the big knucklehead would be able to make out was the silhouette of a man brandishing a blade—a very large blade. He hoped that would be enough.

It worked. After a pause, Clarence slowly backed toward the street, then called, "You ain't gonna trick *me,* mister!" and then bolted across the street, to the relative safety of the Seawitch's front porch. He stopped, in fact, just inside the front door, and stood peering across the street from inside the lobby.

Blowing out an enormous sigh of relief between fluttering lips, Grady turned toward Maggie. "It's all right," he said. "He's gone. Run for the hills. Turned tail. Maggie?"

Wonderful. Just peachy. She'd fled back to the Seawitch while he was busy with Clarence, and he hadn't even told her about Trini's Uncle Sutter!

He supposed he'd just have to chase her down, which meant he had to move fast. He grabbed the basket and started down the alley, trotting away from the Seawitch and Clarence—he'd circle it, as Maggie apparently had. He was halfway to the other end when he remembered his britches.

Cursing under his breath, he dropped the basket and pawed through it, pulled out the largest napkin and shook it open. Quickly, he tucked it into the back of his trousers, beneath his jacket. It hung a good four inches past his backside. Not at all fashionable, but at least it was modest. He could carry the basket in front.

Quickly, he scooped it up and was nearly to the far end of the alley, when from behind, Maggie hissed, "Grady! Where on earth are you going?" She paused, then pointed at his britches. "What *is* that? A kilt?"

Without breaking his pace, he spun around and headed back, ripping the napkin out of his trousers as he marched.

"Will you please stop appearing and disappearing?" he said angrily. "Criminy!" He covered the distance between them and plopped on a barrel, glaring at her.

"You don't have to get huffy," she said, folding her arms. "If you must know, I ducked behind these boxes when Clarence started toward us."

"You abandoned me!" Grady broke in. "I could have been killed!"

"You were fine," she said. "Anyway, after you chased him off, I had this sudden urge to . . . Well, they've been making me drink an awful lot of coffee, Grady. An *awful* lot, if you get my drift."

Grady turned his head to the side and looked away from her. He couldn't argue with that. He wanted to, but he couldn't. And he didn't want to tell her about Sutter, but he had to. Life, he thought for not the first time, was not fair. He took a deep breath. He supposed he'd better get this over with before she had some other crisis of bodily functions.

"All right," he said, "Get a grip on yourself, Mags. Remember Trini's Uncle Sutter? Quincy's dearest friend in all the world? The merry prankster who wallpapered over the door to the convenience at the Yale Club? Formerly the lad who bobsledded down Wilson's Hill in record time and landed in the creek, with Quincy and the governor's plucky son right behind him?"

Maggie frowned and said, "Is there a point to this?"

"He's here," Grady said. "In San Francisco."

She held a finger to her lips. "That's odd. I wonder why Quin didn't tell me he was going to contact him?"

"He didn't. I mean, he's not with Quincy, Mags. I'm reasonably sure Quincy doesn't know he's here."

Maggie cocked her head. "Sutter came on his own? How in the world did you find out? Did he—No, he wouldn't have known to contact you. Would he? Grady?"

Best give it to her straight. "I found out," he said, "because I was following your Sister Mae and Brother Michael when they met him at the depot.''

Maggie stared at him. Not a word, not a gesture. Just a stare.

"They took him to the Palace," Grady continued. "He's registered there under the name of John Dobbs, out of Chicago. I haven't told Quincy yet. Haven't told anybody except you."

"Suds," said Maggie finally. Then, "Hell and damnation!" She took a step toward him and propped her hands on her hips, enunciating every syllable of, "This complicates *everything!*" as if he were the one who'd complicated it!

"Fine," he said, leaning away and remembering, too late, that she was testy when she didn't feel well. Through smudged spectacles, he looked down his nose and added, "Go ahead, shoot the messenger."

"Don't tempt me," she grumbled.

FOURTEEN

M AGGIE HOISTED HERSELF ATOP ONE OF THE RAIN barrels in back of the hotel, reached for the gutter, and pulled herself up to the Seawitch's rear overhang. She swung her leg a bit too far in, and the little roof creaked. She froze, holding her breath and silently cursing herself for making such a stupid mistake.

When there was no sign of activity from within, she carefully moved on, working her way toward the third window. It was her own, and it was still standing open.

She peeked through the opening. Darkness. Everyone was still asleep. Good. Slithering over the sill and through the window, she quietly made her way through the darkness to her bed. She slipped off her shoes, then the blue dress, and in her underwear, burrowed beneath the worn counterpane.

She lay there a moment, listening to the other girls' breathing, letting it lull her heartbeat back to normal. She was tired. Not just worn-out from the long day and the day before that and the day before that—normally, she wouldn't have given that part a second thought. Sneaking out second- or third-story windows and hiding in alleys and scrambling up and down drain spouts and evading those who sought to catch her was, by now, second nature.

But as good a show as she'd put on for Grady, as much as she'd belittled the entire situation, Maggie was sick and exhausted from her much-too-near experience with the afterlife. Her bones ached, every one of them, and she had the curious notion that they weren't quite solid, that they were made of plaster which had been exposed to the liquid of the drug for too long, and were turning to mush. Her head pounded unmercifully, and every square inch of her skin alternately itched or burned or felt nothing at all. At least it had stopped itching madly, as if there were ten thousand ants waging a war under her hide.

If she hadn't been on a case—if she hadn't been on *Quincy's* case—she would have just thrown in the towel and gone directly to the nearest hospital.

Well, no, she probably wouldn't have. She probably would have done exactly what she was doing. But the thought of a nice hospital bed and cool crisp sheets seemed soothing. She'd have given anything for a nice alcohol bath.

She kicked away the covers, suddenly hot again. Good grief, when was it going to stop?

And now this new hickory stick in the spokes! What in the name of all that was holy was Sutter Malone doing in San Francisco?

It might be a scheme whereby Sutter planned to get Brother Ascension himself, she thought. After all, he was registered under the name of Dobbs. Perhaps Mae and Michael didn't know his true identity. Perhaps Sutter planned to insinuate himself into the Children of Golgotha somehow and—

No, that didn't wash. For one thing, the man was in his thirties. He was far too old to be a follower. And he was staying at the Palace. If he were going to enlist in Brother Ascension's flock, Mae and Michael would have brought him to the Seawitch.

Maggie supposed that Sutter could have once again hired his own detectives—Mae and Michael. While the Pinkertons were out, there were certainly other agencies to hire. But if Mae was a detective, why in the world would she have done what Grady said she had—set out on her lonesome, sniffed out Otto, and told Ascension? And why would she have come ahead to San Francisco to do Ascension's point work, when she could have kidnapped Trini back in Conquistador, hopped a stage, and never looked behind her?

Another possibility occurred to her. Perhaps Trini and Sutter had worked this out together, somehow, and planned to—No. Why would Sutter have told Quin that whole involved story about Trini running off after Ascension again?

Maggie realized her teeth were chattering. She pulled up the covers again, hugging them to her. *I'm running a fever,* she thought, and wished she had a thermometer. And then she was glad she didn't. It was best not to know some things.

She had a horrible suspicion growing within her like a cancer—she wasn't going to find an honorable explanation for Sutter Malone's sudden appearance in town. She could make excuses, certainly. Sutter was rich, Sutter loved his niece, Sutter was a decent man. She knew this, because Quincy had told her it was so.

But how long had it been since Quincy had actually seen his old friend? Since college? A man's morality could change a great deal in twelve or thirteen years. He could spend or gamble away a fortune, that was certain. She'd seen all too often what the lack of money, where it had never been an issue before, could do to love, what it could do to decency. And Trini had, if nothing else, money.

Hot again, she kicked away the covers and rolled on her side. The air came as a blessing, cooling her back and shoulders, and pressing a metaphorical ice pack to the back of her sweating scalp.

Knives, she thought. *I'd kill for a nice set of knives to throw. Or balls to juggle. Even a chance to stand on my head!*

Anything to take her mind off her body and put it back on Sutter Malone, where it belonged.

Whether she wished to admit it or not she'd already decided he was up to no good. He'd come here to oversee the murder of his niece, or make certain that he got his cut, or perhaps to pat Brother Ascension on the back and say, "Well done, old boy!" In any case, he was throwing a royal wrench into the gears of her plan.

Maggie flopped onto her back again and stared upwards at the soft shadows on the ceiling, ignoring the raucous noises from outside.

What she would have liked to do was to just shove Trini into a cab and climb in behind her and let the rest of them go hang. But then, nothing would be tied up, would it? Nothing would be tidy and neat. There'd be no explanations, no theories proved or disproved, no one sent to jail, no one declared innocent or guilty. And Brother Ascension would be free to murder some other open-faced, bean-brained postadolescent.

If there was one thing Maggie Maguire couldn't stand, it was a loose end.

Good gravy, she was so cold! She snatched the covers up around her again, and shivering, forced herself to concentrate on the coming day. It was supposed to have been Brother Ascension's day of reckoning, but now, what with Sutter's appearance, she didn't know. It called for an expansion of her plot, somehow, to take in Sutter's part.

But how could she know what changes to make if she couldn't be certain—absolutely certain—of his motives?

If she guessed incorrectly, she'd lose Quin. It was just that simple. She knew him all too well. He'd known Sutter since they were both boys, and to a man like Quincy, that bond was nearly as strong as brotherhood. If she should mistakenly accuse Sutter of being in the wrong—worse: not just being in the wrong, but helping to instigate it—Quincy would never forgive her.

Not only would she lose his friendship, which was almost as dear to her as that of Grady, but she'd lose his business.

Another sobering thought.

So tomorrow she'd play it out as if she'd never heard Sutter was in town. Just like they'd planned. She'd keep this Sutter business between herself and Grady, and tackle it when the time came. Not the best solution, but the only one she had at hand.

Brother Ascension was probably in his room, trying to decide whether she was the real McCoy or a fortune hunter—a clever twist, she'd thought at the time, having her own people doubt her and telling them to say someone had sent Hardy Obermyer's watch all those years ago when he had supposedly died. Give Ascension a bone to gnaw and keep him busy—and away from the other morsels of her story, more easily chewed to bits. Except that at the moment, she wasn't certain it had been such a clever idea. At the moment her brain was in such a sludgy state that she couldn't remember half the pieces.

And then there was Trini. Gad, was the girl trying to drive her stark raving mad? She thought she'd warned her not to sign anything, but she had no idea if the girl had heard her or taken her seriously. She wasn't even certain she'd really said it, or just imagined it.

A fine kettle of fish you've got stewed up, here, Miss Magdalena, she thought she heard her papa say as, at last, she drifted into sleep. *It'll never work on the road, daughter. With all those fire-eaters and dancing ponies, they'll never even* see *the high-wire act!*

Quincy Applegate lay in the dark, staring at his bedroom ceiling. *What's Maggie doing now?* he wondered. *Is she awake? Is she plotting and planning?*

He was so lucky to have found her! Smart, beautiful, as brave as the day was long. Candid—well, outspoken, really. Almost dangerously so. And not afraid to do a man's job.

He cupped his hands behind his head and screwed up his face. Hers were not exactly womanly virtues, except for the "beautiful" part.

He doubted she could cook or bake, and he'd never heard her play a musical instrument. He'd never heard her make mention of any watercolors or porcelain she'd painted, any needlework she'd done. Did she sew or knit or darn or tat? He didn't believe so. Probably couldn't even mend a sock.

Hardly a paragon of femininity, was his Maggie, hardly a woman one could take home to Mother in complete confidence, let alone honesty. But there was something about her, something so forthright and—

I shouldn't be thinking about this, he told himself. *Not now. Not when it's—what had Grady said? Not when it's "going down" tomorrow.*

Really, he was picking up a whole new vocabulary.

He'd discovered a great deal about himself today. That lying was very easy, for one thing. Well, lying to a liar. He wasn't at all sure he'd have been able to pull it off if he'd been dealing with anyone other than Brother Ascension.

But it had been fun! Rather like putting on a play or some such frivolity, except that at the end, nobody stood up and applauded. You got your satisfaction from pulling the wool over your—what had Blevins called Ascension? Ah, yes, the mark! You got your satisfaction from pulling the wool over the mark's eyes.

He'd never dreamt that Maggie could pull together this gossamer, this fantasy, this . . . all right, this web of deceit. And she'd put it together so quickly!

A clever girl, his Maggie, even if she'd be out of place in his mother's house, even if she couldn't tat or bake or paint or play the piano. Well, perhaps she could learn.

No, hang it, she didn't have to! His Maggie had qualities all her own. And perhaps he wouldn't take her home to meet his mother, not that he'd actually considered it before. The thought of them in the same room shot him through with something akin to horror. He saw his mother in the drawing room at home, wearing one of her high-necked matron's dresses, always conservatively fashionable. She was an officer in the Ladies Temperance League and the

Garden Society, a woman who thought that "darn" was an unpardonable swear word, and whom he had never, not once in his life, heard raising her voice.

He pictured walking into that room with Maggie on his arm. They'd probably be just fine for five minutes, but the first time Maggie mentioned her father, or her work, or the first time Mother asked her a question?

Involuntarily, he shuddered.

Then, just as quickly, he smiled. *Father would like her just fine,* he thought. *After he got used to her.*

He wondered, for a moment, if he had a right to call her "his Maggie," but pushed it from his mind. Her reports, those were the amazing things. To think that he'd read them without understanding them, *really* understanding them, for these past three years!

Rufus Haggarty was located in a remote cabin, along with three thugs, he recalled she'd written in one of them. *The thugs were dispatched, and Rufus was summarily bound and brought in for trial.*

Amazing! He'd just read it before, but now it seemed a thing of wonder that, all alone, this slip of a girl had tracked Rufus "Split Lip" Haggarty and his gang to an isolated cabin, and then managed—all on her own, mind you—to "dispatch" his minions and bring him to justice.

How in the world had she *done* that? Set fire to the cabin? Walked in the front door with a pistol pulled? Ambushed them one at a time? Roped one, shot another, cracked yet another over the head? She'd never said, and he'd never asked.

Never asked! He felt the heat rising in his face, belatedly embarrassed for so many oversights on his part, so many times when he could have celebrated her processes as well as her results. So many more times to have been proud.

So many more times to have been afraid for her after the fact, when it did absolutely no good whatsoever.

Slowly, he shook his head. He'd have to add modesty to

her list of virtues. And he'd have to ask about Rufus and all the rest.

No, perhaps he wouldn't. Perhaps it was all in a day's work to her, risking life and limb. Her father had owned a circus, and she'd been with the Pinkertons for a short time before coming west. He supposed that had equipped her in an odd sort of way, but still!

An amazing woman.

Dimly, for he was more asleep than awake by now, he became aware that downstairs, his telephone was ringing. Muttering a soft curse under his breath, he roused himself, sat up, and fumbled for his robe and slippers, then stumbled toward the door.

Out in the hall, down the front stairs, and toward the phone cubby he went, only stubbing his foot once and grumbling all the while. In the lower hall, the light of a single candle and muffled but heavy footsteps approached steadily from the opposite direction, but he held up his hand.

"Go back to bed, Mrs. Lovejoy," he said sleepily as the housekeeper, a candle lighting her round, nightcapped face, clumped nearer. "I've got it."

"Somebody's got a lot of nerve, ringin' up decent people in the middle of the night. Them machines ain't natural," he heard her growl as she headed back toward her room, the candlelight glowing dimly around the edges of her not inconsiderable bulk.

The phone rang again. Expecting it to be Grady, reporting some urgent and ghastly new turn in the case, he picked it up gingerly, cleared his throat, and said, "Applegate here."

He stood, dumbfounded at first, then jubilant, then angry. At last his expression settled into one of anxious curiosity, and he said, "But—Yes, of course. Of course I'll meet you, Sutter."

FIFTEEN

>─┼─◆─┼─❍─┼─◆─┼─<

N O NEED TO BE NERVOUS, GRADY TOLD HIMSELF AS
he dismissed Tommy Two-Tone and took up the
watch outside the Seawitch Hotel. It was noon,
bright and sunshiny, and the birds would have been singing
had any songbird been daft enough to perch in the Barbary
Coast. As it was, for company he had the chatter of bick-
ering sparrows and the cries of seabirds, mixed with the
usual sounds of hooliganism.

But he couldn't help but be a little shaky. It was nearly
time for Brother Ascension to accompany Maggie to the
Majestic and Otto, and he wanted to be there, in case anything went awry. But no, Maggie had said he was to watch
the Seawitch and keep an eye on Trini. And Tommy Two-
Tone had said she was still in there. At least, he'd said no
girl matching Trini's description had marched out at seven
with the others, or had come out since. So Grady waited.

This day, he was disguised as a sailor. Sporting an earring and clad in a worn turtleneck and patched trousers held
up by suspenders, he leaned against a barrel outside Best
Dry Goods.

He was beginning to feel like an employee.

He scratched at his ear—he'd had it pierced years ago
in a fit of jovial drunkenness, and had only worn the gold
hoop long enough to drive his father half crazy. And for
the hole through his lobe to heal open. It wasn't noticeable

now except with a magnifying glass, its diameter having significantly decreased over time. In fact, it was barely large enough to accommodate the tiny wire. He scratched at it again, and for the fifth time considered taking it out, and for the fifth time thought better of it.

He hoped Maggie wouldn't mind that he'd taken on a couple of new men. Actually, on second thought, he didn't care whether she minded or not. The whole thing was getting out of hand, swelling beyond all proportion, and he simply couldn't cover all the bases by himself. Thus, Tommy Two-Tone and Carpface Gershwin. Carpface was over at the Palace right now, probably reading a newspaper in a cushioned lobby chair, sipping a lime fizz, and watching for any signs of life from Room 332.

And no one had phoned this morning. He'd expected word from Quincy, anyway, if nothing more than to cackle about the "adventure of it all." But nothing. And when he'd phoned Quincy's office, they'd said he wasn't coming in today. Odd. Quin Applegate was so wrapped up in actuarial tables and appraisers that Grady'd been surprised he'd actually made it to the hotel yesterday.

"Back again?"

Grady flicked his eyes skyward before he turned round.

"What you doin' here, anyway?" the storekeeper, the champion bad speller of all time, asked him.

"I warn't here before, mate," Grady growled. "Ye be mistook."

"Yeah?" the man said without expression. He heaved his burden, a sack of flour, off his shoulder and to the ground. "Well, if I was you, I'd stand different. You mighta been out here in three different outfits, but you gots the same kinda slouch. Why you watchin' the Seawitch, anyways? You gots somethin' t'do with them Bible-thumpers in blue?"

Grady gave up. If he couldn't even fool this ape, he was sunk. He said, "Why? What do you know about them?"

"Know they're a buncha pests," the storekeeper said,

folding his arms. "They was all over the place last night, handin' out papers to folks what didn't want 'em."

"Last night?" Grady hadn't seen one of them while he was waiting for Maggie, and he'd waited a long time.

"Evenin', more like," the man said, bending to snatch something blue up from the sidewalk. "They went away round nine, into that hall yonder." He pointed across the street, to the one-story side wing of the Seawitch. "You could hear 'em prayin' and singin' halfway up the block," he said with disgust. "Ain't decent on a Wednesday."

Grady considered this. It fit. He said, "You have a name?"

"Best," said the owner of Best Dry Goods. It figured. "Zeke Best. And I might be askin' you the same?"

"Grady Maguire, at your service, sir." Best to be polite with these earthy types. Besides, it didn't really matter.

But Zeke Best said, "Maguire? Your papa wouldn't't've been old Conner Maguire, would he?"

Grady paused before he answered. If he replied in the affirmative, Zeke Best was liable to either give him a bear hug right here on the street, or pull out a pistol and shoot him in the stomach.

Neither possibility held a great deal of charm.

But at last he answered, "Yes, he was my father."

"By gum!" Zeke roared. "By diddly-damn gum!" And went with the first alternative: he swept Grady into a humiliating (not to mention rib-crushing) hug that lifted him off his feet and spun him around. "Ol' Conner ran the bestest floatin' craps game this whole town has ever see'd!" he shouted, once he'd set Grady down. He wiped away a tear.

Perfect, Grady thought as he attempted to pull a little air back into his lungs. *Just what I need right now: an illiterate hysterical gorilla.*

"Why, you jus' tell me what you're after, young Grady, an' ol' Zeke Best'll do his best!" He grinned widely, his eyes still moist. "That there was a joke, son!"

Grady forced a chortle, although he was hampered by the fact that his chest still felt like a compressed accordion. Zeke pounded him good-naturedly on the back, knocking the wind out of his sails again and pitching him forward, to his knees.

"Aw, sorry, boy!" cried Zeke, hauling him up by one shoulder. "I didn't know you were sickly."

As Zeke brushed him off, Grady caught sight of Maggie, just emerging from the Seawitch in the company of Brother Ascension. Well, two of each actually, for that last unexpected "friendly" blow had shaken his brain and now he was seeing double. On the other hand, it could have been because he was oxygen deprived, and as the air rushed back into his lungs with a *whoosh*, he grabbed hold of Zeke Best's arms and said, "Stop dusting me off!"

Zeke stopped, and quickly Grady checked his watch. Twelve-thirty, on the dot, read both the watches in both of his hands.

He snapped them closed and stuffed them in his pockets as he watched the two Maggies and the two Brother Ascensions walk away past two Harris's Saloons and two Jimmy Dale's Frolics and two Fieldings's Girls Girls Girls, and then he lost them in the crowd of doubled toughs and floozies and hawkers.

"What's a'matter, boy? You all right?" Zeke was still beside him, worry furrowing both his brows.

"Afraid that last one banged my brain, Zeke," Grady said. "I'm seeing double." He wished he could follow Maggie. He *should* follow her, but then who would look after Trini?

"That's all?" said Zeke. "Why, just give your head a good shakin'. Works for me ever' time. And if that don't fix it, I got a bottle back of the counter that'll have you happy t'see two of everythin'. Might even make you see three or four, if you get deep enough into it."

He started into the store, apparently to fetch the bottle, then stopped. "Oh. Here," he said, handing Grady something blue. "This is what them kids was foistin' off on ever'body last night. Reckon the streets is full of 'em, but at least this 'un ain't been crapped on by a horse yet."

Grady took the paper blindly, holding out one hand and shaking his head violently. When he stopped, Zeke had gone inside, he supposed, and things looked a little better. At least the images overlapped now. He smoothed the tract flat on his knee and tried to read it, but his vision was still fuzzy. He glanced across the street, more to check his vision than anything else, and just caught sight of Trini, stepping off the sidewalk!

Hurriedly, he shoved the paper into his pocket and took off after her at a jog. Why did everything have to happen at once? And why did every meeting with one of his dad's old friends always end with him being crippled or knocked silly or drunk or worse?

He slowed his gate to a walk. Trini was half a block ahead now. Two men accompanied her. He hadn't noticed them at first—his eyes being locked on that blue dress— but one of them was Brother Michael.

The other was Brother Clarence, or so he assumed from the fellow's height and bulk. He hadn't turned around yet, but he was attired in a tight-fitting dark grey suit. The two men bracketed her like bookends all the way out of the district, each one alternately taking her arm when the other let go.

He realized his vision had cleared—just one of everything, thank goodness—a moment before Michael flagged down a cab. Grady heard him give the driver instructions, then turn to Clarence and grumble, "Help her get in the damn thing, will ya?"

The cab had pulled away and was out of sight before Grady could catch the attention of a hack looking for a fare, but he had the address. He gave it to the driver and settled nervously back in the seat. He certainly wasn't attired for the particular section of town into which he was heading, but he'd just have to make do.

The earring was still itching, and it was with a great deal of relief that he slipped the wire out and stuffed it into his pocket, only then remembering the leaflet. He pulled it free again and smoothed it, and this time he could read it:

FREE!!
Come all ye seekers!
CAMP MEETING THIS SUNDAY
9 A.M.–9 P.M.
SEAWITCH HOTEL DINING HALL
FREE!!
Hosanna in the Highest!
Let Brother Ascension and the Children of Golgotha help
you rest your burden at the feet of the Lord God
Almighty through his Only Son and Servant Jesus the
Christ Everlasting! Let His Precious Blood wash away
your sins! Let his Blessed Resurrection lift you from the
sorrows of your day-to-day life! Come one, come all! Be
healed! Be whole!
Behold the Son of God
for He is All-Powerful!
FREE!!
(offerings received at the door)

Brother Ascension was reasonably pleased with himself.
Last night, he'd sobered up Magdalena—not too sober, mind, but sober enough to walk, and sober enough that he was certain she wasn't going to croak on him—and this morning, after a breakfast containing a little "hair of the dog," she was in a perfect state to meet that old fool of a grandfather.
Rich old fool, he corrected himself, and stifled a smile.
He flicked his eyes toward Magdalena—sitting quietly across from him in the cab, gazing dully out the window— and then he glanced at his watch. It was 12:35.
Clarence and Michael were on their way to Ingram's office with Trini by now. He'd used Ingram once before, for

the Morton girl, and he could be trusted. Gambling debts did that to a man. Ingram would have the papers all drawn up and ready, and all Trini would have to do was sign her name.

And, in roughly an hour and a half, he'd be on his way there himself. He'd have Magdalena sign on the dotted line. He'd be set. That was, almost set. Still the little details of two deaths to be unfolded.

It was all planned. Of course, they'd have to take care of Obermyer first. A heart attack would be nice, and he had the drugs in his arsenal to push the old man over the edge, once he'd redrawn his will. No one, not even that meddling lush Dr. Hedrick, would be the wiser.

Today was Thursday, so the old kraut-eater would have three days to fix his will—the rest of today and Friday, maybe Saturday if that obnoxious pup of a lawyer worked weekends. And so, come Sunday, when he was in full and glorious sight of everyone at the camp meeting for twelve straight hours, he'd send Clarence to the docks with three girls.

Three, because it would look too suspicious, even to him, if just the two girls who'd left him all that money died. Therefore, three. He'd have loved to wave good-bye to Polly, too—the grasping little fishwife—but that would have been foolhardy.

Besides, Polly was a strong swimmer, drat the luck.

No, he'd send someone else. Sister Hester, perhaps? She was tiny and easily weighed down by wet skirts and petticoats, she had no family—no money either—and she couldn't swim.

No. Hester had only serviced him twice, but she'd serviced him well. He wanted another taste or two before he got rid of her.

Sister Edwina, then. She was equally poor and without relations, and chubby. He didn't care for chubby women, and he was practically certain she didn't swim. Yes, Sister Edwina would do nicely.

Of course, he didn't know whether Magdalena could swim or not, but he thought it was doubtful. Most females, being basically uncoordinated, couldn't. And she'd been raised inland, where there'd be no need to learn. But if, by some chance, she could? Clarence would have little trouble with her. And the boy would enjoy it so.

It was unusual for Ascension to take action so quickly. Usually, he'd let a youngster cleave to the group quite a bit longer before he made it to the will stage, and longer still before there were any "unexpected" deaths.

He'd let Amy Proctor follow for almost two years before he'd "let" her make a new will, leaving him everything, and waited another six months before he'd had Clarence push her out that window.

The Anderson boy followed him for ten months before he signed, and it had been another ten before Clarence held him down in the bathtub until he was dead.

The Morton girl had trooped after him for more than a year, gladly signed her will, then trooped after him for almost another year and a third before he killed her himself, one night in bed. They'd dressed the body and thrown it in an alley, and the death had passed as a mugging.

Will Sempler followed him for nearly a year and a half before he'd had the boy make a last will and testament. Of course, he'd taken care of Will only ten days later, but that was necessary—one of the others had confided to him that Will was considering marriage to a girl in the flock.

He couldn't have that, now, could he? A marriage would invalidate the will and snatch over one hundred and fifty thousand right out of his fingers!

Except that after he and Clarence had thrown Will under the wheels of that beer wagon, not one of the girls had so much as made a peep.

He scratched his head. Odd. Perhaps the informer had been mistaken.

Well, never mind. No one had complained. He'd collected the cash with no problems, then moved the group to the next town, as usual. His little chicks.

He checked his watch again, then looked out the window. Almost there. He supposed he'd best get to work.

"Magdalena?" he said softly.

The girl raised her head and stared at him with fuzzy adoration. It was a shame he couldn't keep her for a bit after she signed the papers. She was really quite lovely, and he'd decided that it didn't really matter if she was the real thing or a con artist, out to swindle Obermyer. Either way, she had the birth certificate, she bore a resemblance to the late Hardy Obermyer, and with his help, she'd have the old man's money.

But she wouldn't have it for long. Clarence would row them out into the cold, cold bay in the boat. Then he'd overturn it, make sure they were all drowned, and swim to shore.

He wondered if perhaps he shouldn't tell Clarence to haul one of the corpses back with him. Magdalena's would be the best, for hers was the largest estate. Besides, if she was a swimmer, he could hold her under on the way in. Best to have her there, anyway, so her body could be identified. Best not to leave it to chance. Or to the sharks.

It would certainly be a lovely effect. The distraught young man, sodden and exhausted and kneeling over the body he'd carried all that way, for nothing. Weeping on the docks and all that. Yes, it made a pretty picture.

Well, best to get started. The south of France, with its clattering gaming chips and glittering jewels and warm Mediterranean breezes, called to him. He could almost smell the croissants. Or was it crumpets? England or France, France or England?

Figure it out later, my dear boy, he thought, smiling just slightly. *Right now, there's business to attend.*

Quietly, and maintaining eye contact, he said, "Magdalena?" The girl leaned forward. She was practically crawling onto his lap!

Concealing his smugness, he continued, "I want you to relax. Rest, my child, in the comfort and care of Jesus the Christ, who loves you, and Brother Ascension, who loves you more. Lean back and let your eyes drift closed. Listen to the sound of my voice, only the sound of my voice . . ."

Across town at the Palace Hotel, Louie "Carpface" Gershwin sat in the lobby, in a deep-cushioned leather armchair, smoking, sipping a limeade—straight, no booze—while pretending to read the paper.

He wiggled his narrow backside in the seat again, searching for a new position, and looked at the big clock over the desk.

A quarter to one! he thought irritably, and put the paper aside for a moment to relight his cigar, which had gone out in the ashtray.

That's near four hours I been here! You'd think the mark'd do something, go somewhere! What's the bloody bastard doin' up there, anyhow? Writin' a book? Hatchin' eggs?

He puffed at the cigar in annoyance, then paused, cocking his head. *Calm down,* he thought to himself. *No good to get all discombobulated, Louie. The mark'll show when the mark shows, and that's that.*

Still, he'd rather have been actually doing something instead of sitting on his butt. Get a line on a good game of cards, say. Or better yet, a rigged one.

"Nothing to it, Carpface," Grady had said last night at Corcoran's Cubbyhole, Carpface's usual haunt. "Just sit there and watch. And if he leaves, follow him." Grady had fed him the skinny on the man upstairs, and then he'd pressed two double eagles into Carpface's hand.

"Well, I needed the scratch," Carpface muttered aloud. He'd lost big last night, and Grady'd paid him—up front, no less—twice what he'd lost. "Good ol' Grady." It was better and cleaner work than cutting purses or fiddling a cash drawer. Besides, you couldn't go to jail for it.

The gentleman across the way lowered his newspaper and frowned at him. Carpface Gershwin frowned back, and the man quickly raised his paper again.

Sucker, thought Carpface, and then he smiled. Not many men could look at him without cowering. That came from being born naturally ugly, he supposed. That, and a kick in the face by a blue-roan plow horse when he was eleven, a kick that had permanently flattened his nose and crushed the bones in his cheeks and over his eyes, also permanently.

After that, companions had started calling him Louie the Fish. He'd come by the Carpface tag later on, after he grew the sparse beard.

His ma had cried and cried, both just after the accident and later on. But to his way of thinking, the kids could call him anything they wanted. At least he was still alive to hear it.

I'm just naturally menacing, he thought with a certain degree of pride, and gave his chin whiskers a self-satisfied stroke.

He was so caught up in complimenting himself that he didn't catch sight of the mark until he was at the front desk.

He gave no sign, however. He remained seated, casually watching the desk clerk check for messages and take the room key—number 332, just like Grady had said—and place it in the same cubby.

And then, after the mark had had time to cross the lobby, he rose, stretching his lanky frame, and sauntered toward the door to the courtyard, on the tail of Sutter Malone, aka John Dobbs.

Finally, something to do. The mark was on the move.

SIXTEEN

>=!=•+•=•=❍=•+•=!=<

MAGGIE WAITED COMPLACENTLY WHILE BROTHER Ascension knocked on Otto's door. He'd told her to be bright and friendly with Otto. He hadn't asked her if she were really Otto's granddaughter, which gave her a momentary qualm. But since he'd then given the suggestion that she loved Otto very much, although she'd never met him, she decided he'd come to the conclusion that he was going for the money. He didn't care if she was the real thing.

She was so relieved she'd almost forgotten to dig her nails into her palms.

Quincy opened the door. He gave no sign of recognition, simply saying, "I see you're punctual, Brother Ascension."

They went inside, Maggie first. Otto was nowhere in sight, but Bedside Blevins waited in the middle of the room, his arms crossed over his little belly. "You're here," he said, by way of greeting. "This the girl?"

Beside her, Brother Ascension nodded. "God bless you, Mr. Halliday. And you, Dr. Hedrick. Yes, this is our little Magdalena." He placed a hand on her shoulder, a fatherly gesture that made her skin crawl. "And where is Mr. Obermyer, if I may be so bold as to inquire?"

"He'll be in later," said Quincy, standing to the side. "First, we'd like to ask Miss Obermyer a few questions."

Ascension was nothing but genteel civility. "Certainly,

Halliday, certainly,'' he said, ushering Maggie toward a chair. "I hope this won't take too long, however. For Miss Obermyer's sake. Magdalena is most anxious to meet her grandfather.''

Blevins said, "I'm certain you wish it to be as short a wait as humanly possible,'' infusing the statement with all sorts of overtones. Grady had been positively brilliant, Maggie thought, to suggest him for the part of Dr. Hedrick. Come to think of it, he had insisted rather emphatically.

The grilling commenced. Quin and Blevins took turns asking about her parents, her upbringing, her schooling, with the occasional nonsequitur tossed in, just to give Brother Ascension the idea that they were trying to trip her up.

Maggie folded her hands and answered as best she could. Between trying to remember the details of a made-up life and fighting the monstrous hangover that had plagued her all morning with no signs of relief, she thought she did a creditable job.

Quincy seemed strange, though. Ascension would never have noticed it, but Quincy appeared a bit distracted—odd, considering that this was a job he'd contracted. Distracted and a bit distanced and, well, short. He was almost, but not quite, angry.

Very odd. But she made the excuse that this was his first stab at acting—his first stab at deceit, to be more precise— and he could be forgiven a little overzealousness. If that was what it was. Perhaps he'd thrown himself into the part with too much gusto.

She didn't have much time to consider it further, because, after only seven or eight minutes of questions, a door—probably to the bedroom—opened, and Otto stepped out.

Maggie gasped slightly, enough so Ascension could hear, and gazed at Otto with eyes full of wonder and hope. At least, she trusted this was the case.

She rose to her feet and said, *"G-grossvater?"*

Without skipping a beat, Otto sternly replied, *"Setzen Sie, bitte.* Is not established yet for sure if I got anything to do with you."

Maggie lowered her eyes and sat again, just in time for Ozymandias, who must have been in the bedroom with Otto, to fly across the room and take a vaulting leap into her lap. Immediately, he put his front paws on her shoulders and began rubbing her face with his, and purring to beat the band. He did everything but yell, "Mommy!"

Good gravy, Maggie thought. *Just what the act needed.* But she said quickly, "Oh, a kitty!" and hugged him and tickled him in all the right places. "What's his name?" She hoped Ascension would just think this was a strange cat who *really* liked her.

"You got a way with animals," said Otto.

She looked up from Ozzie, who had fallen into a purring, slit-eyed trance, his gigantic paws going large and medium and large again into the air.

"Well, yes, sir," she answered shyly. "My papa, he had it, too, but it was aimed more toward horses and dogs. I like whatever critter takes a shine to me, I reckon."

Otto seemed to consider this. He was ad-libbing quite nicely, she thought. She turned toward Brother Ascension, who she noticed, too late, was leaning away, and said, "You wanna pet him?" and held the cat out.

Suddenly Ozzie hissed and spat, startling them all, then calmly backed up onto her lap again and resumed his kneading and rubbing.

"He don't like everyone," a smiling Otto offered to Ascension, who had vaulted to his feet and was now standing two yards away and staring at the cat with a none-too-loving expression.

Otto turned his gaze on Maggie. "Young woman, I listen through a crack in the door to all the questions of these men, and I hear all your answers. You answer fine and dandy, but the questions? *Nicht so gut.*"

Blevins was perfect. He had the exasperated expression

of a man who was a doctor and a scientist, for God's sake, and wanted facts, not frippery. She couldn't see Quincy.

"Now I got some questions to ask," Otto continued. "Your papa. He dies when you are seventeen, no?"

Maggie said, "Eighteen," and kept stroking the cat. She noticed that the couch looked a little frayed. Tacky of the Majestic, she thought, until she noticed that the tatters had a certain familiarity. *Ozzie, you little rat!* she thought.

Otto was speaking. "Was there anything he used to do?" he asked. "Anything unusual?"

Maggie cocked her head. She couldn't for the life of her figure out where Otto was leading. "Unusual?"

"*Ja.* Anything strange, like what the other papas didn't do. Or say. Or sing. To make a joke sometimes."

There's a trail in here someplace, Maggie thought, *if only he wouldn't be so blasted obtuse about it!*

Affecting embarrassment, she offered, "Well, gosh! All those little family things, you know? They were just silliness. Every family's got 'em."

But like a feisty dog, Otto wouldn't drop the blasted bone. He said, "I'm not caring 'bout everybody else. What they do in *your* family?"

She sighed. She'd just make up something. Otto would say he recognized it, by jingo, and she could rake him over the coals later. She lifted her chin and said, "Well, my mama used to fold up the linens, straight from the line, and put 'em on her chair and sit on 'em. She called that ironin' by the cold process."

Behind her, Quincy snorted, but she didn't dare look round. Blevins had sucked his cheeks between his teeth.

Otto, however, looked at her quizzically, then shook his head. "*Nein, Liebchen.* About your *Vater.*"

"Well," she said, hesitating, "Papa used to talk German sometimes. He taught me some."

"Hmph," growled Otto. "Anybody can speak *Deutsch.* Is easy language. What else?"

Easy for you, Maggie thought. She was growing annoyed

with him. But she continued softly, "Sometimes he used to go round the barnyard and—No, it's awful silly."

Blevins was leaning forward. Otto cocked a brow. He said, "Tell it anyway."

Doing her best to exude embarrassment—and think quickly—Maggie said, "He'd put the chickens to sleep, all right? He'd just walk round and catch 'em, one at a time, and stick their heads under their wings and rock 'em and sing to 'em and pretty soon there'd be a whole yard full a hens, all tranced."

Otto looked like a hunting dog on point. He said, "This song he sings. What was it?"

It had to be something unusual, something odd. Suddenly it came to her, and she said, "It was church hymns, all right? Except all like . . . like a what-you-call. Silliness."

"A nonsense song? A parody?" offered Blevins.

"Yes, sir, that last one." She made a point of glancing over toward Brother Ascension, and made herself think of something embarrassing, like standing in the middle of the street with no clothes on at high noon. The blush pushed heat into her cheeks almost immediately.

She turned back toward Otto, just in time for him to demand, "Well? What is it?"

"I don't like to say." She flicked her eyes at Ascension again. "My mama raised me to be a good Christian girl, and—"

"Speak up! *Heraus!*" Otto barked.

Letting her eyes go wide, she said, "It was 'Gladly, the Cross-eyed Bear,' all right?" She lowered her gaze then, and staring blankly at the cat, said, "I'm real sorry you had to hear that blaspheming, Brother Ascension."

There was silence all around her for what seemed the longest time, and she realized that she didn't know whether the hymn had even been written for the imaginary Hardy to learn it, let alone subvert it. She wished she could see their faces to get some sort of an inkling . . . but then Otto spoke.

"That Hardy," he began, his voice cracking. "Always he sing that church song like that, since he was little boy. *Und ja,* always he puts the chickens to sleep. Ducks, too. Even back home in *Deutschland,* before we came . . . came to . . ." He lifted his hands to his face, unable to continue.

Dropping an annoyed Ozzie to the floor, she rose to her feet. "Grandfather?" she whispered. *"Grossvater? Opa?"*

"Liebchen," he blubbered and held out his arms.

She raced into them to hide the fact that he hadn't any real tears, and was surprised to find he was really weeping! She had no idea he had such a talent!

Somehow, he'd turned his back toward the room during their embrace, and when he released her with his back to the room, he said, "You wait and see, Magdalena Obermyer. Everything gonna be hinky-dinky." And hiding her for a moment with his bulk, quickly squeezed two drops of liquid into her eyes.

The old faker, she thought proudly as he moved away.

"This here is *mein Grosskind,"* he said, getting out his handkerchief—and, she noticed, dropping the little bottle into his pocket at the same time. "Halliday, we make a new will right away."

"But, *Opa,"* Maggie protested, just for show, "I don't want your money! I was only coming to see you!"

Otto took her arm and turned her toward him. She could see Ascension. He had gone a lovely shade of green, and Blevins seemed to be having a very difficult time of it not to laugh. Quin looked, well, distant, as if he hadn't heard a thing that had gone on in the room. Maybe he was thinking about the couch, and how much the hotel was going to charge for reupholstery.

"This is true?" Otto said, wiping one of Maggie's cheeks with a big, flat thumb. "You don't the money want?"

"No," said Maggie softly. Maybe she should have hung on to Ozzie, for his own protection. "Just you, *Opa."*

Out of the corner of her eye, she spied Ascension, sinking into the chair she'd vacated. His green hue had gone to grey.

She hugged Otto and whispered, "You old poop. You'd better leave it to me now, before somebody faints." She didn't know if Ascension could stand any more.

Otto thrust her out to arm's length, a big grin on his face. "Just what I want to hear. *Liebchen*, whether you want this thing or not, you are one wealthy *Mädchen*. Halliday, get cracking! I want this . . ."

Suddenly, Otto's hand went to his left arm, gripping it savagely. "I want you should . . ." He fell, uttering a weak, *"Scheisse!"* from between clenched teeth. Maggie caught him, lowering him to the floor.

"Grandpa?" she whispered, Otto's magic "tears" glistening on her cheeks. Then louder, *"Opa!* Please," she implored the men, "won't somebody help him?"

Ten minutes later, Ascension found himself on the sidewalk, alone.

"Magdalena *must* stay with him, you idiot!" Dr. Hedrick had called to him from the bedroom. Actually, he'd yelled it, and rather angrily, too.

What could he do? He couldn't make a scene, could he? So he'd left, wringing his goddamn hat in his hands like some stupid farmhand and telling Halliday that his prayers—all the prayers of his flock—were with Obermyer.

For once, that wasn't a lie. Obermyer had to live long enough to change his will. Tonight, the Children of Golgotha would pray their little hearts out if he had to thrash them into it.

The last thing Ascension had heard as Halliday shoved him into the hall was Magdalena, back in the bedroom, praying over her grandfather.

He'd call back for her at seven: he'd told this to Halliday while that sanctimonious bastard was busily slamming the door on his backside. Well, he'd take Maggie down to see the lawyer first thing in the morning. If Obermyer was still alive tonight. Even if he wasn't, surely Magdalena would at least get *something* out of the estate!

Except Ascension didn't want just a slice of the pie—he wanted the whole thing.

Christ Almighty! he thought as he climbed into a cab and pulled the door shut with a *bang* behind him. *Why does everything have to happen to me?*

SEVENTEEN

>─┼─◆─○─◆─┼─<

CARPFACE GERSHWIN BRUSHED THE PEANUT SHELLS off his trousers before he stuck a long leg down to the road. Flipping a coin to the driver with one hand, he asked him to drive down the block and wait. This wasn't a neighborhood accustomed to hired hacks. The one he'd been following—the one which waited around the corner and down the block for Sutter Malone—had provoked enough excitement for one day. Children hung from it like monkeys.

From the safety of the same lilac hedge that hid his horse and driver, Carpface studied the neighborhood. This was the run-down residential kind, the sort where the mothers took in laundry, fathers held down two or three jobs if they worked at all, and the kids passed down patched clothes from Jimmy to Johnny to Hank to Bill.

Not a slum, Carpface thought, but the next thing to it. The houses, built about forty years back, cried for paint, needed work on the roofs or gutters or both. Roughly every third house had a "Room to Let" sign tacked up in a window. Carpface was familiar with this kind of neighborhood. Some folks were clawing their way up from the bottom, others were slipping down. It was the kind of neighborhood Grady had lived in when Carpface first met him. Of course, Grady had been just a boy, then, perhaps sixteen or so, but he was already a decent pickpocket. And

Grady's father, Conner, had been alive and kicking. Conner had a suit with little bells tied all over it that would jingle at the slightest brush, and he'd put it on to school Grady in the fine art of purse-lifting. Carpface and Tommy Two-Tone or Slipfinger Pete or Joker O'Banyon (or whoever was out of the pokey at the time) would sit in the kitchen and kibbitz and drink the warm beer one of them had brought up from O'Malley's.

Those were the days, he thought with a sigh.

Carpface watched as Malone strolled from his cab and up the walk of a two-story house. Half the home's once-white paint was peeling. *Definitely somebody slithering down the old drain in that one,* he thought as he watched Malone walk through the weedy front yard and knock at the door.

Carpface waited for Malone to be invited in. Once the door opened and Malone disappeared inside, Carpface relaxed a bit and dug the peanuts out of his pocket. He opened the sack and cracked a shell, and had the first nut halfway to his mouth when he thought he saw something beside the house Malone had gone into. Was there someone in the bushes?

Stuffing the peanuts back into his pocket, he parted the lilacs. He leaned forward.

Ah, you're gettin' crazy in your old age! he told himself after a bit of staring. And then the shrubs rustled again, just slightly.

"Well, call me Mabel and make me late for supper!" he whispered, brightening as he caught a quick glimpse of the top of a man's head as it surfaced from the bushes, then ducked again. "There's somebody down there peekin' in the side window!"

His glee at the day being broken up in this unexpected way was further amplified when Sutter Malone, red of face and quick of step, burst from the front door and stormed down the walkway, yelling at the kids to get off his blasted cab, goddamn it. He was in the hack and clacking away before they could all scramble off. Children, laughing, dropped like falling leaves from its fenders all the way to the corner.

Carpface had to race to jump into his rig and get the driver turned round.

Maggie sat in the overstuffed parlor of Otto's suite and gratefully took a tall glass of iced tea from Quincy. Her head was still thumping dully from yesterday's overdose. Unconsciously, she rolled the glass against her forehead, and only caught herself when she looked up to find Otto—miraculously "cured" the moment the door closed behind Brother Ascension—staring at her quizzically.

"Headache," she muttered, and lowered the glass. She took a long drink, then set it aside, mostly to make room for the cat. "Quincy?" she said, scratching Ozzie's ears. "What's wrong?"

"Nothing." The answer came too quickly. All his talk of enjoying this to the contrary, Quincy was a lousy liar. He dropped his eyes, for one thing. She hoped he'd put on a better show than this for Ascension.

"Quin," she said, putting the cat down (an unpopular choice, so far as Ozymandias was concerned) and standing up, "can I talk to you in private?"

She led the way past Otto and Blevins to the small study, Quincy following.

"Close the door," she said.

He did. In the privacy of the study, he looked absolutely stricken, as if the showing he'd made in the other room had taken everything out of him. He cleared his throat and said, "What is it, Maggie?"

She tilted her head to one side. She was fairly certain what the problem was, but she wasn't about to tip her hand first. After all, she might be wrong.

She said, "Quincy, talk to me. Something's got your long johns in a twist."

He scowled, which was the reaction she was looking for.

"Maggie, do you have to use such vulgar language?" And then he seemed to read the twinkle in her eye, and added sheepishly, "Oh, Maggie. This is all a mistake. We've got to call the whole thing off."

For a moment her mind stuttered, and the resulting surge of adrenaline went straight to her pounding head. It felt like ice picks behind her eyes. Call off *which* thing? Stop seeing her?

Then she took a deep breath. Strangely enough, he was far too grief-stricken for the subject of all this hand-wringing to be her. Besides, she knew him—his love life would be the last thing on his mind at a time like this. She thought it should have been the last thing on hers, too, but there you were. Her mouth twitched slightly in annoyance. Well, she'd worry about that later.

Right now, there was Quincy. And whatever was on his mind would have to be far worse than losing her—in his estimation, anyway.

Without expression, she said, "Quin, is this about Sutter?"

Just the mention of the man's name seemed to stagger Quincy. *Bingo,* she thought as he fairly fell into a chair. She might have gone to aid or comfort another fellow, but not Quin, no matter how she wanted to. The wound to his dignity would far overshadow what comfort she could bring him. So she simply sat down, watching helplessly and waiting.

At last, he looked up. Softly, he said, "You knew."

She nodded, even though she wasn't sure what she was agreeing with. There was an accusation in there somewhere, but she chose to overlook it. She hated to do it, but she had to find out exactly how he'd been tipped to Sutter's presence, if indeed he had. For all she knew, he could have received a letter from Sutter. A man could beat a letter from coast to coast any day, usually by a week or so, and Sutter Malone hadn't shown himself to be exactly trustworthy.

"When did you find out?" she asked. She couldn't leave a question any more open-ended than that.

"Last night." Quincy didn't look at her.

"Last night?" she repeated. What had Sutter done, anyway? Come calling at three in the morning? Frankly, Quincy was so upset that she wouldn't have been surprised to learn that he'd sent someone to Quincy's house with the news that he'd been run over by a milk wagon, and the funeral was the day after next.

She found her distaste for Sutter Malone growing by leaps and bounds.

She leaned forward slightly. "And?"

Quincy seemed to get a grip on himself—she knew he would, sooner of later—and faced her. "Last night, the phone rang. It was Sutter. He's here, in town. He asked me to meet him, and I went. It seems . . . it seems I've made a terrible blunder, Maggie. We have to call off this sordid mess. I've got to tell Sutter what I've . . . Lord, I've made a muddle of it all! All these people!"

He stood up and went to the room's tiny window.

Maggie turned in her chair. To his back, ramrod straight, she asked softly, "What did he say to you, Quin?"

"It doesn't matter, does it? It only matters that I've got it all wrong. I . . . well, I didn't tell Sutter about hiring you and this . . . this vast crew of shady characters. I was too humiliated."

Brows furrowed, Maggie broke in, "Quincy? Slow up a minute. What did Sutter tell you, anyway?"

He slowly turned to face her. "Why, that Trini has come to her senses, of course. She wired him. He's come all the way to San Francisco to fetch her home."

Grady let the cab go and walked the rest of the way into the Coast. Not that he was in much shape to travel by shank's mare. Those filthy bushes had poked him every which way. He hopped on one foot, pulling another twig out of his britches. *This had better be the last time Maggie has the bright idea to put me in the field,* he thought as he walked ahead, limping slightly and feeling in his pocket for his earring.

At least Carpface was still on the case. He'd seen his cab flash by the house right after Sutter's pulled out. No mistaking Carpface, even from a distance, even if all you glimpsed was the edge of his profile. A non-profile, really.

He shuddered, as much at the thought of Carpface's profile as at the earring, which slid into his itchy lobe.

He kept his eyes on the street, watching for Carpface. He'd lost him in the crowds, but he knew the old cheat had followed Sutter like a bloodhound. If he found one, he'd find the other. And on the Barbary Coast, Carpface wouldn't stick out at all. Down here, they were used to that face, and liked it. He'd probably get three invitations to a "really good game" within the first block.

He didn't spot him on the way up, but he found him across the street from the Seawitch, leaning against old man Best's apple barrel. He was just about to cross over to him, to tell him to go on home because he'd take it from here, when someone tapped him on the shoulder.

Grady turned around, took in a vast amount of air quite suddenly at the shock of it, and yelled, "What the hell you think yer doin', mate?"

Sutter Malone, in the flesh, shrank back against the Seawitch's facade and held out his hands, palms up. "I didn't mean," Sutter started in trembling tones, "that is, I wasn't aware, that is . . . I meant no offense, sir, I assure you!"

Grady scowled menacingly and fought the urge to mop his brow. Malone had nearly startled him out of his skin.

He snarled, "Well? What'd ye want?"

Sutter opened his mouth a few times, looking for all the world like a hooked fish on the dock, before he stammered, "I . . . I wanted to ask a favor."

Grady tipped his head and looked at Sutter as if (he hoped) he was out of his mind. He growled, "I'll do ye the favor of not guttin' you like a scrod,'' and turned to leave.

But Sutter was a persistent cuss. It was a good thing he'd picked Grady to corner, for on the Coast many a fool had had his throat slit for grabbing a man's arm. Which was exactly what he did.

Grady eyed the hand on his sleeve until Sutter, gulping, took it away. ''I—I'll pay you?'' Sutter said. He brought out a monogrammed handkerchief and wiped at the back of his neck. ''I'll pay you, uh, two dollars,'' he added nervously.

Grady appeared to think this over. Actually, he was taking stock of the man. Dressed in a hundred-dollar suit, gold watch chain gleaming, it was stupefying that he hadn't been rolled and murdered within a half minute of setting foot on the Coast. And when he suddenly pulled out his wallet, Grady shoved him back against the wall again.

''Ye stupid git. Put that back!'' Grady whispered gruffly. ''You wanna get your throat cut? There's them that ain't so honest as me.''

One of the local riffraff had lingered on the sidewalk, probably to pick up the crumbs if Grady was about to perpetrate a crime. Grady wheeled and roared, ''Get off with ye!'' The man ran up the sidewalk, and Grady turned back to Sutter. ''So what's this favor, mister?''

Sutter swallowed hard. He handed Grady a slip of paper, which Grady squinted at upside down.

''My card,'' explained Sutter, who appeared to have retrieved some small part of his superiority. ''I want you to go into the hotel and find a man named Brother Ascension and give it to him. Tell him I'm here.''

Grady pursed his lips. ''If this feller's your brother, why can't you tell him yourself?''

''He's not *my* brother,'' said Sutter, suddenly all Boston, a trait which, in this part of town, would land him stone dead in an alley quicker than you could say, ''Patty pours the porridge.'' He sniffed and said, ''He's *a* brother. A religious gentleman.''

''Like a preacher?'' Grady growled, lifting the card again and squinting at it sideways.

''I suppose so,'' said Sutter, lifting an eyebrow disdainfully.

So disdainfully, in fact, that Grady was tempted to slug him himself. *Who does he think he is?* Grady thought. *The bleeding Prince of Persia? Two minutes ago, he was practically on his belly!* He stuck the card in his belt and said, ''I'll do 'er, but not fer no two dollars. Five.''

Sutter appeared aghast. ''Five? Five *dollars*? For a simple—''

''A five spot for fetchin' your friend, and also for seein' that you don't get shanghaied or worse while I'm inside diggin' him up.'' Without waiting for a reply, Grady stuck two fingers in his mouth and whistled up Carpface, who was now standing in the street, watching them intently.

Carpface came running, and when he reached them, Grady didn't give him a chance to speak. ''Keep an eye on this fool, mate,'' he said gruffly. ''There's a drink in it for you.''

Carpface caught on immediately, for which Grady was immensely grateful, and smiling, put a bony hand on Sutter's shoulder. All of the Boston fled Sutter's face directly. He appeared mortified.

Who wouldn't be? Grady thought happily as he crossed the threshold of the Seawitch. Carpface had put a lot of practice into that particular smile, which he usually used as he was crossing a barroom floor, broken bottle in hand. There was a delightful touch of the maniac in it.

Grady asked at the desk for the whereabouts of the good Brother, was told he had just come, and was referred upstairs, to number 14. He knocked at the door.

From inside came the words, ''Clarence, I thought I told you to—'' The door opened. Brother Ascension's countenance changed dramatically when he found Grady at the door instead of Clarence. Leapfrogging from stern to beneficent, he folded his hands and placidly inquired, "May I help you, my son?"

Grady scratched his neck. "Ye be Brother Pretension?"

Ascension smiled. Just his mouth, Grady noticed. He nodded and said, "Close enough."

Grady dug under his belt. "There's a puffball downstairs says I should give ye this." He handed Ascension the card. "Says you're t'come down."

With that, he turned and walked back down the stairs, mulling over the expression on Ascension's face when he'd read the card. It had been a surprise to him, too.

Seconds later, he found Sutter and Carpface much the same way he'd left them. He bit his cheek to hold back the smile, straightened his shoulders, and then thrust himself between them.

"All right, chum," he said. "The deed's done. Me money?"

Relief that he hadn't been murdered in broad daylight dripping from every pore, Sutter pulled out his wallet and began to open it.

"Coin, if ye don't mind," Grady said. "I ain't trustin' no paper."

Sutter put away his wallet and got out his coin purse. Five silver cartwheels clinked into Grady's palm.

Just then, Ascension appeared in the doorway. "Here's yer friend now," said Grady, pocketing the money and throwing an arm about Carpface's shoulders. "Whatcha say we take ourselves down to O'Hanratty's, mate?"

Carpface eyed Sutter. "I can't kill him?"

Grady clucked his tongue. "Not now, friend. But maybe later?"

Carpface brightened, and he and Grady strolled down the sidewalk, leaving Brother Ascension and a shaky Sutter Malone behind.

EIGHTEEN

>—I—‹•›—◦—‹•›—I—‹

"**T**HAT'S AS THICK A SLICE OF BALONEY AS ANY-
body's tried to feed me for a long time," said
Grady. He stood in the fading light beside the window, watching the street below. "In town to fetch his niece,
my aunt's pajamas!"

Maggie glanced at the clock, then over at Bedside Blevins. He was snoozing on the sofa, the tent of an opened
newspaper covering his face. The last thing he'd said before
he dropped off was "So much bourbon, so little time . . ."

Quincy had left an hour ago. She knew he was confused,
although he wouldn't—couldn't—admit it. She knew he
was worried, too, but most of all, he was angry. Angry with
Sutter, for popping up out of nowhere and complicating
everything even more than it was already complicated, angry with Trini for starting the whole mess. And angry, most
of all, with her.

It had hurt, the way he had lashed out—well, more the
way he *hadn't* lashed out. Because she knew what he was
feeling. Knew what he had stoppered up inside him. He
was the next thing to exploding, and if he did, it wouldn't
be pretty. And he'd detest her for having seen. So she'd
soothed and agreed and soothed some more, and eventually
he'd calmed down.

A little.

He hadn't yet moved on to the point where he'd be angry

with himself. That would come in time, and she knew he'd
be an ungodly mess about it—all stiff upper lip on the
outside and a quivering mass of bludgeoned nerve endings
on the inside—but she could handle it. *He* could handle it.
For the moment, she had to make certain he wouldn't tip
their hand to Sutter.

And he'd agreed, finally. Grudgingly, haltingly, and with
numerous misgivings, yes. But he'd agreed.

She said, "Grady, Sutter's really got Quin convinced."

"Well, I'm convinced, too," Grady said, turning his
back to the window and stepping toward her. He slid into
a chair. "I'm convinced that your dreamboat's old buddy
is about as crooked as a corkscrew. Crookeder, if there is
such a word."

"He's not my 'dreamboat,'" she said angrily, "and
there isn't. Any such word, I mean."

"Now, *kinder* . . ." Otto soothed from across the room.
She'd forgotten he was there.

Maggie made a face at him, then said to Grady, "You're
certain? I mean, are you certain you didn't miss part of the
conversation?"

Grady sighed. "Mags, I told you. I followed Trini and
the boys to Ingram's house. 'Festus Ingram, Attorney at
Law' is what his sign said, although I should think the law
would want little to do with him. As an advocate, anyway.
No sooner than those three left, Sutter pulled up. He had
an argument with Ingram, and then tore out of the house.
I hooked up with Carpface, and—"

Maggie held up her hand. "Back up. You never did tell
me what the argument was about."

"The will," Grady explained, none too patiently. "The
will that Trini had just drawn up. She left everything to
Ascension. All right?"

"You don't have to get snappy about it," she said.

Grady eyed her disapprovingly. "I'm. Not. Snappy," he
said.

She gritted her teeth, and when she failed to rise to the

bait, he continued, "So Carpface followed Sutter to the Coast and I followed Carpface, and after that business I told you about—the business at the Seawitch—we went back to the alley behind the dining hall and had a listen. That was where they went, the dining hall." He scratched at his ear for the tenth time since entering the suite.

"For God's sake, Grady, just take the blasted thing out!" Maggie said in exasperation. She'd never known anyone to take as long to tell a story as Grady. "Ascension's going to walk in and shepherd me off before you get even halfway through this."

Grady stopped to work the wire free of his ear, and grumbled, "Some people . . ."

Otto, his hands full of cat, said, "Maggie, tell him again how good I have the heart attack."

From beneath the newspaper, Bedside Blevins's voice boomed, "Hush, Otto. Grady, my darling boy, won't you please get on with it before I perish from old age?"

Maggie closed her eyes. Maybe she should just go to sleep, as she thought Blevins had been. Maybe when she woke up, she'd find she'd been dreaming all along. Perhaps Brother Ascension and the drugs she'd ingested and Trini's plight and this growing cast of participants—and now Sutter's appearance—were only the by-product of too much chocolate mousse too close to bedtime.

She gave the back of her wrist a good pinch, just to make certain.

No such luck. It hurt like the devil, and now she had a red mark to boot. She turned her attention back to Grady, who was carefully poking the earring into his pocket.

"Better," he said, rubbing at his earlobe again. "And now, if the peanut gallery will please calm the hell down, I'll proceed."

Maggie cupped a hand over her sore wrist. "*Please* do."

He nodded at her. "It was an argument. Sutter, it seemed, was most displeased with Ascension, because our little Trini had made out her last will and testament incorrectly."

Maggie lifted a brow. "Incorrectly?"

"Right. She left everything to Ascension, as said before."

The newspaper moved again. "What's wrong with that? Setter or Sutter—or whatever his name is—is in the clear. He can settle with Ascension afterwards."

"*Ich bin* confused!" broke in Otto. "I thought all the money was what Ascension wanted, and now you got this uncle coming in town! Who the hell's bells is this person?"

"Oh, gad!" cried Grady in exasperation, and Maggie clamped a hand over her mouth. As much as she wanted to be angry with him, she had to admit that they'd made it hard on him.

"Go on, Grady," she said at last. "And you two, be quiet."

Grady closed his eyes and took a deep breath. "Ascension wanted all the money to be bequeathed to him, because he doesn't trust Sutter. Sutter wanted all the money, because he doesn't trust Ascension. The plan was Sutter's not Ascension's, although Ascension certainly planned to do Trini in—but Sutter decided to take a cut and push the matter forward."

Otto opened his mouth, but Maggie threw him a look that said *don't you dare,* and Grady picked up speed.

"Sutter was supposed to stay back in Boston, but he didn't. He wired Ascension, and the two kids—Michael and Mae—picked him up at the depot. He wasn't supposed to leave his hotel, but he did. I got the feeling that Ascension was not in the least amused by all this, and that Sutter might find himself strangled in an alley and trying to explain himself to St. Peter. Although Sutter didn't get that impression at all. Pompous idiot."

He paused a moment, staring at his hands. "Maggie," he said, looking up, "if I were you I'd be having second thoughts about Quincy, if this horse's ass is his best friend. Plotting to kill his own niece!"

Maggie's eyes narrowed. "We'll discuss Quincy later, if I choose to discuss him with you at all."

"Atta girl, Mag-pie," came from beneath the newspaper.

"Oh, shut up," she grumbled, and then pointed a finger at Otto, who was about to add his two cents. "Not a word from you, either. And honestly! Bringing Ozzie up here! Somebody's going to have to pay to have that couch recovered, you know."

Otto's mouth quirked to the side. "New drapes, too," he mused. "*Und* I forget to mention about the sandbox . . ."

"Well," said Grady, standing and heading for the door, "I've had enough. I don't imagine anybody's interested in where and when the foul deed is supposed to take place. Just get the damn sofa reupholstered, that's the important thing . . ."

"Grady, stop!" Maggie came out of her chair.

"First," he said, ignoring her completely, "it's 'Grady, don't lollygag' and 'Grady, get to the point,' and when I do, everybody has to put their two cents in—about every five seconds, I might add—about the draperies and the sandbox and those long uncomfortable nights in the Majestic Hotel—"

"Grady?" Maggie put on her sweetest face, which was exactly the opposite of the way she was feeling. She could have strangled everyone in the room and several people outside of it. Sutter Malone and Brother Ascension, for starters. "Grady, please?"

He stared at her for some time before he said, "Ascension plans to kill you and Trini the day of the tent meeting or whatever you call it. Clarence is going to row you out in the boat, then capsize it."

Maggie snorted, then flopped back into the chair. Drown her? Not by a long shot! Not Clarence, not anybody.

Grady eyed her, then took off his glasses and began to clean them. "Clarence," he said, "is a very strong swimmer. He's supposed to drown you, if you don't do him the favor of drowning yourselves. Oh. And he's going to drag your body back to shore with him. Just for show, I take it." The glasses went back on his nose again.

Maggie thumped her head backward, into the chair's upholstery. She'd expected an "accident" in the street or a push from a window. She knew she could take care of herself, but she began to have second thoughts. Could she take care of Trini? Wet skirts weighed a ton, and Trini was already weak.

And what would Trini think of all this, anyway? Had she known Sutter was coming? Had they cooked up some sort of plot between them? It seemed doubtful, but what other possible reason could she have for staying when she was in such danger?

She looked up at the sound of Grady's voice. "He's taking a third girl, too." He scratched at his head. "What's her name. Sister Edwina. You know her?"

Maggie nodded, frowning. She knew Sister Edwina on sight. She'd eaten dinner with her that first night, back in Conquistador. Chubby and dour-faced, she didn't appear as if the thought of swimming had ever, once in her life, crossed her mind.

"I know her," Maggie said at last. "Gentlemen. We're in trouble."

Ascension called for her at seven on the dot. Everything was in place when he arrived. Otto was stretched out on the bed, grey of face (due to a last minute dusting with talcum powder) and appearing to doze fitfully. Maggie knelt beside him, hands clasped, head bowed, her lips moving in silent prayer as she clandestinely watched everything that went on in the room. Blevins, who did all the talking, appeared in his shirtsleeves.

Haggard of face, he whispered to Ascension, "I hope you're happy. He spent himself dictating that new will. Wouldn't rest until he was finished."

Ascension placed a hand over his heart and did his best

to look wounded. "I assure you, sir, I haven't the foggiest notion—"

"Shhh!" Blevins hissed. Then he went to Maggie's side and took her elbow. "Magdalena? Magdalena, time to go. Your grandfather needs his rest.

"If indeed he is your grandfather," he added, looking straight at Ascension.

Ascension ignored the dig. He gathered Maggie under his arm, which set her to shivering with abject loathing. He said, "Come, my dear. God bless you, Doctor."

As they neared the stairs, she began to weep, a trick she'd taught herself long ago, but which, in this case, was brought on more by sheer exhaustion than anything else. Brother Ascension said, "There, there, child. Jesus will watch over your dear grandfather."

She raised tear-filled eyes. "Brother? I prayed so hard for him."

"And we will continue to pray, child," he soothed. "All the Children of Golgotha will pray for your grandfather, and for you."

She hoped that Jesus was listening.

Back at the Seawitch and alone in her room, Maggie divested herself of the paraphernalia she'd had Grady hastily scrape together. A small knife with a short blade. Forty small snaps. Two spools of thread, some elastic, and two seam rippers. Two apples and two corned beef sandwiches, wrapped in paper.

She slid the knife beneath her mattress, along with twenty of the snaps and a spool of thread, and one of the apples and sandwiches. She divided the elastic in half, stuck one half under the mattress and coiled the rest tightly, stuffing it deep into her pocket along with the remainder of the items.

Just in case, she told herself as she stood and smoothed her skirts. *Just in case.*

The door opened without preamble, and Sister Polly

stuck her head in. "Sister Magdalena?" she said, smiling that insufferable smile. "Do you feel like coming to meeting?"

Maggie, drawing the fog over her features, said, "Certainly, Sister Polly. God bless." And followed after her out into the hall.

Grady had been a busy boy. First, that visit to police headquarters and the talk with Doohan. It had taken quite a bit of explaining, but now Doohan was on their side. *For what little good that does,* he thought. He had a low opinion of the police, but Maggie had a high one, and it had been her idea.

Then he'd run by the stable where Maggie kept that nag of hers and dropped off another check. Nickel was the horse's name, but he should have been called C-Note, considering what they paid for board and farriers and the like. Horses were such filthy, uncomfortable things, anyway. He had no idea what Maggie saw in them.

Next, to the Coast, to touch base with Tommy Two-Tone and to tell Carpface to go on home for the night, and also to tell him what they wanted him to do next.

And lastly—this was the hard part—to Quincy's house, across from which he presently stood.

At last, he made himself cross over the cobbles and walk up the steps of the Victorian. He rang the bell. A woman on the down side of middle age opened the door, and Grady presented his card. *Mrs. Lovejoy, I assume?* he thought, watching her generous backside amble down the hall.

A moment later he was ushered into the study, where he found Quincy waiting expectantly.

"Well?" was the first thing out of Quincy's mouth.

Grady sat down in a chair near the fire and leaned forward, elbows on his knees. "Well, what?" he said. "Well, how's Maggie, or how's Trini, or how's good old Sutter doing?"

Quincy poured himself a brandy before he seemed to

remember his manners, and asked Grady if he wanted one, too.

"No thanks," Grady said, before the words were half-way out of Quin's mouth. "You see, I've been standing outside for some time, trying to think of a way to break this to you. I ducked into that tavern on the corner a couple of times. Building courage, you know." Quincy stared at him. "If I have another right now, I might lose my concentration altogether. Later, you can offer again. If you're still of a mind."

Quincy came forward, carrying his brandy snifter, and sat down next to him, in the other fireside chair. He didn't look at Grady, though. Grady thought his hands were shaking: a slight quivering of brandy painted the sides of his glass. He cupped the snifter in both hands, as if he'd noticed, too, and then he said, "It's bad, isn't it?"

Grady said simply, "Yes."

Quin sat for a moment, staring ahead, then suddenly twisted toward Grady. "It isn't Maggie, is it?" he asked, and Grady was secretly pleased to hear the faintest note of hysteria in his voice.

"No, no," he said quickly, waving his hands, which reminded him that he was still in his seaman's getup. Filthy thing! "Nothing of the sort," he added. "Well, not immediately, anyway. It's . . . it's Sutter, I'm afraid."

"Sutter," Quincy repeated. "What about Sutter?"

Grady told him. He didn't pull any punches, just told him flat out and as unemotionally as he was able. Told him the whys and the wherefores of what they'd speculated, and then he stood up. "I'll take that drink now." Quincy started to rise, more on instinctive good manners than anything else, Grady thought, and he waved him back down. "I can find it myself, old man."

When he'd poured himself a whiskey—brandy seemed too tame for the situation, somehow—and turned back toward the fire, Quincy was still sitting in exactly the same position: one hand on the arm of his chair as if preparing to rise.

Grady took his brandy, which was tilting slowly and about to spill onto the rug, and put it on the little table between the chairs. Then he took a rather large gulp of his whiskey.

"Quin, I am truly sorry," he said quietly. He had expected shouting, or perhaps tight-lipped acceptance—verbal, anyway—but not this. He didn't quite know how to deal with it. He wished Maggie were here.

"Sutter," whispered Quincy. "Sutter, all along."

Grady studied the other man's profile and waited.

"I . . . I think I knew," Quincy said finally. "I think I knew he was leading me down the garden path. I just . . ." He looked to his hand for the brandy and found it empty.

"Table," said Grady.

Quincy lifted the glass and drained it in one gulp, then blew air out, slowly, through pursed lips. "These past years, it's been . . . Well, I suppose I knew he had money troubles. A little too much dancing around the subject in his letters. I just didn't want to believe it. And when he announced this thing with Brother Ascension and Trini, I . . ." He looked up. "Maggie thinks I'm an utter fool, I suppose. How could I have been so stupid!"

"Not at all, Quincy," Grady said quickly. "If anything, she believes you've been a loyal friend to Sutter and his family." When there was no change of expression, he added, "Maggie values loyalty quite highly."

He was afraid Quincy was going to crush the empty snifter in his hand, unaware, and he rose. Unfolding the man's fingers from the glass, he said, "Whiskey?" and without waiting for an answer, proceeded to the little bar.

He topped off his drink and poured one for Quin. Then, reevaluating, he dumped Quincy's shot glass into a large tumbler and filled it to the top. This, at least, had been the worst thing he had to do tonight. Now he was over the hump. He brought Quincy his drink and sank, once again, into the upholstery.

He'd never been in Quincy's home before. Quin had been to their place quite a few times, but never the other way around. It was quite nice, actually. Dark paneling, gold-stamped book spines crowding the shelves, paintings of horses and ships here and there on the walls. Elegant, and not too gingerbready. Nothing too bizarre. Tasteful. Just the sort of home he would have expected the man at the helm of Western Mutual to live in.

Especially when Western Mutual, among other companies, was owned by his father.

Frankly, he'd always suspected Quincy of being a bit of a twit, of leaning too much on the good graces of nepotism, although he'd certainly never hinted as much to Maggie. But now? Quincy was loyal, he'd proved that with Sutter. But now, as Quincy took a large drink of his whiskey and said, "What do you want me to do next?" he proved he had a head on his shoulders, too.

Bully for you, old fellow, Grady thought.

"For now," Grady began, "proceed as we agreed. But come Sunday, here's what we have planned . . ."

NINETEEN

T HE NIGHT, AND THE NEXT MORNING, TOO, MAGGIE
had no chance to talk to Trini, let alone give her the
notions in her pocket, for Ascension accompanied
her to the Majestic the first thing after breakfast. He stayed
with her until midday and took her downstairs to the dining
room.

He'd gotten rather bold about adding her ''vitamins''
right in front of her, and she had to oblige him by partaking
at least a little. Now was not the time for him to catch her
shoving a drug-laced bit of apple cobbler into her napkin.

After lunch, he took her for a drive—for a taste of fresh
air, he said—which ended at the home of Ingram, Attorney
at Law. There, he had her sign some papers. She signed
everything set before her without reading (not that she
could have made sense of a Mother Goose rhyme, she was
so blurry from the drugs) and after, he drove her back to
the Majestic.

He left her for the afternoon, content that she was
drugged to a state just shy of a stupor, when in reality she
was making herself vomit into a thunder mug until her poor
stomach was empty, and then downing a gallon of strong
room service coffee.

She was sick to her stomach, wobbly in her legs, and the
headaches never went away: they just pounded with less or
more intensity. She was beginning to feel that if Ascension

didn't kill her quickly, she might just do it herself.

Grady came in the afternoon. He just stuck his head in the door, said, "It's set," then left. Neither did Quincy show himself. She knew the wheels were turning out in the world, knew that people were working away for her and for Trini, but somehow she was feeling too punk to draw much comfort from it.

Stanley "Bedside" Blevins was beginning to cloy at her, too, what with his unrelenting attention to the never-ending convoy of bourbon and scotch bottles delivered to the room. He never seemed to get really drunk. But then, he never appeared to be entirely sober, either.

At least Otto had the foresight—and thoughtfulness—to somehow get a set of throwing knives delivered. So after she finished vomiting up what was left of her lunch and downing her coffee—and if she never saw another pot of the stuff, it would be too soon—she spent the rest of the afternoon tossing knives at the broad side of a suitcase.

"You gonna ruin that," commented Otto. Ozzie on his lap, he was reading the part of the newspaper Blevins hadn't propped over his face. As usual, the good doctor was asleep on the sofa.

"Already ruined," Maggie replied, and tossed another blade. Her aim was off, and the knife fell outside the chalked circle and next to the stitching. It was probably those blasted drugs, a lingering aftereffect that loused up a person's coordination.

"I'll buy you a new one," she added slowly, carefully forming each word. Her mouth tasted of cotton and rubber.

Otto shrugged. "Some friend of Grady's suitcase." He raised the paper again, then lowered it. "You want I should call downstairs for some cards? We have a game of gin rummy? Old Maid?"

Maggie threw the last knife in her hand, and this one, missing the suitcase entirely, landed in the front leg of the table it was propped against.

She stared at the quivering knife. Carefully, she said, "Cards would be fine, Otto."

From the sofa, from beneath the newspaper, Blevins cleared his throat. "Hold on, you two," he said, pausing to yawn. "I'll call. Otto's supposed to be dying, remember?"

That evening, Ascension picked her up again. She wept all the way back to the Seawitch, ostensibly because her dear *Grossvater* was growing weaker with each passing hour. In truth, she wept because she detested Ascension and hated her circumstance. She wept because she was worried about Trini-the-silent and that little boat ride Ascension had planned for them.

Most of all, she wept because the drugs were creeping into her system, little by little, no matter how she purged them. She felt powerless, victimized. If only she could have just taken a swing at Ascension or Clarence! She was certain that punching one of those two—or a good old-fashioned catfight with Sister Polly—would perk her up immensely.

She wanted to kick somebody in the ribs, jump on them from a rooftop, sweep their legs out from under them, pound them, thrash them.

But she couldn't. Her hands were tied, if they wished to close down Ascension for good and all. No, she had to wait for him to try something, had to wait so that the police would have enough evidence. She found herself longing for the good old days, when all you had to do was get up an angry mob and find a hanging tree. . . .

When they reached the Seawitch and Ascension sent her, bleary and red-eyed, up the stairs and excused from evening prayers, she quietly set to work sewing her half of the elastic into the waistband of her skirt.

While she worked she hoped against hope that Grady would be able to pull it off. They should have done it all along, right from the start. Maggie was so disoriented that she had no idea whether this sudden change of plan would work, or if it even made sense. Her brain had been so battered by a wall of drugs that she couldn't trust her own thoughts, but Grady had agreed wholeheartedly that it was the only thing to do now. She'd just have to trust his judgement.

She focused what was left of her concentration on the waistband of the skirt, although by now she scarcely remembered why she was sewing all this elastic and all these blasted snaps into place.

All else fell from her mind, and later, when her fingers had gone numb from countless pricks and she had finished the skirt and Sister Polly came up from the meeting to offer her a cup of hot chocolate, she took it and drank it down.

Grady and Carpface slunk quietly through the back alleys of the Barbary Coast, although Grady was thinking they really didn't have to sneak to avoid detection. The fights were still going, here and there. The sounds of breaking bottles and out-of-tune piano music, of moaning whores and coarse laughter, were still thick in the air, even at two o'clock in the morning.

"This one?" whispered Carpface. They had just stopped at the rear of a building, and he was pointing to the second story.

Grady looked up—ten feet up, to a short, fragile-looking overhanging roof—then down at the hard-packed dirt of the alley and the broken glass that crunched beneath his feet and glinted dully in the moonlight. This was what Maggie had been navigating? Good God.

He swallowed and said, "I'm afraid so."

"Which window is it?" said Carpface, still looking upward.

"Second from the right." Grady felt his pockets for the fifteenth or twentieth time since picking up Carpface. Everything was still there.

He sighed heavily, made the sign of the cross, and said, "All right. Boost me."

A moment later, he was silently cursing and hauling himself onto the rickety roof. Somehow, he made it to the window and clung to the sill with both hands, panting and gathering his thoughts, and hoping the damn thing wouldn't give way under his weight.

At last, he rose unsteadily. One-handed, he carefully raised the window higher. One leg over, crouch, then two legs.

Don't think of it as a kidnapping, old boy, he told himself as he slipped inside. *Think of it as a college prank. A knickers raid run riot.*

While his eyes adjusted to the dimness of the hotel room, he pulled the bottle of chloroform from one pocket and the rags from another, trying to count how many corners this blasted case had turned since they took it up. And what had it all come down to? Doing the one thing that had popped into both his and Maggie's minds first. Well, it was a lot more complicated than that, but kidnapping was what it boiled down to.

He was well aware of the reasons Doohan had to stay out of it for now, but he was amazed to find himself thinking that he'd have given anything to hear a police whistle and the thuds of footsteps mounting the stairs. A good, old-fashioned raid! Let Doohan's boys pick everyone up and sort it out later.

He shook his head. Grady Maguire, actually *wishing* that the bulls would lower the boom! My, my, how times had changed. But if the police turned up now, he'd be the only one they would arrest. There was no evidence to hold Brother Ascension or anyone else. Anyone else but him, that was.

With a sigh, he uncorked the bottle. Holding it well away from his face, he soaked the rags.

Quickly, he went from one bed to the next. Two of the girls woke a little and fought—probably the two who would have awakened when he snatched Trini if he hadn't dosed them with chloroform first. But they only struggled, weakly, for a matter of a few seconds. The rest went like lambs, Trini included.

The sweet stink of the anesthetic was beginning to affect him. Satisfied that all the girls were unconscious, he threw the rags out the window and stuck his head outside for good measure. The room was beginning to reek of it.

Carpface called, "Well?" in an elaborate stage whisper.

Scowling, Grady held a finger to his lips. After he'd gone to all this trouble to incapacitate the residents of this room, he didn't want Carpface waking up the rest of the hotel.

Ducking back inside, he went to Trini's bed and picked up her clothes, neatly folded at the foot. These he threw out the window before he went back to scoop her up. By God, the girl was practically weightless! She was an armful of nothing but hollow bones, like a bird.

With one hand, he pulled the top sheet from the bed, and cradling the unconscious Trini, straddled the windowsill. Looping and tying the sheet beneath her arms, harnesslike, he then began to lower her across the short overhang, and down to Carpface, who waited with upstretched arms.

A minute later he was on the ground, too, and rubbing his backside, which he'd had the misfortune to land on. Carefully, he pulled a stray sliver of broken glass out of his britches and cut his finger in the process.

He swore softly and stuck his finger in his mouth, then snatched up her clothing. Around the coppery taste of blood, he said, "Wrap her up and let's get out of here."

Saturday dawned weakly, through a thick bank of fog that showed no signs of diminishing. At breakfast, Maggie didn't see Trini, and it took her a moment to realize what had happened, and that Grady had been successful.

Brother Ascension was in a snit, however, casting his blue eyes over the room, sending withering stares to this follower or that. Sister Polly went along the breakfast tables, from acolyte to acolyte, asking everyone how their breakfast was today. And, oh, and by the way, had they seen Sister Trini this morning?

At least Ascension was so distracted that he paid no mind to what anyone was eating. Maggie had the presence of mind not to eat, and for the most part left her breakfast in her napkin.

She shouldn't have drunk that chocolate last night. She could tell she shouldn't by the way her hand was slow when she went to reach for a new napkin, by the way she kept half-stumbling over her own feet and knees, and by the numbness in her lips, which made her speak as though she had a mouth full of marbles.

It seemed to her there were probably other signs, but she was still too woozy to think what they might be. And strangely enough, it didn't worry her. Although the fact that she wasn't worrying *did* bother her.

Humming a hymn, she pushed back from the table and carried her plate to be scraped. Then, as usual, she took a seat toward the back of the hall and waited for the last few stragglers to finish their breakfast so that Brother Ascension could start morning prayer meeting.

But Brother Ascension wasn't there. He'd left when she wasn't looking, and Brother Clarence took over the proceedings. Now, what in the world . . . ?

Ah, yes. Now she remembered. Trini. Grady had boosted Trini during the night. Stolen her and got straight away. She hoped.

"Amen," she said, along with the others, and rose. She checked the wall clock as she shuffled with the others to the lobby. An hour had gone by? She shook her head. This stuff didn't only fuddle your thinking processes, it ruined your sense of time, too.

Someone tapped her shoulder, and she turned around to face Sister Polly. "God bless you, Sister," she said automatically, although it came out thick and fuddled.

"And you, Sister Magdalena," Polly replied. Tiny creases furrowed her brow, although the ever-present smile was in place. "I was sitting in back of you during Meeting. I couldn't help but notice that you were mumbling something."

Maggie blinked. Wonderful! Now she was talking to herself. She didn't know which was worse—that, or the fact that she'd been completely unaware of it. She seemed all right—well, comparatively—on the inside of her head. She just couldn't control what happened on the outside of it. For instance, what words passed over her lips.

"You said 'Trini' several times," Sister Polly went on. "Would you happen to know where she's gone?"

Maggie blinked again, frantically trying to think what she might have said, and holding her face as blank as possible. "I did?"

Sister Polly frowned slightly, then appeared to catch herself. The smile was restored. "Did she say anything to you, Sister Magdalena? About where she might have been going, I mean."

Maggie slowly shook her head. "Did she go away?" she asked, and her mouth felt as if it were full of cotton. But even in her stupor, she could tell that Polly was gritting her teeth behind that smile.

Slowly, Maggie added, "I like Sister Trini. God gave her green eyes."

Polly looked as exasperated as was possible for someone who was trying hard to appear beneficent. "All right," she said, adding a "God bless." She quickly moved on to another acolyte.

Brother Ascension appeared from out of nowhere, or so it seemed to Maggie, who was having a hard time keeping track of people. "Are you ready to go to your grandfather, Sister?" he asked.

Even she could tell he was nervous. His usually serene blue eyes flicked in his skull, glanced quickly about the room, then out the door, then toward the stairs, and over again. All at once it struck her that she was looking not at a man, but at a death's head. With no awareness that she was moving, she brought her hands to her face, covering her eyes. "Stop," she whispered.

She heard someone hiss, "You're giving her too much!" Polly?

And then a whispered but terse, "Shut up." Brother Ascension.

His hand was on her arm, and she looked up from behind her fingers. The death's head smiled at her. "Let's go," it said, the jaws moving, the eyes staring from their sockets.

She shivered, and the death's head was Brother Ascension again. She'd been wrong about the inside of her head being relatively free of cobwebs. It was as thick with them as a deserted barn. She said, "Go see *Grossvater*?"

"Yes," he said, fairly dragging her from the Seawitch. "For God's sake, hurry along, Magdalena!"

TWENTY

>━┤━◆┿◯┿◆━├━<

G RADY CLOSED THE DOOR BEHIND HIM JUST IN TIME
to hear Trini's plate collide with the other side.

Carpface looked up from his makeshift bed, on
the sofa. "You wouldn't think nothin' that tiny could be
so mean, could you?" he said with a yawn.

Grady took the question to be rhetorical and said, "I'm
done cooking. I think that three breakfasts are enough for
any person to throw against a door." He felt in his pocket
for the key.

Carpface sat up. He'd borrowed a nightshirt—at Grady's
insistence—and it hung on his bones. "Now that you got
her, whatcha gonna do with her?"

Grady locked the door. Clever idea, putting her in Maggie's room.

Something else shattered on the other side. He didn't
want to think which of Maggie's treasures it had been. He'd
had, at least, the presence of mind to haul out all the weap-
onry last night, while she was still unconscious.

"Grady?" Carpface was waiting for an answer.

"Don't know exactly what I'm supposed to do with
her," Grady said. "Wait, I guess. Eventually, I suppose
we'll ship her back east, to her family. Or what's left of it.
I just wish she'd tell me what's going on!"

An odd look came over Carpface's countenance, although it was difficult to tell, what with it being kicked in

and all. "You want I should make her talk?"

Quickly, Grady held up his hands, palms forward. Carp-face seemed a little too eager. "No, no! Nothing like that, old man. Nothing of the sort."

Dish hurlers, Grady thought testily. *Dish hurlers and crockery smashers. Why do I merit this treatment? You try to save someone from sure and certain death, and all you get for your trouble is—*

Another piece of bric-a-brac shattered against the door.

Grady sighed. He'd try one more time, but that was his limit. Bending to put his lips to the keyhole, he said, "Trini? Trini, I've been trying to tell you that—"

Something else hit the door and smashed. Her coffee, he thought, for a drop of liquid came through the keyhole. He scrubbed his face with his handkerchief, though. You never could tell. She might have hurled the chamber pot.

"Damn it, Trini!" he said, putting his handkerchief away. "Brother Ascension was going to kill you tomorrow!"

Another thud and shatter, although smaller this time. Maggie was going to be awfully upset if the little snip had broken those cheap porcelain cupids she was so crazy about.

"Your Uncle Sutter was in on it, Trini," he continued. He was going to get this out. "He made a deal with Ascension to split the money."

Another crash, just like the one before. Maggie's cupids.

That did it. Cruel or not, he played his last card. "Trini, they killed your mother."

This time there was silence, and Grady added, "They killed her so that all the money would be yours, so that Sutter would have a nice big chunk of change."

Still, the silence.

From the couch, Carpface said, "Maybe she ran outta things to throw."

Grady ignored him. "Trini?" he said more softly.

Nothing.

He stood up and, against his better instincts, unlocked the door. He opened it just a hair and peeked inside.

Trini was crouched on the opposite side of Maggie's bed, her back to him, the nubs of her spine pushing against the cotton of her nightgown.

"Trini . . ." he began.

"Go away!" she sobbed, curling into a tighter ball. "You're hateful! I don't believe you!"

"Believe me or not," Grady said, opening the door and sagging limply against the frame. *I don't believe you* meant that she did. He was relieved, but sorry, too. "It's the truth, Trini. Maggie tried to talk to you, but, well . . ."

At last, Trini turned her head. Those beautiful green eyes were bloodshot and swollen. "Magdalena?" she sniffed, and pushed red, tear-dampened hair away from her face. "You're a friend of Magdalena's?"

Grady nodded. The particulars could wait.

"They killed my mother, too?"

Again, Grady nodded.

Trini covered her gaunt face with her hands and wept.

Shards of cupids and dinner plates crunching under his feet, Grady stepped outside and closed the door behind him. He'd leave her alone for a bit.

"It's all right," he said to Carpface, who was staring at him quizzically. "I'll fix you some breakfast. Her, too, I suppose. Maybe she'll eat it this time."

As he made his way to the kitchen, however, he kept turning Trini's last phrase over in his mind. *Too,* she'd said, as in "also." As in "as well."

They killed my mother, too.

Strange, but she didn't have the slightest recollection of the cab ride to the Majestic. She must have fallen asleep, because the next thing she knew, Ascension was patting her hand and saying, "Magdalena? Magdalena, my child, wake up," and helping her down to the sidewalk. And the next thing she knew, she was in Otto's suite with Blevins, and he was saying good-bye to Ascension.

The second the door closed behind Ascension, Blevins was tugging at her arm. Anyway, he was doing something with it. "Come on, get up," he kept repeating. "Don't make me carry you."

But she kept falling down, slithering down his leg. Curious, that. And he kept holding on to her arm. With an enormous effort, Maggie (who was now on the rug beside the cat-clawed couch) yanked her arm free and slurred, "Unhand me, villain!"

She fell back against the sofa, scarcely noticing that one sleeve was unbuttoned and rolled past her elbow. "Where's Otto?" She pushed, without effect, at her skirts, trying to straighten them. "He dead yet? S'posed to be deader'n a . . . dead thing." The effort it took to talk was enormous.

"Nein," came a voice from the bedroom, and Otto emerged, looking fuzzy. Actually, he was completely blurred around the edges. In the middle, too.

She squinted her eyes, and when that didn't help, said, "Go in and come out again. Maybe it'll be better next time." Except that her lips didn't move at all and there was no sound. Had she only thought it?

"Get into bed," demanded Bedside Blevins, completely ignoring her inability to speak. Come to think of it, he was a little on the blurry side, too. He leaned down into her face and said, "I mean it, Maggie. Come on. Be a good girl."

"I can't," she said, blinking. Why had she never noticed what a tremendous effort blinking took? All of a sudden, she realized she couldn't feel her legs. She pounded at one calf ineffectually. "Why didn't, uh, why . . ."

Blevins muttered something under his breath that she didn't catch, then said, "Otto, throw back that top sheet, will you?"

"Was already back," Otto replied, thumbing his suspenders indignantly. "You both say I am gonna die this morning. I am all ready *mit* the makeup, and the face is grey. But no, look at me!'' He slapped his barrel chest. ''Standing up I am, by God! Do I look to you like a corpse?''

Having lost track of the conversation, Maggie started to say something intensely relevant—although she wasn't sure what—but Blevins scooped her up in his blurry arms. She wouldn't have thought he was capable of it, being so out of focus and all.

''Oh, shut up, you old blunderbuss,'' he snarled, walking past Otto toward the bedroom. It seemed that he was floating, though, floating without moving his feet, and she was gliding along with him.

He said, ''She's completely incapable of standing on her own, let alone swimming away from that boat tomorrow. Get Grady over here. No, don't. I'll call in a minute. What she needs is bed rest. And lots of coffee.''

''No!'' Maggie protested. She pinched Blevins's arm to distract him, and with a bigger burst of energy than she knew she had left, wriggled free. She landed half on a chair, half off it, and slithered the rest of the way to the floor, smack in the middle of the bedroom doorway.

''On the other hand, perhaps not,'' observed Blevins, making a face and rubbing at his arm.

''Say,'' said Otto, leaning down, his caterpillar eyebrows working. ''What you think they do to her, anyway? She gonna be all right?''

Maggie was studying the upholstery. Ozzie had been at this one, too. Rats. What's-his-name was going to be mad. Quincy. Sweet Quincy. She fingered the cat-shredded chair lovingly. Quincy, Quincy, Quincy.

Somebody was pulling at her again, and suddenly she remembered. She pulled herself up on one elbow. ''You were supposed to tell . . . that man.'' She paused, and tried again. ''Supposed to say he's dead,'' she said, using every ounce of energy in her body, and pointing an accusing fin-

ger at the blurry shape across the room that she assumed
to be Otto.

She turned back toward Blevins with great effort—why
was it taking so much energy, for goodness sake?—and
said, "Where's my kitty?"

She fell back to the floor, exhausted, her torso in the
bedroom, her legs in the parlor. The last thing she'd had to
eat or drink had been that cocoa, last night! Why was she
so weak this morning? Why did everyone look so odd, act
so strangely?

Suddenly, cold terror coursed through her veins. This
wasn't normal. None of this was right. There was a great,
unforgiving wrongness in the world, of which she was the
center. *I've gone mad,* she thought with surety, and just as
quickly thought, *No, I've been doped again!*

But the thoughts left her mind as quickly as they came
to it, and left behind only fear, fear that she was going to
be this way forever, fear that she was a prisoner inside her
own body, and fear, most of all, that she was not in control,
that she'd never be in control again.

With effort, she said, "Grady . . ."

Otto said, "He telephoned. Said everything is A-OK and
hinky-dinky *mit* Trini. Happy this makes you?"

What was wrong with him? Couldn't he see she was
begging him to find Grady? Grady could fix this. Grady'd
send somebody a wire or something and fix her right up.
Good old Grady.

"And now," said Blevins, "will someone please make
me happy? Will someone please follow Dr. Hedrick's orders and go the hell to bed?"

She couldn't move. Why didn't someone move her?
Why didn't they pick her up and put her on the sofa? If
only Grady were here, Grady would make them put her on
the couch, Grady would . . . Grady would . . .

Grady stood in the doorway to the bedroom, clenching and
unclenching his fists around a beaver hat which had, up to

this moment, been his favorite. Maggie looked so frail and grey lying on that big hotel bed, helpless in sleep.

"Let her sleep," said Blevins, behind him.

Otto took his arm. "*Ja, kommen Sie,* Grady," he said quietly. "She been through a lot today."

He followed Otto to the couch and sat down. He looked over at Blevins, slouched in a chair. "She looks like death, Stanley," he said in a low voice. There was a threatening tone to his voice, which he did little to hold back.

Blevins didn't blink. He folded his hands in his lap and said, "They're injecting her. I found two puncture marks and bruises. I suspect she was given one sometime last night, and another this morning. She doesn't remember. She barely remembered her name when he left her here this morning."

Grady frowned. "Why the hell would he dope her that much when he—"

"Knows she has to appear normal to outsiders?" Blevins finished the question for him. "Because Maggie is particularly susceptible to drugs, that's why. It's probably tangled up in her unusual reaction to liquor."

Grady mumbled, "Never gets drunk, but her hangovers are murder."

"Precisely," Blevins said. "I don't claim to understand it, just as I can't claim to fathom why you can get drunk as a lord at night and not suffer for it the next day. Whatever the reason, Ascension's drugs seem to treble their effect in Maggie."

Blevins picked up the tumbler at his side and swirled the liquid in it. Scotch, Grady thought. Studying it, Blevins continued, "I managed to get my hands on some stimulants. Oh, I still have friends who don't mind that the great state of California lifted my license. Actually, they probably wouldn't care if I'd never had one . . ."

He pursed his lips, staring at the ceiling for a moment. "Well, anyway, I injected her—used a vein in her leg, so nobody'll be the wiser—and then we walked her and poured coffee into her. Got her evened out. What you're seeing in there''—he poked his thumb back toward the other room—''is sheer exhaustion. Hell, I'm exhausted, too, and nobody pumped me full of narcotics.''

He paused for a moment, then added in a gentler tone, ''Grady, she's all right. Really. I made her up a little packet of powered cocaine to take with her. If she gets in trouble, all she has to do is take a pinch, like snuff. It'll wake her right up, make her feel wonderful.''

Grady frowned. ''Are you sure it's—''

Blevins waved a hand. ''Perfectly safe. I use it all the time myself.''

Somehow, this didn't make Grady feel any better, but he held his tongue.

''I have half a mind,'' Blevins continued, ''to hold on to her for the night. It'll keep Ascension from administering another intravenous cocktail overnight, at any rate.''

Grady nodded. Blevins was right. If Ascension doped her again, she'd never survive the little boat ride he'd planned for her, let alone remember the details of the plan they'd made.

He said, ''All right. You can tell Ascension that she was overcome with shock at the death of Grandfather, here.'' He tilted his head toward Otto, who was at that moment muttering, ''*Nein, Liebchen,*'' and removing Ozzie's claws from the side of a chair.

Otto looked up. ''*Was?*''

''Are you dead yet?'' Grady inquired.

''*Nein.* They don't kill me this morning,'' the toy maker grouched. He scooped up the cat, kissed the top of its head, and added, ''I was all ready *mit* the grey makeup on the face. *Und* I practiced holding my breath! Up to a minute I got,'' he added proudly.

''Well, you can kick the bucket in about three hours, Otto,'' Blevins said, checking his watch.

Otto brightened somewhat, and then, almost as an afterthought, asked, "You do what Maggie tells you, Grady? You make everything in the rows?"

Blevins lifted a brow, and Grady said, "He means, did I get everything set up."

Blevins said, "Oh," and took a sip of his drink. "And did you?"

Grady nodded. Now he was wondering if Maggie had been in her right mind when she gave him all those instructions. She'd been on the woozy side, but if there was one thing he could always count on through hell or high water, it was Maggie's brain. Marvelously cunning, adorably devious, and unrepentantly honest, it went *click-click-clicking* along, through broken limbs and exhaustion and sickness and bad times and fever. It was the one steadfast thing in his life. The fact that Ascension was muddling it with narcotics made him want to throttle the man. Throttle? Pound him into the ground!

"Does that mean yes?" asked Blevins.

"It does," Grady replied, his mind on the slender, dozing figure in the next room. "Doohan and company, Quincy, me, everybody. And Trini, I suppose. She's not talking much, I'm afraid, but at least she's stopped throwing things." He looked up. "Why does everybody *throw* things at me? That case in Bent Elbow, the Lemke murders, the kidnapping up in Montana . . . I could go on, you know." He could have, too.

Blevins shrugged. "You just have that kind of face, I suppose. For a small fee, I could change that for you, you know. A nip here, a tuck there . . ."

Grady gave a small snort. "No thanks, Stanley. I'll put up with the vases."

"Never hurts to ask, old sport," said Blevins pleasantly. "And what's our lovely Brother Ascension up to, other than no good?"

"Running around like a headless chicken, so far as I can tell. I've got the storekeeper across the street watching him. Set that up first thing this morning."

Blevins lifted a brow. "Can you trust him?"

Grady scowled, remembering the newest bout of back-pounding. "He used to know Dad."

Out of the corner of his eye, he saw Blevins smile. "And he didn't pull a greener from behind the counter and shoot you on sight?"

"Very funny," said Grady dryly. "He's trustworthy. And I couldn't very well use Carpface. Ascension's seen him, and once you've seen Carpface . . . Well, you know. I left him back at the office, watching Trini."

Blevins nodded. A snore came from Otto's chair, and Grady turned to find the corpse slouched, hands over his belly, sound asleep. Ozymandias had followed suit and was curled in the crook of Otto's arm, his tail blissfully tucked over his nose.

"Some people," said Grady as he stood up to take his leave, "can sleep through anything."

Blevins went with him to the door. "When's Quincy showing up?"

"About an hour before Ascension," Grady replied. He pushed down on the latch. "That ought to give you time to get him calmed down."

"Calmed down?"

"About Maggie. And when she wakes up, tell her I'll be by again late this evening and fill her in on all the details."

Blevins looked as if he had a bug in his undershirt. Grady said, "What, Stanley?"

"I wish she hadn't called in Doohan, that's all," he replied. "The bulls make me nervous."

Grady knew just how he felt, but said, "Maggie wants the cops, Maggie gets the cops. This is her game."

Blevins started to say something else, but Grady cut him off before the first word could emerge. "Remember that, Stanley. It's Maggie's game, and nobody—*nobody*—plays it better."

TWENTY-ONE

> ⊱—┊—◆⟩—❍—⟨◆—┊—⊰

ASCENSION SAT IN THE EMPTY DINING HALL, SCOWL-ing and drumming his fingers on the worn plank table. He'd looked everywhere. Talked to shop-keepers, stopped people in the streets (and very nearly got himself shanghaied), scoured the railroad depot. Well, he hadn't exactly scoured the railroad depot. Not personally. Michael and Mae had seen to that. He hadn't actually talked to the shopkeepers either—that job had gone to Clarence. But he trusted them as far as he trusted anyone, and he'd told them to do it, so he'd *practically* done it. Besides, if they hadn't turned up a clue to Trini's whereabouts, there wasn't one to be had.

It was most infuriating, to say the least.

He heard someone entering the dining hall, but he didn't look round. He knew Polly's footstep.

She walked round the table and slid onto the bench across from him. "No luck?"

He shook his head and thought, *Go away, go away, go away* . . .

But she didn't. She just sat there, staring at him. Cold, heartless old bitch. He could have strangled her just for looking at him like that, a look that said, *What are you going to do now, Mr. Big Shot?* and *This is what you get for hovering over Magdalena and forgetting all about Trini,* and *Who's going to pull your tit out of the wringer this time?*

"Shut up," he said, although she hadn't spoken a word of condemnation.

She rose then, glaring down at him. Her, with her solid figure and her Minnesota peasant's face and her smug Nordic superiority. Why, what was she when he picked her up? What was she when he married her? Nothing! Nothing but a hick farm girl. All right, a very smart girl, but a hick nonetheless. What would she have been without him?

Nothing.

Absolutely nothing.

She'd probably be stealing laundry or shoplifting trinkets or hoochy-kooing in a burlesque for the middle-aged, that's what. Lord knew she was no good in the sack. If she had to make a living on her back, she'd starve.

She was still staring at him.

"What?!" he snapped.

She pressed her lips together tightly for a moment, as if she was considering using that smart tongue of hers—and she'd better not, not if she knew what was good for her—and then she said, "Are you going to tell the uncle yourself, or should I send Clarence?" She leaned forward slightly and, with a hint of a sneer, said, "Just what do you want me to do?"

"Do?" he answered immediately, without giving himself time to think. "You're not going to do a damn thing. What makes you think it's your business to *do* anything? I'll take care of this. And I'm not sending anybody to see the uncle. Got that?"

Slowly, Polly drew her arms up and crossed them, cupping her elbows in her palms. "Fine," she said, her tone holding no clue to what she might be thinking.

"Get out!" he barked, quite a bit more forcefully than he'd planned.

Without changing her expression, Polly said, "I love you, too, you great, thundering ass," and marched from the hall before he had time to register what she'd said. By the time he'd realized it and turned to reply, she was already gone.

Mouthy Valkyrie bitch.

In truth, Trini's disappearance was unfortunate but hardly a disaster. Had she been the only fish on the line, he would have been a great deal more upset than he was now, that was certain. But he still had Magdalena, and he intended to keep her.

The grandfather had still been confined to bed when he dropped her off at the old man's hotel this morning. He'd have to find out if Hedrick stayed there at night. Otherwise, he'd have to send Mae or Michael to decoy him downstairs on some excuse or other, so that Clarence would have a clear field at finishing off the old coot.

Clarence did have his uses at times.

Well, this was the last time good old Clarence would come in handy. The last time that that Scandinavian fish-wife, Polly, would nag him. The last time—well, not last, but *almost* the last time for any and all of it—that he'd have to give another sermon or look into any of those sheeplike, moronic faces. Gad. People were such idiots. They practically went around with "sucker" painted on their foreheads.

The south of France. Just keep thinking about the south of France. You and all that lovely money and no Clarence, no Polly, no Mae or Michael, no Sister-This and Brother-That—the little piglets. No more God bless you's, and no more praising the Lord. If anyone's going to be praised from now on, it'll be me.

He would go to France and find himself a blushing young girl to entrance. Someone to help him spend his money. And when he got tired of her, he'd find another.

And Sutter Malone? That Boston prig could go hang, for all he cared. In fact, he might just hang him himself. They'd say it was suicide, once the truth about Malone's financial situation came to light. . . .

He snorted. There he went again, trying to have a little
fun when he should be plotting his future. He pushed Sutter
Malone from his mind, and turned it toward the Majestic
Hotel, and Magdalena Obermyer. And of course, her dear
Grossvater.

Both of them, soon to be dead.

And himself, soon to be much richer.

He stood up and smoothed his suit jacket, then ran his
fingers through his hair. It was time to pick up Magdalena
and scout the terrain for Clarence.

By the time he'd walked to the edge of the Barbary Coast
and flagged down a hack, he was humming a little tune.

Quincy was furious—with Ascension, with Grady, with
Blevins, with Otto. Most of all, with himself for starting
the whole business.

"How dare you let it get this far!" he shouted for the
tenth time. "They've been drugging her for days, and you
knew it! They could have killed her!"

Blevins, for once without a drink in his hand, stared at
him flatly. "Look," he said. "If you don't calm the hell
down, and very quickly, I'm going to give you a little of
what Maggie's been having."

"Don't do it, Quincy," ventured Otto, shaking his head.
"She throw up plenty."

The side of Blevins's mouth quirked. "Just once, Otto,"
he said. "And I'm fairly certain it was more from the coffee
than anything."

Quincy wouldn't be put off, though. "I want her out of
here, and now. Call the whole thing off! I—I won't pay
you!"

It seemed to him that Blevins considered this threat for
a moment, but by the time Otto had said, "Nobody pays
me a cent to help Maggie! I help from my kind nature!"
Blevins had regained his composure.

"Quincy," he said in what Quin took to be a patronizing
tone, "we have approximately three minutes before Brother

Ascension knocks on that door. Maggie and Grady know what they're doing, I assure you. However, if you have no faith in them, if you want to throw all their hard work out the window, then go right ahead. March into that study and pick up Maggie and march right out of here. I won't stop you.''

Quincy's hands balled into fists, relaxed, balled into fists again. If he put a stop to it right here and now, Maggie would be safe. But would she ever forgive him, ever trust him again?

It was a terrible decision, especially for a man to whom everything was stamped in black and white. From the beginning, Maggie—and the people who surrounded her— had been nothing to him but various and confusing shades of grey. Perhaps it had been what attracted him to her in the first place.

He could be certain she was safe (and be just as certain she'd never speak to him again, for fouling up her well-laid plan) or he could leave things as they were.

His hands stopped fisting at his sides. He said, ''You're sure . . . that is, you said she'd be safe here? Guards posted?''

Blevins said, ''Quincy, there is no need for a guard. As I've been trying to tell you, she'll be as safe as a babe.''

Quincy opened his mouth to say a grudging, ''I suppose so,'' but he never spoke it aloud, for just then there was a knock on the door.

Blevins stepped forward. ''That's him.'' He put his hand on the latch, then theatrically flopped his head back on his shoulders to stare at the ceiling. ''Otto!'' he hissed. ''Get in the bedroom and look dead!''

The old German's brows shot up. ''Oh! *Ja, ja,* I go now!''

The moment the bedroom door clicked closed behind Otto, Blevins signaled Quincy to look sober. He opened the door, ushering in Ascension.

Buck up, old boy, Quincy thought, *and get a grip on yourself. You must do this part right!*

He put a hand to his forehead and slid into a chair just as Brother Ascension said, "My dear sirs! Why so glum?"

Quin let out a low moan, and Blevins said, "Mr. Obermyer has . . . passed."

Once again, Grady was late. Too much racing around to do, that was all, and not enough time to do it in. Everyone was alerted, from Old One-Eye and Broom and Tommy Two-Tone down at the docks to old man Best at Best Dry Goods. The police were watching Sutter Malone's hotel, although not the Seawitch. Police stuck out like a sore thumb on the Coast, even when they were disguised.

A little like me, he thought sheepishly as he raised his hand and knocked on Otto's door.

Blevins opened it. "About time," he said crankily.

Grady winked. "You work for me, Stanley, remember?" he said, and stepped inside. The parlor was empty, the lights turned low. "Where is everybody?"

"Bedroom," Blevins said. "Maggie's moved from the study back to Otto's 'deathbed,' and she's holding a conference." He started for the bedroom, but Grady took his arm, holding him back.

"How is she?" he whispered.

Blevins snorted. "Oh, she's fine. She's so goddamn fine that I'd spank her if I weren't afraid she'd toss me out the window."

"That's my Mags," Grady said, and he found himself beaming. He hadn't realized how worried he'd truly been. If anything had happened to her . . .

When they stepped into the bedroom, Maggie (who was sitting cross-legged on the edge of the mattress) looked up and snorted. "Nice of you to show up," she said.

He smiled wider. Ah, she was back to her cantankerous old self! "Just one man, doing the work of six," he said. "As usual." He took a seat on the end of the bed, since

Blevins and Quincy had the only chairs. Otto was stretched out on the floor, his head nestled on a cushion. Ozymandias was curled in the small of his back.

"Bring me up to date," commanded the small empress, who was swathed in a white linen nightgown. Three apples rested in her lap.

Grady commenced to tell her everything, repeating what had been said while she was under the influence. "Yes," she said, picking up the apples. "Yes," she said a few paragraphs later, and starting them moving in the air. "And Trini?" she asked, still juggling, when he got to that part.

"Weak as a kitten," he said over Otto's snores, "but not so weak she couldn't sling a few dinner plates at my head." He decided—wisely, he thought—not to tell about the cupids until later. Much later. Say, the turn of the century. He continued, "She was quite shattered when I told her about her mother, actually."

Maggie's mouth twisted slightly. To all intents and purposes, she looked to be concentrating on the apples. "And she still didn't explain why on earth she came back to Ascension after the Pinkertons had brought her out?"

"No," he said, half-shouting over Otto's snoring that time. "We didn't exactly get that far, Mags. I've been away from the office all day. Carpface is still baby-sitting. Stanley, be a good chap and roll Otto over on his stomach again."

"Everything else peachy?" she asked.

He recounted all the dribs and drabs—he hoped—and when he was finished, she sat staring at the wall, the apples at rest in her lap.

"Good," she said at last. "Excellent. I was afraid there were parts I'd missed, but everything seems to be in order." She took his hand in hers and squeezed it briefly. "Thank you, Grady," she said with a smile that warmed him through.

"And now, gentlemen," she continued, still grinning as

she turned toward Quin and Blevins, "just one small alter-
ation, and we'll be ready."

"Because I couldn't, that's why!" shouted Ascension.
"Damn it, Polly! Leave me alone!"

They were alone in the dining hall. He wouldn't have
raised his voice upstairs, where those idiot children could
hear, but down here was different. Thank God. Or whoever.
He'd be delighted to get rid of Polly. No, thrilled! He
couldn't stand the sight of her anymore.

"All right," she said in that cool, even tone he'd grown
to hate. That Viking Princess tone. "You don't need to get
so worked up. I was just asking a civil question."

"I couldn't take her because she collapsed when her
grandfather kicked the bucket, and that doctor was hovering
around," he said as calmly as he could in his agitated state.
"The attorney, too. That civil enough for you?"

Polly calmly folded her arms. "Yes, dear. Did you see
him?"

"Who?"

"Obermyer."

He bit the inside of his cheek to keep from snapping.
She was always checking up on him, always carping on
some detail or other. "Of course I saw him," he said, drawing the words out. "They had him laid out on the bed. He
was as dead as a flank steak."

Polly cocked her head. "You saw his face?"

"Yes, damn it!" he exploded, then took control of himself. He wiped his brow on his cuff. "I saw his face. He
was dead, all right?"

"Thank you," said Polly, exasperatingly cool. "Is
everything signed?"

Just like a woman to nitpick it to death.

"Yes," he said, trying not to clench his teeth. "Everything's ready. The old fossil signed the will last night."

"Then you'll pick her up in the morning."

"Of course." He nearly spat it at her, but checked him-

self just in time. Best to keep this relationship fairly harmonious—well, what was harmonious for them—until he
was ready to play his last card. "I've already told Clarence
his services won't be needed, and he can go to bed.
Happy?"

She nodded. "Lovely," she said. Why did she always
have to wear that same icy smile? She looked to him like
a Nordic priestess about to happily sacrifice a bull to Odin.
"Good night, then."

He watched as she left the dining hall and passed into
the lobby, then turned to take the stairs. *Stupid cow,* he
thought as he, too, left the dining hall.

At least she wasn't harping on Trini anymore. He
couldn't for the life of him figure out where she'd gone,
what had happened to her! You'd think one of the lads
would have turned *something* up.

He'd given up on finding her. In fact, he hadn't told
Polly, but he'd already sent Michael and Mae off to scout
the next city. They'd caught the seven o'clock train, bound
for Portland. Of course, it didn't matter where he sent them.
He wasn't going. By the time they arrived in Oregon, found
a lodging suitable for thirty young morons and wired him,
he'd be long gone.

Trini had simply vanished into thin air, he mused as he
stepped out into the foggy night and took a seat on the
hotel's porch, surrounded by a community intent on picking
its own pockets dry by morning. One corner of his mouth
quirked up. Well, he supposed it wasn't unusual, a thing
like that happening in the Barbary Coast. Girls probably
disappeared every day and were never heard from again.

Just a few square blocks of real estate, shrouded by fog,
but a very dangerous place to be, particularly if you were
a frail young girl like Trini, particularly if you'd been im-
bibing his little "remedy" for any time at all.

He lit a cigar, twisting the match. Well, he hoped whoever had Trini would have the courtesy to leave her body
in a ditch somewhere, with identification. That way he'd

get the money—well, half of it. He still had to decide what to tell Sutter Malone. But if Sutter was following instructions, he wouldn't try to get in contact until Tuesday. With any luck, he'd be gone by then, having left instructions with the correct people to transfer his Obermyer inheritance to Geneva.

Ah, the pleasures of a Swiss bank account.

Tomorrow, he thought, trying for a smoke ring and losing sight of it before it was a yard away. The fog was thick tonight. So thick that he couldn't see the dry goods store or the bar across the street. Hell, he couldn't even see the middle of the street.

Just a little weather. A little local color. Tomorrow he'd pick up the grieving Magdalena, let her wander around the hall for a bit, working with the others to set up for the revival meeting, and then he'd send her and Edwina off with Clarence. And then he'd preach, business as usual.

Until someone brought him the awful news, of course.

He didn't need Trini's money at all, he rationalized. He'd be fine, just fine.

He blew another smoke ring, settled back, and smiled. Eight o'clock, Obermyer's doctor had said. Pick her up at eight. Actually, he'd said quite a bit more, and most of it unpleasant. A very suspicious sort, that doctor, for what little good it would do him now. Obermyer had signed the final papers. That prig of a lawyer had said so.

A chuckle escaped him, although there was no one close enough to hear. Besides, the brawl at the Gartered Thigh, two doors up, was quite noisy. For a second, he was tempted to go up and join in the melee. But no, he was getting too old for that sort of thing. Too rich, too.

Come eight o'clock the next morning, he'd pick Magdalena up—he'd likely have to dope her for later—and by ten it would be finished. They wouldn't be able to get away with a needle this time, he thought, rolling his cigar's excess ash off against the sole of his shoe. His concoction would have worn off and she'd be too alert for the syringe, although there'd still be some residual effect.

Well, he thought, taking a puff and slowly exhaling through an open, smiling mouth, *there's always breakfast.*

TWENTY-TWO

A T EIGHT ON THE DOT, BROTHER ASCENSION AP-
peared at the Majestic Hotel. When he climbed the
stairs to Obermyer's suite, Magdalena was waiting
for him: her head down and her eyes glassy and her skirt
rumpled, she sat on the sofa with her grandfather's cat in
her lap. Horrid animals, cats.

"She's still in shock," Dr. Hedrick said quietly, although
no more kindly, Ascension noted, than last night.

"The Lord heals all wounds," he said piously. Maybe
Polly was right. Maybe he *was* giving her too much dope.
Twenty-four hours after the last dose, she was still woozy.

"I've given her a sedative," the doctor went on, his
brow furrowed. "I suggest that you put her to bed the minute you get back to—Where are you people staying, anyway?"

Ascension gave him the address, and as he recited it, he
thought how nice it was of the doctor to have doped her
for him. Very tidy, indeed.

The doctor looked up from the paper where he'd just
scribbled the address, and his frown deepened. "This is in
the Barbary Coast, isn't it?"

Ascension, who was by that time helping Magdalena
limply to her feet, nodded. "Yes, it is. Where better than
the devil's playground to find the Lord's lost lambs and
bring them back to Him?"

"Brother?" Maggie seemed to realize he was there for the first time. She looked up at him with those huge, brown, tear-stained eyes, the lashes damp with tears, and said, "Poor Grandpa's dead. I had . . . had . . ." She slumped against his side, and he bore her up under his arm.

"There, there, Sister Magdalena," he murmured, just loud enough for that nosy doctor to hear. With a voice full of fatherly concern, he added, "Trust in the Lord, my child. Your grandfather is with Him now, resting in the heavenly arms of Jesus. Come now, and take solace in the comfort of your earthly family."

Ignoring Hedrick's scowl, he helped Magdalena from the room.

So far, so good, Maggie was thinking as she slumped back and forth across the dining hall at the Seawitch, carefully placing a handbill at each seat. So carefully and precisely, in fact, that Sister Polly had finished six tables to her one, and Sisters Mavis and Edwina—who was scheduled to drown, along with Maggie—had set out all the water pitchers and glasses.

Ascension had disappeared for the moment. Just as well. During the cab ride she'd feigned sleep, because if she kept her eyes open and looked at him the whole time, she would have been sorely tempted to—well, perform a highly unladylike maneuver which would have had him doubled over for a week and blown her cover. As it was, she'd had to remain still, with her eyes closed, while he put his arm around her and petted her hair and her arm. And her breast.

She shuddered at the memory of it. Gad. She'd forced herself to play possum while he petted her, thinking daggers at him the whole time and counting the minutes until the police would have their evidence and she could deliver a swift kick to his tender parts. She pretended to rouse when he finally shook her. She'd wanted nothing better than to run straight upstairs and take a bath, but instead plodded dully into the dining hall like a sheep on the way to the slaughterhouse.

"Just you wait," she muttered under her breath, again picturing Ascension in the hands of the constabulary, and picturing herself walking up to him, bold as you please, and administering one good kick to his—

"Did . . . did you say somethin', Sister?" Sister Edwina was behind her, her round face smiling stupidly. Doped to the gills.

"No," Maggie muttered, then took a quick look around. Lowering her voice, she said, "Edwina, can you, by any chance, swim?"

Edwina just stared at her dully. She might as well have asked if Edwina dressed in buckskins and drove the stage. She would have received the same blank stare.

"Never mind," she said, turning again to the handbills.

"Won the Bentley Medallion," Edwina mumbled as she began to wander off. "In '79. Or maybe '80? Forget."

Maggie stood up straight. "*What?!*" she hissed, then just as quickly, checked to see that Polly's back was still turned. It was.

She grabbed Sister Edwina's arm and spun her around. The girl wobbled. "Edwina," she whispered, hoping against hope, "what's the Bentley Medallion?"

Edwina's head was still wobbling. "Prize. For swimming . . . Monongahela River. Pittsburgh to, um . . . um . . ."

"That's nice. God Bless," Maggie said quickly. Polly was heading their way. "Did you see my handbills?" She held them up. "Aren't they pretty?"

Polly was beside them. "Hello, sisters," she said with that unbearable trademark smile. "Hasn't the Lord made a glorious day today?"

Both girls nodded. And smiled.

"Brother Ascension has a surprise for you," Polly continued, clasping her hands before her. "A special outing. Brother thought it would be nice for Sister Magdalena, in light of her recent troubles, and he has decided that you may accompany her, Sister Edwina.''

Edwina blinked slowly, her smile widening. ''What is it?''

''You'll see,'' said Polly. ''Now run along with Brother Clarence.'' She lifted a hand to point, and Maggie's gaze followed it to the doorway, where Clarence slouched against the frame. ''Go on, now,'' Sister Polly chirped, much too cheerfully for a woman sending them to their deaths. ''Have a good time, and God bless.''

And the same to you, lady, Maggie thought sarcastically as she and Edwina joined Clarence.

At least Edwina had the Bentley Medallion in her favor, whatever that was. But it would have had to have been swimming upriver, against the current, because Pittsburgh was where the Monongahela and Allegheny rivers joined to form the Ohio, if she remembered her geography correctly. It meant that Edwina was a strong swimmer. Or had been, a few years ago.

Maggie watched as Clarence took Edwina's arm and steered her out of the street. ''Stay on the sidewalk, will ya?'' he muttered.

''Yes, Brother,'' Edwina murmured stupidly.

Good God, thought Maggie, closing her eyes. *This is a swimming champion? Well, back to square one.*

The hall was filling up, and Brother Ascension, resplendent in his sky blue robes, stood just out of sight, in the kitchen. He checked his watch and smiled. Clarence should be reaching the docks by now.

Just as he snapped the timepiece shut, Polly appeared at his elbow, carrying a pitcher of water and a glass.

She smiled at him. ''It's time.''

He started to scowl, then remembered that very soon Polly would be only a distant, unpleasant memory. He could afford to be magnanimous.

He returned the smile, as loving and kindly and caring a

smile as he'd ever given anyone. "Thank you, my dear," he said. Was there a little tremor in her expression, a millisecond of bedazzlement? Ah, he still had it if he could charm an old fishwife like Polly.

He kissed her on the forehead, distasteful as it was, and said, "Bless you." He took the pitcher and glass from her. One of the boys, Brother Jim—wasn't he the one who'd brought in Magdalena?—was at the head of the room, speaking to the crowd. Getting them ready for him.

"Go sit down," he said to Polly, whose smile was back to normal.

"Don't forget your water," she said. "You know how thirsty you get at these things." And then she was gone.

Sutter Malone answered the knock at his hotel room door. "Yes?" he said with a slight air of superiority. The two men who stood in the hall were obviously not of his social caliber.

"Sutter Malone?" said the taller of the two. He wore a cheap suit, and he was reaching into his breast pocket.

"You're mistaken," said Sutter, as a small shiver of foreboding raced up his spine. He had suddenly realized that this was the beginning of a very bad day. "The name's Dobbs," he said, bluffing it out the best he could. "John Dobbs. From Chicago."

The tall man opened the wallet he'd just fished from his pocket and opened it, displaying a badge. "Well, Mr. Malone or Mr. Dobbs or whatever you're calling yourself these days, I'm Detective Mulrooney. If you'd just come with Sergeant Cullen and myself?"

Panic seizing him, Sutter tried to slam the door, but Sergeant Cullen's foot was in the way. The officers caught his coattails and hauled him back just as he was halfway out the window, not caring that his room was three stories from the pavement below.

Death was infinitely superior to jail, infinitely superior to the social disaster which had just fallen down about his shoulders.

"Tsk, tsk," clucked Detective Mulrooney, his hand like a vise on Sutter's arm. "There'll be none a that, now, laddie."

Cullen produced a pair of cuffs and secured his hands behind his back. Sutter didn't fight. It was too late for that, too late for anything.

"But why?" he asked dully. "What are you arresting me for? I haven't done anything!" And that was the truth. He hadn't done anything yet, not yet, and even then it would be some minion of Ascension's who'd do the actual killing.

"Land sakes!" said the sergeant, speaking for the first time as he shoved him toward the door. "If I might, Detective Mulrooney?"

"Speak freely, Sergeant Cullen," said the detective, closing the door behind them and taking Sutter's arm.

"Well, we've all manner of charges waitin' for you," said the sergeant with a happy lilt as they moved down the hall. "Toppin' the list, of course, is conspiracy to commit murder. Oh, that's a lovely charge, isn't it, Detective?"

"That it is," said Mulrooney, as disgustingly chipper as Cullen. "And shame on you, Mr. Malone. A lovely little lass, your very own niece!"

Insanity, Sutter thought dismally, *is the only plea left.*

"Let's not be forgettin' conspiracy to perpetrate a fraud," Cullen added. "And—"

"I want to see my lawyer," Sutter said, tears of frustration suddenly streaming down his cheeks. "I want to see him now."

"Pretty sailboat," commented Maggie. She said it to Clarence, but it was really for the benefit of the battered sailor at the end of the dock—Grady's pal, Old One-Eye. He didn't look at her, just shambled past them, scratching his elbow through the hole in his sweater. She hoped it was a signal that he'd seen her. If it was, Doohan would know where they sailed from, and Old One-Eye could give a description of the boat.

Clarence had rented, for the occasion, a small sailing craft, perhaps all of ten feet long. Just the right size, she supposed, to capsize easily.

He helped her down to join Edwina on the deck, then jumped down himself. Distantly, she saw Old One-Eye stop at the head of the dock and flag someone down. A policeman? No, someone dressed in brown. Whoever he was, he spoke with Old One-Eye for a second, and then he took off running.

Clarence said, "You ever sailed before?"

"No," said Maggie, jerking her attention back. "Water scares me." That, at least, wasn't a lie, for today she was dreading it. She even felt a little seasick, but she knew it was more the effects of Blevins's stimulants than anything else. He'd warned her that she'd probably collapse before afternoon, and she was beginning to believe him. Her stomach had turned over, and her head was already starting to buzz: not with the grogginess she'd felt before, but angrily, as if there were irate bees caged behind her eyes.

Edwina opened her mouth lazily and said, "I used to—"

Maggie grabbed her arm and said, "Sit down, Sister," and thought, *Gad, don't start bragging about that medal now!*

Edwina sat down—fell down, actually—and remained there, blissfully staring out over the waves.

"Why don't you join her, Sister Magdalena?" said Clarence. He'd untied the last line and was pushing them away from the dock. He'd probably have to row out a bit before he put the sail up, she imagined. Too many boats, too much traffic. She wondered how far out he'd go before he thought it was safe to capsize them.

TWENTY-THREE

GRADY SNAPPED HIS POCKET WATCH SHUT AFTER checking it against the wall clock. Two minutes fast: the Seawitch's lobby clock, that was.

Brother Ascension had taken the floor some thirty minutes prior. The fire and brimstone he'd started with had gradually lessened, become more gentle, more intimate, until it had gone from a thunderstorm to a gentle but all-pervasive rainfall; the kind that soaked you through to your bones before you realized you were more than slightly damp.

The audience or the congregation—or whatever you called the people who came to these things—was certainly mesmerized. The promise of free food had brought them in, but they were staying strictly on account of that voice. Prostitutes, sailors, and street toughs mixed with opium smokers, drunkards, and pickpockets were wedged into their seats, and he hadn't heard so much as a cough in the last fifteen minutes. Heard and not seen, because he was standing around the corner, in the lobby, with his back toward the meeting.

Maggie had insisted he be here this morning. He'd fought her on it, feeling that his place was at the docks. But she'd assured him that she'd be fine, what with Doohan and all, and that Ascension would bear close watching.

Frankly, Grady thought this was a load of horse manure.

Ascension didn't need watching. What was there to watch? Besides, if you wanted to nitpick, he *couldn't* watch. She'd forbade him to look in on the meeting lest he fall under Ascension's hypnotic spell.

Ascension was off on a tangent again, which was—to the best of Grady's reckoning—some sort of twisted interpretation of scripture which would eventually allow Ascension to lay claim to being the son of God. At least, Grady figured that was where he was going, the sick bastard. But then, he had to lay a modicum of blame on the crowd, too. Some people would believe anything.

He was about to sit down on one of the wooden chairs lined against the wall, when Quincy burst through the door.

"Gone!" he panted, once Grady had dragged him out of Ascension's line of sight and propped him in a chair.

"Who's gone? Not Trini!"

Quincy nodded. "I went to the office according to plan, except I found Carpface just getting up off the carpet. She cracked him over the skull," he said, and winced. "With a brass lizard! Oh, I'm afraid it's a terrible mess!"

Maggie's Chinese dragon, Grady thought, cringing. He hoped Carpface's skull hadn't dented it. "How long ago?" he hissed.

Quincy scowled, thinking. "An hour? Lord, if only I'd gotten there earlier! I had one last simple job, to guard a slip of a girl . . ."

Where would she go? Grady thought frantically. And then he suddenly felt very calm. Here. She'd come here, of course. Something had made her go back to Ascension when the Pinkertons got her out the first time. She'd come back again.

But he hadn't seen her in the group of Ascension's acolytes. In the crowd, perhaps?

"Stay here and watch the door," Grady said, and slipped into the dining hall. Ascension was just putting down his water glass. The members of the crowd all sat at attention, their eyes glued to him. The Children of Golgotha stood round the perimeter, also mesmerized.

"When our Lord and Master came upon John at the place of baptism," Ascension was saying, "John's heart was filled to overflowing. He had known from the start that the Christ was born again, as He had been born before and would be unto eternity."

Grady, making no more editorial comment than an unspoken *Drivel!* began to search the crowd with his eyes, looking for a slim figure, a slim figure with red hair.

The sail was up, and they were out in the middle of the bay, and Maggie was nervous. Edwina, alternately dozing and rousing to look at the scenery and say, "Nice," before nodding off again, sat beside her. Clarence was guiding them away from the water traffic.

The last of the fog had long since burnt off. Maggie looked out over the waves, squinting against the sun for a glimpse of Doohan's boat, but the glare was impossible. She wouldn't be able to tell which one it was anyhow, she reminded herself, even if she could see clearly. What did she expect him to do, bring a boat emblazoned "San Francisco Police" when he was supposed to be keeping a low profile?

Clarence apparently felt he was far enough away from any water traffic to avoid detection, at least until the deed was done, because, without warning, he gave the sail a mighty heave and sent it swinging wildly across the boat.

Maggie ducked in the nick of time, but it caught Edwina in the head, sweeping her over the side and into the water. Maggie barely had a chance to hear her splashing before Clarence was upon her.

His hands were on her throat. He lifted her up and off the deck before she regained the presence of mind to knee him in the groin, but the sail swung back and took them both over the side before she had a chance.

She went under the water, Clarence still holding her by

the neck and pressing her down at arm's length. Her skirts were the enemy as much as Clarence, dragging at her, sucking her down. She held her breath and thought, *For God's sake, don't panic!* and stopped trying to pry his hands away.

Instead, her hands went to the waist of her dress. Three quick rips, and the snaps she'd sewn into place gave way.

Madly, she kicked the elasticized waistband downward and felt the skirts finally drift free, but she was nearly out of air. She grabbed Clarence's hands by the thumbs and abruptly twisted them outward. His hold was broken immediately, and she kicked away from him, surfacing gratefully to take a big gulp of air.

Behind him, the boat was sinking. She caught a glimpse of Edwina, awake at last and fighting the heavy skirts that were surely dragging her down.

And then Clarence disappeared. Maggie twisted and turned in the water. Nothing. He couldn't be beneath the boat, for as she searched for him it upended and slipped beneath the surface, nearly taking Edwina down with it. Suds! Where was he?

Maggie shoved her trepidations aside when Edwina sputtered, "Help!" But she hadn't taken two strokes toward her when hands grabbed her ankles from below and yanked her down.

She kicked violently and freed one ankle, and used that foot to grind at the hand that still restrained her, pulled her down. Clarence surfaced just as she did. With a sputtered, "Bitch!" he came for her again.

But this time, when he shoved her head down under the water, she didn't fight him. Instead, she reached inside the bodice of her dress and pulled free the short blade she'd hidden there.

Gripping it firmly, she shoved it upward, into Clarence's side.

The water was immediately clouded with blood, and Clarence let go of her shoulders. She didn't stay around to watch him grip at his flank. She just put one foot against his hip and used it to shove herself away, toward Edwina.

But Edwina wasn't there. Taking a huge and desperate lungful of air, Maggie dived downward, swimming deeper into the cold murk of the bay until she spotted something in the murk. She grabbed Edwina by her hair and jerked her up, swimming to the surface. While Edwina coughed and sputtered, Maggie took the blade to Edwina's skirt.

"Glurp!" cried the drugged Edwina, and tried to climb on top of Maggie's shoulders.

"Stop pushing me down!" Maggie sputtered after she swam out from underneath, half choking on a mouthful of brine.

Edwina flailed and knocked the knife from Maggie's hand.

"Kick!" Maggie commanded, spitting out water as she ripped free the last shreds of Edwina's skirts. "Kick, damn it! Think of the Monongahela!"

This must have gotten through to Edwina, because she began to kick her chubby legs like a champion. Maggie got clear of those pistoning legs just in time to avoid having her kneecaps pummeled, and she aimed Edwina toward the shore.

But where was Doohan? And where, come to think of it, was Clarence? That one stab wouldn't have killed him, for the blade was only three inches long. She wanted him alive. She turned in the water, thinking to dive for him—she'd drag him back to shore if she had to—but Clarence was up to his old tricks. Hands grabbed her again, yanking her down.

This time she spun in the icy, blood-tinged water, twisting against him, twisting her ankle from his grip and leaving him with her empty shoe. He was weaker this time, and when she kicked against him he tumbled backwards as if in a dream, slowly arcing back in the water.

"Maguire!" It came as a distant shout, then "Maguire!" again, closer.

She turned back toward shore, and she could see the tug coming toward her then, and see the uniformed men on deck. Not the uniforms of sailors, but of San Francisco's finest. Doohan!

She was lifting a chilled hand to wave at them when Clarence caught her wrist—didn't he ever give up?—and hauled her onto her back, then under the water.

This time, the angle of her descent filled her nostrils with water. *Help!* thought Maggie, and forced herself to fight her natural impulse, which was to claw her way to the surface immediately. Instead, she tore her wrist free and swam deeper, righting herself below the water and beneath Clarence's silhouette. And then, with a burst of energy, she came up hard underneath him, ramming his midsection with her head.

She saw the belch of bubbles as his lungs emptied. And then saw his expression turn to panic when he realized it. He fought to swim to the surface, but by that time she'd surfaced above him. He was weak. Easy enough to hold him down, lock him between her legs and hold him down a little longer, a little longer . . .

But at the last minute she reached down and hauled him up by his collar. "You're not worth it, you bastard," she said, as hands reached down from the tug to take him from her, and then lift her from the water.

Blankets, towels, coffee, an ocean of them. She took the blankets and towels, spurned the coffee. She'd been weaker than she thought—that struggle in the cold waters of the Bay had left her exhausted and shivering and sick as a dog. Those buzzing bees in her head had multiplied tenfold, and she was certain that if she tried to stand again, she'd fall over. *I'd have to get better to die,* she thought dejectedly.

"You all right, Maguire?" Doohan's voice, close to her ear. "Maguire? Maggie, darlin'?"

She looked up through wet hair to see his worried face—chubby, flooded with Irish freckles, and ruddy from the excitement. Those pale blue eyes peered from beneath his

russet brows like ice from a volcano. She'd kept company
with him for a short while, once upon a time, before
Quincy. The sound of his voice still comforted her. Not
that she'd let him know that, of course.

"Yes," she lied, and was surprised to hear her teeth chattering. "I'm fine. You get Edwina?"

"She's below. Soggy, but fit as a fiddle," he said softly.
"What the devil's the Monongahela?"

Doohan's face began to recede, then come into focus
again, then fade. Maggie forced herself to ask, "Did you
get Ascension?"

"Don't know yet," said Doohan, standing up, his hands
on his hips. Now that he was sure she was more or less
alive, he was all police officer again. "Get yourself dry.
And tie a blanket around yourself, for the love'a Mike.
Ain't decent, showin' your limbs like that!"

Quickly, Grady searched the rows of parishioners. Five
rows up from the back, his gaze stopped on a narrow
cloaked figure. Just as he recognized the cloak as one of
Maggie's, the cowl lowered, exposing a long red braid. And
just as suddenly, before he could decide what to do next,
let alone take any action, the figure stood up.

"Brother Ascension!" Trini announced.

He stopped, halting the sermon mid-parable. He stared
at her for a half second before his smile broadened in a
predatory way. "My child," he soothed.

Trini's hand came up—with one of Maggie's pistols
clutched in it and aimed directly at Brother Ascension.

"No!" Grady started forward, pushing people out of his
way, knocking them to the ground. "Trini, don't!" One
row, climbing over the lady in purple; two rows, kicking
the man in the pinstripe.

"This is for Amy Proctor and Will Sempler," Trini said,
cocking the pistol.

Grady got his ankle caught in an umbrella in the third
row and fell into the lap of a sailor reeking of opium. He

shouted, "Trini!" again, but nobody was listening: not Trini, not Brother Ascension, not the people in the room, sitting glaze-eyed.

Brother Ascension held up a hand. "The Lord commands that you put down the gun, daughter."

"Amy was my friend," she said. "And Will was on to you."

Grady put his foot through a chair in the fourth row and kicked his way free, shouting, "Stop it!"

Paying no attention to Grady, Ascension held up both hands then, wide apart, palms out. He frowned, with the gentle disapproving expression of a disappointed father. "My child, I haven't the slightest idea what you're—"

"My mother," said Trini, her voice breaking as Grady regained his feet and pushed forward. "On top of everything else, why'd you have to kill my mother?"

She pulled the trigger just as Grady reached her. Ascension looked vaguely surprised, then crumpled. None of the attendees seemed to notice. They still sat there, as if waiting for someone or something. None of the Children of Golgotha moved, either, with the exception of Sister Polly.

While Grady took the pistol from Trini and police whistles blew outside, Polly slowly walked to the front of the room, then knelt beside her fallen husband. Trini sagging against him, Grady called, "Is he . . . ?"

Polly stood up. "He is alive," she announced with an eerily pleasant lilt to her voice, "but he won't be for long."

The police appeared from nowhere, it seemed. First they weren't anywhere in sight, and then they were crowding the dining hall's exits. Grady recognized the one headed toward him, and slipped Maggie's pistol into his pocket. "Morning, Kelly," he said to the thick, redheaded bull. "Where's Doohan?"

"Mornin' yourself, Maguire," replied the sergeant. "He's at the docks. And would that bulge in your pocket happen to be the firearm we just heard go off?"

Grady looked offended. Shifting Trini's weight under his

arm, he said, "You don't mean the gun that just shot Brother Ascension?"

Kelly looked toward the front of the room and, cursing under his breath, swatted the head of a seaman two seats over in the next row. "Damn it, Officer Carnes!" he shouted, giving the seaman's scalp another swipe. "Wake up! You put men in the crowd, and they go to sleep! What's wrong with everybody?" He turned toward some of the uniformed officers. "Well? What're you waitin' for? Somebody see if that man's still alive!"

As Grady scooped up Trini, who had fainted, and carried her into the lobby, he heard Kelly shouting orders behind him. He saw Sister Polly—rather, the hem of her dress—at the top of the stairwell.

Quincy rushed to his side, immediately taking Trini and cradling her. Grady said, "Let's get out of—" He stopped. He blinked twice, very slowly. He said, "I'll be fiddled!"

He grabbed Trini from a bewildered Quincy and shoved her at an officer. "Whatever you do, don't lose her," he said, and popped back into the dining hall. Over the crowd, which was just beginning to show signs of life, he called, "Is he dead, Kelly?"

The sergeant rose and brushed his knees. "As a post," he said, perplexed. "Damnedest thing. Only nicked in the shoulder."

"Whatever you do," called Grady, "don't drink the water!"

Kelly looked up and shouted, "What?" but by then Grady was already back in the lobby, pistol drawn, and grabbing a puzzled Quincy by the arm. "This," he shouted, taking the stairs two at a time and dragging poor Quincy along, "is the fun part!"

TWENTY-FOUR

GRADY APOLOGIZED FOR THE THIRD TIME AS HE opened the office door.

The doctor, who had come in grumpy and was leaving even grumpier, said, "Sir, do not call me again," slammed his hat on his head, and walked stiffly down the stairs to the street without another word.

Grady closed the door behind him. "So much for the Hippocratic oath," he said, and then called loudly, "Well, you scared off another one."

Maggie mumbled something that he couldn't make out. He picked up the glass of orange juice he'd left on his desk and walked across the office, past the semicircular window, to her door. He stuck his head around it. "What'd you say?"

"I said, I don't need a doctor now." She was sitting up, her dark brown hair fanned out against the pillows propping her. Her face, heart-shaped, looked like a child's with her hair down. Grady was, for the moment, touched.

"I'm perfectly fine," she continued. "Nothing a little rest won't cure. Besides, that quack was going to bleed me."

"Imagine," said Grady.

Maggie made a face. "Oh, shut up. You knew very well he was awful when you called for him. Just my luck Dr.

Sykes is out of town the one time I need him for something besides setting your bones.''

Grady came in, handed her the juice, and pulled up a chair. ''Well, you did have his partner yesterday, but you punched him in the stomach.''

Maggie blinked. ''I did?''

''You did. I figured that you were going to be all right if you were hitting, but just to be safe, I sent for Dr. Roberts this morning.''

''What was wrong with Sykes's partner?''

''He declined. He was afraid you'd punch him again. Feel up to talking?''

She sipped at the orange juice. ''Nothing I'd like more, especially since I slept through most of yesterday and half of Sunday before that and missed all the fun.''

Grady shrugged. ''Blevins said it would take a while for all the narcotics to leave your system. Considering yesterday, I'm shocked you managed to handle the boat caper on Sunday. That you even stayed awake for it, I mean.''

Actually, the cocktail of stimulants Blevins had fed her and injected her with were what had kept her going, and Grady was more surprised that she was still alive than anything else. He'd already given Stanley a sound tongue-lashing—actually, once he found out what Stanley had *really* given her, he was inclined to just take him out to the alley and shoot him, but better sense (and Otto) prevailed. If he had lost her, well . . .

''—statement?''

Grady looked up. ''Sorry. What?''

Maggie clucked her tongue, then smiled. ''Woolgathering, Grady? I thought that was *my* annoying little habit. I asked about Polly.''

Grady pursed his lips. ''She gave a statement. She wasn't in very good shape.''

''Why?'' Maggie asked, frowning. ''You and Quin didn't have to get rough with her, did you?''

It was his turn to frown. "Nothing of the sort! What do you take me for?"

"Sorry," she said.

"She was in bad shape because of the drugs."

Maggie rolled her eyes. "Of course. She would have been having something like the same reaction I had, I suppose. She was on them for so long, and—"

"More," Grady cut in. "She was taking a good deal more. Not only was she eating meals with the group, but Doohan's men found a syringe with her belongings. It seems she was addicted to heroin, as well."

He waited while Maggie mulled this over. Finally she said, "Heroin. Related to opium?"

Grady wasn't entirely sure, but for the sake of expediency, he said, "Yes. She was awfully shaky by the time they got round to taking a statement. Sweating. Shivers. It wasn't very pretty."

"What did she say?"

He leaned back. "Basically, she dumped everything in Ascension's lap, just as I thought she would. Except toward the end, things got a little confused. That is, she got a little confused."

Maggie cocked a brow. "How so?"

"She changed her story entirely. Apparently—if you want to believe her ravings, that is—she was the one who thought the whole thing up. The Children of Golgotha, I mean. I thought it was all poppycock at first, but now . . . Now I don't know. I'm inclined to believe her."

Maggie folded her hands and waited, the very model of patience, but her eyes were dancing with curiosity. He thought about drawing it out and making her suffer, then decided she'd already suffered entirely enough, all things considered. And so he explained what Polly had said in her statement.

She'd latched on to Brother Ascension—Darby Halstead, he was called then—not long after he was released from prison. Palming herself off as a farm girl from Minnesota, she was in truth an experienced confidence woman who, under the name Nancy Swenson, had quite a long and interesting record. "The old cut and run, the badger game, you name it. Including," he added, "two years spent as a druggist's assistant during her teenage years. Not illegal, certainly," Grady said. "But it came in handy later."

"She was the one who had the idea of doping the flock?" Maggie said. He couldn't tell whether she was shocked or delighted. Knowing Maggie, probably delighted. And then a bubble of laughter escaped her. "Oh, Grady, this is rich!"

He nodded. "Not only was it her idea, but she was the one who actually mixed Ascension's potions. She was addicted to them, and she just gave the children whatever dosage she was craving at the time. Of course, the heroin was on top of that. You're lucky she didn't decide to share."

Maggie nodded. She was looking not at him, but at the wall. She said, "It's rather expensive, isn't it? Heroin, I mean."

Grady nodded. "Another thing. She claims to have dug up Sutter for Ascension, too, and acted as liaison between them."

Maggie frowned. "What?"

"Something about a tryst and blackmail, and, well, it was a tad murky—her condition, you know. I mean, I couldn't even figure out who Sutter had the tryst with. But they had their hooks deep into his hide, too. That's why he was letting them get away with such a big chunk of the proceeds. Of course, they all planned to backstab each other."

Maggie's face was working, and he patted her on the wrist. "I'm certain it will all come clear in time."

Suddenly, she turned toward him. "The murders. And the cash they got from them. Polly had to buy drugs, but what on earth did they do with the rest of it? Where was it stashed?"

Grady noticed she was nervously twiddling her fingers, and as he spoke, he rose and went to her knife cabinet. "Foreign accounts, mostly. Ascension thought everything was in Switzerland, but it seems Polly thought ahead." He pulled out a pearl-gripped set and held them up. "These all right?"

Maggie beamed. "Perfect! She was planning to kite out on Ascension, then. Before she decided to murder him."

He handed her the case, and as she opened it and settled the knives in her lap, he said, "Strange, that. Doohan said there was enough poison in his water pitcher to kill the whole room, and a few besides. I suppose she'd just had enough."

Maggie paused, her hand cocked back to throw. "Highly understandable. Besides being a multiple murderer and a cheat—not to mention a blasphemer—Ascension was a certified rotter."

Grady wasn't certain what she meant, but decided to leave it alone for the time being. "She planned to leave from the first, it seems. For every dollar she transferred to Switzerland, she sent twenty to Toronto, to an account held by one Mrs. Paula Hamilton."

Maggie hurled the first knife. It stuck in the already ruined paneling just below the window, in a small circle of splinters. "And Paula Hamilton was, of course, Sister Polly," she said.

"Correct."

A second knife joined the first, still quivering in the wall. Maggie was back on her game. She paused, the third blade in her hand, and grinned at him. "It's almost a shame we picked her up. Who got her, by the way?"

"Quincy."

"Quincy?"

Grady nodded, a wry smile on his lips. "Actually, she sort of tripped over him while she was running away from me, but he's taking all the credit."

Maggie tipped her head slightly, her smile broadening. "You're sweet, Grady Maguire."

"I know," he said, turning away so she wouldn't see him blush. "Is that somebody coming up the stairs?"

It turned out to be Quincy and Trini, bearing an enormous three-bean salad. Grady greeted them in the office.

"I tried to tell her not to," Quincy said, "but—"

"My mother raised me to always bring food when someone was ill," Trini broke in. She had certainly changed from that little ragamuffin in Ascension blue. She was far too thin, still, but her emerald gown played up the green of her eyes and set off her hair. Grady found himself wishing they'd met under very different circumstances.

"I'm so sorry," he said, taking the bowl and putting it down on a table. "About your mother. If there's anything Maggie or I can do . . ."

Trini, newly elegant, waved a narrow hand. "No, you've done enough already. Really. It's just that I'm at rather loose ends at the moment. What with Mother gone and Uncle Sutter in . . ." She colored slightly, and it was impossible to tell whether it was from sorrow, annoyance, or disappointment. Perhaps all three. "I mean, what with Uncle Sutter being away . . ."

"Quincy?" he heard Maggie shout from the bedroom. "*Grady!* What's going on out there?" Ah, Maggie. Always the lady.

"You'd best go in before she has an apoplexy," he said to Quin and Trini, then had an idea. He supposed he might as well get it all over with at once.

Excusing himself, he went to his rooms, back through the study and the bedroom and finally the workshop, and stopped at a green-painted, half-glassed door in the floor. There was no need to knock. Otto Obermyer's mutton-chopped face was already there, staring up at him.

Grady leaned down and lifted the door back on its hinges. Otto emerged, but not before Ozzie scampered up the stairs and between his feet.

"She is *gut, ja?*" Otto said.

"Fit as Murphy's mouser," Grady replied, picking up the cat. "Not yet, fluffy britches," he said, putting Ozzie on the stairs and closing the door between them. "Quincy's here," he said to a curious Otto, by way of explanation. "I don't think he's quite over the repair costs yet."

Otto shook his head. "A good idea. Mad, he was. I think that hotel charges too much for the upholstery. Three hundred dollars!"

"Well," said Grady as they left his rooms and walked across the office, "just don't bring up the subject."

They found Maggie grinning, with two new ceramic angels in her lap and a third in her hands. "Look what Quin and Trini have brought me!" she exclaimed. "Dresden china!"

Trini, at the foot of the bed, colored. "To replace the ones that I broke," she explained.

"And I believe we still owe you a set of dishes," Quincy added glumly. Then he said, "Oh. Hello, Otto."

Quincy was sitting in the bedside chair, Grady noticed, and appeared to be itching for Maggie to put down the angel so that he could hold her hand. "Only half a set," Grady said, taking up residence on the window seat, just to the left of the knives Maggie had thrown earlier. He pulled them out of the wall.

"It looks as if all the principals are here," Maggie said. "Except for Bedside Blevins. Where is the old quack, Grady?"

"Seattle, I should imagine," Grady said. "We had another little argument about Maggie's medication, and he hopped a train. Not before I paid him, though."

"I wanted to meet him," Trini said. "Quincy's told me quite a bit about . . . about what you did. All those people! If I'd known, well . . ."

"I doubt it would have made any difference at all," Grady said.

"No," Trini concurred. "I suppose it wouldn't have.

Amy Proctor and Will Sempler were all I was thinking
about." She turned toward Maggie then and said, "You
see, Amy was one of my best friends from school. When
she died, her cousin told me about this religious order she'd
attached herself to. It sounded, well, fishy, to use the ver-
nacular."

"So you went straight away to join up," Maggie said,
looking as if she understood completely.

"Yes. Yes, I did. Except that I didn't know the food was
doped, and I—" She stopped and sighed deeply. "It was
like being spellbound. But then, Will was there, and I . . .
I . . ."

"You became accustomed to the drugs a little, didn't
you?" Maggie said quietly. "And you fell in love."

Trini lowered her eyes. "Yes," she admitted softly.
"Will weaned me off the drugged food, and we stuck
around, trying to find some evidence that would put Ascension in jail. Will was going to go to the police, except,
well, you can't imagine how it was. They suspected him,
you see. They watched him all the time. Even after he
signed the papers and he thought they'd ease up, they still
watched him."

Maggie shook her head, and Grady knew what she was
thinking: that Will Sempler had been a colossal fool to sign
any papers in the first place, that he should have just
grabbed Trini and gotten out, and the hell with the evidence. But youth was impetuous and thought it was im-
mortal, despite all proofs to the contrary: Will had got his
evidence after all. Unfortunately that evidence was his murder.

As if she was reading his mind, Maggie said, "And then
they killed Will."

Trini nodded. "Yes. And not long after, the Pinkertons
picked me up and sent me home. I suppose I should have
told them what I suspected," she said, raising her chin,
"but I couldn't exactly prove that Will's death had been
anything more than an accident. And you have a hard time

trusting people who grab you and throw you in a cab and then lock you in a hotel room, even if they say they're on the side of right.''

"Still, Trini . . ." Quincy said.

"I know. But I thought I was the one who was going to have to do it. I mean, get rid of them for good. It sort of turned into a . . . I don't know. A crusade, I suppose. When you came, Magdalena, I didn't know what to think. At first, I thought you were just another poor convert, and then I thought you were Ascension's spy. And after that? I don't know what I thought." She dropped her head again. "I'm sorry."

Grady, who had been raptly watching Trini's face during all this, and who had decided that with about twenty more pounds on her frame she'd be a stunner, suddenly stood up. "Anyone for lunch?" he asked.

Maggie made a face at him, but Trini said, "Yes!" right away.

"You three run along," Quincy said, never taking his eyes from Maggie's face. He was holding her hand now, Grady noted. "Maggie and I have some catching up to do."

"What catching up?" said Otto, leaning in the doorway. "Brother Protection stole the money, Polly steals it from him, and the police get the money back from Polly. And Trini is now free, so everything is hinky-dinky."

Grady slid an arm around Otto's shoulders, turning him. "Correct, old man," he said, gesturing to Trini to come along. "But I don't think Quincy is talking about the case, exactly."

"*Was, dann?*"

"Come along, Otto."

As Trini and Otto started down the front stairs and Grady lingered on the top step, he heard a soft giggle from Maggie's room.

Smiling, he pulled the door closed behind him.

If you enjoy the Maggie Maguire mystery series,
you will also want to read

The Dumb Shall Sing
BY STEPHEN LEWIS

C ATHERINE HAD JUST come out into the garden with
     Phyllis to see what vegetables might be gathered for
     supper when she heard a confused cacophony of
voices rise from the road that skirted the hill on which her
house sat. She and Phyllis hurried around to the front, and
there she saw a crowd heading toward the northern edge
of Newbury, where the town ran abruptly into the untamed
woods. The voices seemed to carry an angry tone. She
turned to Phyllis.

"Catch up with them, if you can, and see where they are
going, and to what purpose."

She watched as the girl hurried down the hill and trotted
toward the people, whose voices were becoming less dis-
tinct as they moved farther away. Catherine strained her
eyes, keeping them focused on the white cap Phyllis wore,
and she saw it bobbing up and down behind the crowd. The
cap stopped moving next to a man's dark brown hat. After
a few moments she could see the cap turn back toward her
while the hat moved away, and shortly Phyllis stood before
her, catching her breath.

"They are going to the Jameson house. They say the
babe is dead. And they want you to come to say whether
it was alive when it was born."

She recalled holding the babe in her arms and seeing that
he was having trouble breathing. She had seen that his nose

was clogged with mucus and fluids, and she had cleared it
with a bit of rag she carried in her midwife's basket for
that purpose. The babe had snorted in the air as soon as
she removed the cloth and then he had bellowed a very
strong and healthy cry. The only thing out of the ordinary
during the birth that she could now remember was how the
Jameson's Irish maidservant eyed the babe as though she
wanted to do something with it. Catherine had seen dozens
of births, and usually she could tell when a babe was in
trouble. This one had given no indication of frailty.

"Come along with me, then," she said to Phyllis. "Just
stop to tell Edward to watch for Matthew."

Phyllis did not respond, and Catherine motioned to the
tree under which Massaquoit had slept.

"You know," Catherine repeated, "Matthew."

"I see, yes, he should wait for Matthew," Phyllis said.

"Edward need not think about going to lecture."

"He does not think about that anyway," Phyllis replied.

"Be that as it may, I do not think there will be lecture
tonight," Catherine said. "Now go along with you."

The Jameson house was a humble structure of two sec-
tions, the older little more than a hut with walls of daub
and wattle construction, a plaster of mud and manure lay-
ered over a substructure of crisscrossing poles. Henry Jameson had recently built a wing onto the back of the house
to accommodate his growing family, and this new room
was covered in wooden shingles outside and was generally
more luxurious inside, having a wood plank floor and
whitewashed plaster walls.

It was in this room that Martha had delivered her babe.
Catherine remembered that the Irish servant girl had a little
space, not much more than a closet, for a bed so that she
could be near the infant's cradle, and that the parents' bedroom was in the original portion of the house. She also
remembered how the girl had fashioned a crude cross out
of two twigs, tied together with thread, and then hung it
over her bed until Henry had found it there and pulled it

off. He had taken the cross outside and ground it into the
mud with the heavy heel of his shoe. There was a separate
entrance to this side of the house, which gave onto a patch
of wild strawberries, and it was before that door that the
crowd had gathered.

As Catherine shouldered her way through the crowd, she
felt hands grabbing at her sleeve. She was spun around, and
for a moment she lost sight of Phyllis. Someone said, "I've
got her," but Catherine pulled away. Phyllis emerged from
behind the man who was holding Catherine's arm. A
woman placed her face right in front of Catherine. She was
missing her front teeth, and her breath was sour. She held
a smoldering torch in one hand and she brought it down
near Catherine's face.

"Here, mistress," the woman said, "we've been waiting
for you, we have."

Phyllis forced herself next to Catherine, shielding her
from the woman.

"Go," Catherine said to Phyllis, "to Master Woolsey,
and tell him to come here right away."

Phyllis pushed her way back through the crowd, which
was advancing with a deliberate inevitability toward the
house. Catherine moved with the energy of the crowd, but
at a faster pace, so that soon she reached its leading edge,
some ten or so feet away from Henry and Ned Jameson,
who stood with their backs to their house. Ned had his arm
around the Irish servant girl, flattening her breasts and
squeezing her hard against his side. She held a pitcher in
her hand. It was tilted toward the ground and water dripped
from it. The girl's eyes were wide and starting as they
found Catherine.

"Please," she said, but then Ned pulled her even harder
toward him, and whatever else the girl was trying to say
was lost in the breath exploding from her mouth.

The Jameson girls, ranging from a toddler to the oldest,
a twelve-year-old, were gathered around their mother, who
stood off to one side. Martha's gown was unlaced and one

heavy breast hung free as though she were about to give her babe suck. Her eyes moved back and forth between her husband and the crowd, seemingly unable or unwilling to focus. The toddler amused itself by walking 'round and 'round through her mother's legs. The oldest girl seemed to be whispering comfort to her younger siblings. Then the girl turned to her mother and laced up her gown. Martha looked at her daughter's hand as though it were a fly buzzing about her, but she did not swipe it away.

Henry was holding the babe, wrapped in swaddling, and unmoving. It was quite clearly dead. He took a step toward Catherine and held out the babe toward her. His face glowed red in the glare of a torch.

"Here she is," he shouted. He lowered his voice a little. "Tell us, then, if you please, Mistress Williams, was this babe born alive?"

"Who says nay?" Catherine asked. She looked at Martha, who stood mute, and then at the Irish servant girl, who did not seem to understand what was happening. Always the finger of blame, she thought, lands on some poor woman while the men stand around pointing that finger with self-righteous and hypocritical arrogance. She recalled how Henry had asked first what sex the babe was before he inquired as to his wife's health. "Henry will be glad," Martha had said as Catherine had held the babe in front of her so that she could see its genitalia. And then Martha had collapsed onto the bed, a woman exhausted by fifteen years of being pregnant, giving birth, suffering miscarriages, and nursing the babes that were born, and always there had been the poverty. She had not wanted to take Ned in, for there was never enough food.

"Just answer the question," Henry insisted. "We have heard how soft your heart is for a savage. How is it with this babe? Here, look at it, which is not breathing now who was when it was born. Was it not very much alive when you pulled it out of my wife's belly not three days ago?"

A voice came from the back of the crowd, strong, male, and insistent.

"An answer, mistress, we need to know the truth."

Catherine turned toward the voice, but she could not identify the speaker. It came from a knot of people that had gathered just beyond Ned in the shadow of a tall tree.

"The truth," the voice said again, and then was joined by other voices, male and female, rising from the group beneath the tree, and then spreading across the surface of the crowd like whitecaps in a storm-tossed sea. "The truth," they clamored, "tell us the truth."

"What says the mother, then?" Catherine demanded. "What says Goody Jameson?"

"Nothing," came the response from the group.

Catherine turned back to Henry.

"Your wife, Henry, what does she say?"

"Nothing," Henry repeated. "She no longer speaks. She came to me not an hour ago, holding the babe in her arms, and handed it to me, and she does not speak."

Catherine studied Martha's face. Its expression did not change as her children moved about her. She did not seem to see that her husband was holding her dead infant in his arms, and she did not hear the insistent cries for the truth. It was as though she were standing in a meadow daydreaming while butterflies circled her head. Every moment or two she extended her hand toward the toddler that clung to her knees, but the gesture was vague and inconsequential, and her hand never found her child's head.

Catherine stepped close to Martha, close enough to feel the woman's breath on her face.

"Martha, you must speak," Catherine said, and Martha's eyes now focused on her, as though she had just returned from that distant meadow. She shook her head, slowly at first, and then with increasing agitation. Catherine took Martha's shoulders in both hands and squeezed and then the nodding motion stopped. Still Martha did not speak.

"My poor wife is distracted by the death of our babe,"

Henry declared. "Can you not see that? Mistress Williams, you must answer for her."

"Well, then," Catherine said, "if Martha Jameson will not attest to the truth, I needs must say that this babe was born alive, and alive it was when I left it. Truth you want, and there it is."

A murmur arose from the crowd. It pushed toward Catherine.

"It is surely dead now," somebody said.

"If Goody Jameson won't speak, we have ways," said another.

"Yes, press her, stone by stone. She will talk, then, I warrant."

"You will leave her alone," Henry said, and the crowd, which had come within several feet of the clustered Jameson family, stopped. Henry held out the babe toward his wife.

"Tell them, Martha," he said. He thrust the babe toward her, but she did not hold out her arms to take it. He shook his head. "She brought the babe to me. It was dead. She said she had been asleep, and when she woke she saw the servant girl leaning over the babe. When she picked it up, it was not breathing. Then she brought it to me. That girl, she did something while my wife was asleep."

Catherine felt the anger rise in the crowd toward the servant. She remembered once, when she was a girl in Alford, how a crowd just like this one had fallen upon a little boy whose family was Catholic, and how they had beaten him with sticks until he lay senseless in the road. She strode to Ned and grabbed his arm.

"Let her go," she said.

"You are now interfering in my household, mistress. Leave be."

"Step away, mistress," a woman in the crowd said. "You have told us what we needed to know."

"She," Henry shouted, "standing there with the pitcher, ask her what she was doing with our babe."

The servant girl turned her terrified and starting eyes toward her master. Their whites loomed preternaturally large in the failing light of the early evening.

"A priest, it was, I was after," she said.

Ned pushed the girl forward she stood quivering in front of the crowd.

"That is it," he said, "that is how we found her, practicing her papist ritual on our babe, pouring water on its innocent face, and mumbling some words, a curse they must have been."

"Its poor soul," the girl muttered. "There was no priest. I asked for one. So I tried myself to save its precious soul."

Henry looked at his wife, whose eyes were now studying the ground at her feet. Then he stared hard at the girl, his face brightening as with a new understanding.

"You drowned it, for certain," he said. "Or you cast a spell on it so it could not breathe. What, a papist priest? In Newbury? You have killed our babe and driven my poor wife mad."

"Try her, then," came the voice from the knot of people, still grouped by the tree. "Have her touch the babe. Then we will know."

The crowd surged forward and Catherine found herself staggering toward Henry, who dropped to one knee against her weight. Henry threw one hand behind him to brace himself, and Catherine reached for the babe so as to stop it from falling. As she grabbed for it, its swaddling blanket fell. The babe's skin was cold. Henry regained his balance and wrapped the babe tightly in the blanket..

"Try her," again came the cry from the crowd.

"Surely not," Catherine said. "Magistrate Woolsey is coming. This is a matter for him."

"We need not wait for the magistrate. We will have our answer now," shouted one.

"Now," said another.

"Right," said Ned. "We will try her now."

Catherine turned to face the crowd and to peer over it to

the road, where day was giving way to dusk. She thought she saw two figures approaching.

"The magistrate is coming even now," she said.

Henry looked at Ned, and the boy pushed the servant girl toward him.

"Touch the babe," Ned demanded.

"Yes, touch it," Henry said. "If it bleed, it cries out against you."

"There is no need for that," Catherine said. "Talk of the dead bleeding. It is surely blasphemy."

"The blood will talk," came a voice from a crowd.

"Yes," others confirmed, "let the poor dead babe's blood cry out against its murderer."

The girl clasped her arms in front of her chest, but Ned pulled her hands out. She struggled, but he was too strong, and he was able to bring one hand to the exposed skin of the babe's chest. He pressed the hand onto the skin, and then let her pull her hand back. Henry peered at the spot she had touched, and then lifted the babe over his head in a triumphant gesture.

"It bleeds," he said. "It bleeds."

He held the babe out for the crowd to see. Catherine strained her eyes as Henry and the babe were now in shadows. Henry turned so that all could view. Catherine was not sure she saw blood on the babe's chest, but something on its back caught her eye, and then she could no longer see.

"Blood," cried voices in the crowd. "The babe bleeds! Seize her!"

There was a violent surge forward, and Catherine felt herself being thrown to the ground. She got to her feet just in time to see rough hands grabbing the servant girl and pulling her away . . .